CARMEN MONICA OPREA

A Novel

Forever Rose is a work of fiction. Names, characters, places, and incidents are the product of the author's imagination or are used fictitiously. Any resemblance to actual events, locales, or persons, living or dead, is entirely coincidental.

DEDICATION

This book is dedicated to my mom, for too many reasons
to name. She is so much a part of me and a part of everything I
do, and I see her in myself more and more every day.
I love you, Mom.

Carmen Monica Oprea, December 2016

CHAPTER 1

Florence, Italy, 2037

Doctor Alessandro Santini loosened his tie then walked briskly to the Santa Maria Novella hotel elevator, retrieving his car keys from his blazer pocket. *Of course,* he thought, when the elevator doors closed just as he reached them. He pressed the down button and glanced back at the empty conference room where he had just spent three grueling hours discussing the latest in medical technology—the laser pen. By using solar energy to recharge, the laser pen replaced the traditional method of closing surgical wounds. The benefits of this new medical instrument were tremendous, reducing the healing process following surgery to just days.

Alex peered out the conference room windows. Night had fallen over the city, and the lights of Santa Maria Nuova, the oldest active hospital in the historic center of Florence, shone with an eerie glow. If he left now, he could be back in his loft on Via Lorenzo before seven, which would give him just enough time to change his clothes and make it to Sophia's memorial mass.

He paced back and forth while he waited for the next elevator to come, and then, growing impatient, he headed for the spiral staircase winding through the center of the hotel. He tossed his keys in the air as he walked down the stairs, caught them, tossed them again and caught them again, only to miss his catch on the third toss. *Great,* he thought when his keys flew from his fingers and plummeted all the way to the basement. *Just great!* He raced down the stairs until he reached the lobby where a group of people sitting on sofas stared at a large flat-screen TV.

"I lost my car keys. They fell into the basement," Alex told the security guard, a burly man who stood next to a door that restricted access to the basement.

"Please take a seat while I call for someone," the guard said, gesturing toward a cluster of sofas and armchairs.

"Please, hurry!" Alex switched his briefcase from one hand to the other and joined the group of people following the news on Canale 5.

"...a phenomenon that happens every fourteen months," the anchor said in a loud, boisterous voice.

"What's going on?" Alex asked a skinny, freckle-faced girl who was watching the news.

"There's going to be a supermoon tonight." The girl glanced from the screen to Alex, then back again.

"A what?"

"A supermoon, when the moon is closest to earth in its orbit, and it looks bigger," she said. "Legend has it that portals to other worlds will open if the supermoon meets two conditions."

Alex cocked an eyebrow. "And what are those conditions?"

"Everyone with Internet access knows what they are." The girl grinned mischievously at him after she said it.

"Of course," Alex muttered. *Everyone knows about this phenomenon except me.*

Alex headed back to the security guard, who was reading a sports magazine. He coughed when he stopped in front of him. "Anything about my keys yet?"

The man shrugged but didn't look up. "It's going to take a while. The maintenance man is doing some repair work on the other side of the hotel."

Alex looked at his watch. It was time to go. He was never late. Never. "Can't I just get them myself?"

The guard shook his head. "No, sir. Hotel policy."

Alex pressed his fingers to his temples, then rifled through the jumble of bandages and papers in his briefcase before grabbing a bottle of aspirin. He popped two pills and placed the bottle next to the laser pen, his reason for being at the hotel in the first place.

"Did you read the newspaper this morning?" the security guard asked, glancing up.

Alex raised his eyebrows. "No. Why?"

"It's all over the news. The supermoon—"

"Don't tell me you believe that nonsense about the supermoon opening gateways to other worlds," Alex scoffed.

"I do," the guard said, nodding firmly before turning his attention to the TV.

As the guard did so, Alex seized the opportunity, stealthily opening the door that led to the basement and descending the stairs. At the bottom, a single bulb barely lit what appeared to be an ample storage room with spider webs covering the walls, broken chairs, and dusty paintings. The air was moist and cumbersome, and he sneezed a couple of times while he looked for his keys.

After a few minutes of searching, he located them next to a canvas propped against a concrete wall. As he picked them up, he gasped as he gazed at a face he knew by heart. Alex tightened his grip on the keys. He took a step back, while his right hand shot toward his mouth, touching his parted lips. If he didn't know Sophia had died in a robbery three years ago, he would have thought it was she in the portrait. Born in 1717—from what the inscription stated—Countess Rose Estes was only twenty when she died. Locks of ruby-red hair spiraled all over her shoulders, wreathing her oval-shaped face. She had lambent, jade-green eyes with a hypnotic quality about them. His heart raced, and for a split second, his breathing was suspended.

Alex moved toward the painting and touched the woman's face. Then he turned around, preparing to leave when the light flickered. The last sparks of life drained from the bulb. *Don't worry,* he told himself. *It's probably just a bad bulb.* He turned on his cell phone's flashlight app and searched for the door.

A ribbon of light came from ahead of him, and he moved toward it. As the glow spilled across the room like a line of glittering fire, he covered his eyes. He tried to step back, but the vortex sucked his whole body in.

Crackling sounds surrounded him, blurring into one long, whirring noise. Flaming arrows hissed from every direction like snake tongues, charging his hair. His hair lifted on the nape and arms, and he tried gripping something. He lowered his arm, staring straight ahead. Dots of light buzzing incessantly with noise lined his passage through what looked like a dazzling bridge. The bright radiance blinded him while the suction tightened his leg muscles. A sudden coldness hit at his core. Eventually, the noise lessened, and the sounds faded into a musical chime.

After just a few strides, Alex walked out of the vortex. His knees locked. Beads of sweat formed on his forehead. He wiped them with the back of his blazer sleeve. The floor was hard and uneven beneath his expensive leather shoes. Except for the curtain of ivy concealing the entrance, it appeared that he was in a cavelike space. He turned around, looking for the portrait, and when he couldn't locate it, he followed the light and stepped out of the cave into a perfectly manicured garden.

Ahead of him, marble statues lined paths that stretched as far as he could see. Evergreens surrounded ponds where lilies floated, and geese swam undisturbed in the dusk. Deep-yellow roses stood out among the vast variety of flowers, their fragrance spicy. A short distance away, amid the greenery around him, he spotted the roof of a house. *Someone must be there and can tell me where I am.* Alex turned toward the cottage—blood pumping fiercely in his veins, his stomach in knots—when the sound of harps and violins coming from the opposite direction filled his ears. He looked both ways and decided to follow the path that led to the house, hoping to meet someone and ask for directions back to the hotel.

Alex had taken just a few steps when whispers coming from the other side of a bush, made him jump. Sharp branches scraped his skin, and he bit his lower lip. He tilted his chin and peeked at the man and woman, who both wore old-fashioned outfits, and goosebumps rose on his skin. They stood facing each other, their faces inches apart. Alex poked his head around the bush, trying to stay hidden.

"Something's off with Count Estes. He said he'd announce his heir tonight," the man said. His face, which was too close to the woman's face, was pale, and his mouth was drawn back in a contorted grimace. "This must go off flawlessly."

"Listen to me. I've suffered enough. Struggling and weeping have been my life up to the present," the woman said, giving her companion an accusing look.

"You know very well why I must do this." His voice jumped up a few octaves on the last words.

"And I don't like it one bit longer," the woman snapped. "Have you not found another way than marrying her? With my plan, we could be far away from Tuscany and your creditors, love. Why can't you wait a bit?"

The man's eyes narrowed into a pair of tiny chunks. "Desperate times, my dear. I shall use whatever means I can to save my estate from ruin. Until we meet again, farewell, my lady," he said, kissing her gloved hand.

"So be it!" The woman heaved a sigh as they walked toward the vibrantly lit villa, following separate paths.

The young man with a square jaw and finely crafted cheekbones wore a satin coat over a shirt with ruffles at the wrists, and his black hair was tied at the nape of his neck. Alex was immediately drawn to the tall, slender woman, with unusually beautiful sad deep blue eyes and raven-black curls. Her wine-colored silk gown rustled elegantly as it touched the leaves on the ground. The freckled girl in the hotel had said the supermoon opened portals to other worlds, and as he looked at the greenery surrounding him, a chill crawled up his spine. He retraced his steps to the cave where the portal had dropped him and stopped at the threshold. A breeze brushed his face. Frightened by his approach, dozens of bats spread their wings. When they flew as one black mass into the moonlight, Alex ducked, hugging his briefcase. His breathing accelerated. His legs stiffened. The only noise he heard was the thunder of the wings beating above his head.

***

Villa Luce Del Sol, Italy, 1737

Rose Estes wished to be in a hundred different places except the villa. Sitting at the window, she studied the horizon until she caught sight of the cottage, a gift from her father, Count Giulio Estes. It was a peaceful moment before her twentieth birthday party. The full moon she waited for every month caught her eye. Maybe the portal to the world she had visited fourteen moons ago had reopened. Not hearing the knock on her door, she jumped when it cracked open, and Lucia peeked in.

"Miss Rose, may I come in?"

Rose nodded.

The woman, who had a dark complexion and hair tied in a bun, carried a tray with fruits, an almond scone, and a vase filled with Rose's beloved flowers—yellow roses. She was thirty and had worked for Rose's family for more than ten years, just like her mother before her.

Lucia set the tray on Rose's bed. "That'll satisfy your hunger before the witch comes and gets you, Miss Rose. Miss Annabella rang her bell the entire night as if a hundred demons were tormenting her. Poor Blanca had to rush to her side each time."

Rose chuckled. At only eighteen, with light hair and eyes reminiscent of violets in spring, her sister, Annabella, wasn't a bad person, perhaps a bit too self-absorbed. Rose picked up the vase from the tray and inhaled the flowers' sweet fragrance. She dropped a kiss on the petals before placing the vase on her writing desk. As Lucia moved about the room, she broke apart the pastry and nibbled on a strawberry. The sweet juice splashed in her mouth while she tried to keep up with the maid's chatter.

"This morning, Miss Annabella threw a pillow in Blanca's face because she pulled the laces too hard. At noon, she was complaining because her food was too hot. I'm telling you, this girl is evil, Miss Rose. She's nothing like you," Lucia nattered.

"I'm sorry for Blanca. She shouldn't have to put up with Annabella's outbursts."

"Miss Rose, you're an angel," Lucia said, as she tidied her room. "At least, you made it, Miss. You showed your family your talent."

Rose paused with a strawberry halfway to her mouth. Her gaze traveled toward the back of the garden, where she thought she saw something move, but the trees obstructed her view. She took a bite of the juicy fruit, shaking her head. Her parents understood her artistic inclination toward painting events in history. It was her grandmother—the only one who never seemed to accept or even love Rose—who decided that it was time for her first granddaughter to settle down in marriage, instead of roaming free all over the continent. Her passing away, at the beginning of last year, slowed things a bit, and Rose had enough time to talk her parents into letting her go to London to paint. They allowed her an entire year to perfect her painting skills, and Rose wondered if tonight's ball would put an end to her independence and her aspirations to become a historical painter as she had always dreamed. She sighed.

"Milady, the red or the green dress?" Lucia asked.

"The red one, and hurry," Rose said, looking down at the front entrance where her friend waved back to her. "Viola has arrived. I haven't seen her in ages. Perhaps, she'll change Annabella's ire."

"I doubt anything can alter her temper."

Rose lifted her arms while Lucia pulled the laces of her corset. She ran her fingers through a pile of curls and finally gave up, leaving the task to the maid.

"Fancy you, Miss Rose," Lucia said, clapping her hands after she restrained Rose's hair with a pin on top of her head. She grabbed the tray before leaving the room, and the issue of Annabella faded from Rose's thoughts.

Rose left her room and descended the spiral staircase connecting the three floors of the villa. As soon as she reached the first floor, Annabella's voice resonated throughout the drawing room. Rose stopped in the doorway. Lucia had been right, and she lacked the energy to deal with her sister's outbursts on her birthday.

"Have you heard the rumors, Viola?" Annabella asked, too loudly. "Papa will announce his heir at the festivities."

"Splendid," the slim brunette, three years older than Annabella said, as she squeezed a slice of lemon into her cup. "I'm sure you'll have a surprise," Viola said the words as if even having them on her tongue disgusted her.

"I certainly hope a good one," Annabella said.

"How is the star of Tuscany?" Viola asked, playing with the pastries on her plate when Rose entered the room.

"Agitated and happy. Father keeps me occupied, and I barely find time to study and travel. Since my arrival from London, I had to postpone my trip to Siena twice because of his failing health. There are paintings I have to finish for the Duchess and the Duke," Rose said, kissing her friend on both cheeks. She poured a cup of tea and took a bite from a pastry filled with chocolate.

"Rose has an unusual ambition to be a female artist. Her aspiration is to become a historical painter," Annabella said. "Don't you know it's the most difficult genre?"

Annabella turned toward Rose, waiting for her answer.

"And the noblest," Rose added. Her father acknowledged her talent, and he supported her decision although the task of a historical painter was a challenging career for a woman. She looked at Viola, who pressed her temples with her long, slender fingers, closing her eyes. "Are you not feeling well, Viola?"

"It's nothing but a headache, my dear," Viola said. "It's been with me since my husband's death."

"What a terrifying experience!" Annabella shook her head. "I'll help you marry into a wealthy family. You're like a sister to me."

"Your compassion is overwhelming," Viola said, patting Annabella's hand.

"I hope a headache won't stop you from attending the ball. I can't wait for the dancing to start. Maybe you'll encounter a companion tonight now that your mourning period is over," Rose said.

"I'm sure Fabio will have no objections," Annabella added.

"Fabio isn't a man fond of balls. Hunting and gambling are his main activities when he isn't tied up in the estate's affairs," Viola said, looking at Rose.

Rose sipped her tea, pretending to study the gardens outside the windows. By the time she arrived at the cave, the portal, if it had opened, would be long gone. She had to leave before it was too late.

"You are preoccupied today, Rose. You're not worried about tonight's party, are you?" Viola asked.

"Oh, I'm concerned that Mother will need my help," Rose said.

"Mother has everything under control, Rose," Annabella said, rolling her eyes.

"I have to check for myself. Stay here, Viola, and tell my sister to behave. I'll meet you at the ball," Rose said, as she scurried from the room into the hallway.

Outside, Rose tiptoed between the evergreens, ignoring the small branches that caught the hem of her dress. She stopped when she spotted a strange man wearing an unusual outfit, ducking to defend himself from the deafening bats storming from the cave.

CHAPTER 2

Alex peered into the cave as the portal shrunk to a single belt of light, a chill crawling up his spine. *Someone is watching me.* He spun on his toes, coming face to face with a woman who barely made it to his chin. She held the stem of a rose with one hand, while the other one rested above her heart, just as the painting in the hotel's basement portrayed her. Ginger curls kissed her delicate cheekbones, her intent look hastening his breathing.

"Come with me, quickly," Rose whispered.

"Why?" Alex asked.

Rose grabbed his hand, pulling him away from the cave. She didn't seem to care that when she picked up the hem of her dress, branches and thorns tortured her now exposed ankles. She stepped on her tiptoes, avoiding the sharp stones protruding here and there from the grass.

"Where are your shoes? You're going to hurt yourself," Alex said, pointing to her feet and waiting for an answer.

"Worry about yourself, not about me."

"We're going in the wrong direction. I can't go with you. I need to go back."

Rose kept to a narrow path thru the garden, determined to put as much distance as possible between them and the cave. She glanced around while she dragged Alex with her, the only sounds on the road coming from their heavy breathing.

"You're not safe here, and you can't return. The magic door to your world is gone."

"What do you mean it's gone?"

"Vanished for a very long time," Rose said, leaving the path and climbing a steep slope. "Hurry, I don't have all night."

"Where are you taking me?"

Alex pulled her arm, wanting her to stop and bring him back to the portal leading to his world. Rose jerked free from his grip. When she stretched out her arm, hoping to catch him in time to break his fall, Alex pulled her with him, and they both fell onto the dirt road. Rose released herself from his grasp and rose to her feet, shaking the dust from her dress. Alex cleared his throat a few times, avoiding looking at Rose while he searched for his briefcase. He wiped a thin layer of dust from the leather briefcase and hugged it firmly.

"Look what you've done. We were almost to the cottage," Rose said.

"I'm not taking one more step until you tell me how to get back to my world."

"Do as you please." Rose forced a laugh. A vein throbbed on the side of her neck. She rocked back and forth on her feet a couple of times before resuming her walk. Alex kept his distance, two steps behind her.

"I demand to know how to return."

"I couldn't help you even if I wanted to."

"Then, take me to someone who can."

Rose shook her head while she continued to walk ahead of him. Alex turned around. The late hour hindered the sight of the cave he had left behind. He had never been good at finding his way in the dark. That was why Sophia had died. He had taken a wrong turn when they were driving home on a street infamous for muggings after dusk. *Hell no, I won't think of that terrible incident when I have bigger things to worry about now.*

Alex sighed and hastened his step until he walked side by side with Rose. He lifted his gaze and stared at the biggest moon he had ever witnessed. The unfamiliar sky made him feel lonely and scared so far from his home. He looked around at the citrus trees and the bushes overwhelmed by newly born buds, and from time to time, he slapped nagging insects attracted by his cologne.

The narrow alley ended in front of a brick cottage that seemed to have two or three rooms at the most. Strings of colorful flowers hung loosely on the windowsills. He watched as the girl squatted and fumbled in one of the pots on the right side of the entrance. Alex guessed she was looking for a key to unlock the front door. His breath was coming in hard, fast patterns. Half of him wanted to run, to get help, to shout out, but he also felt an overwhelming desire to sort this out. The hinges squeaked when she opened the door, echoing through the house and stopping the trail of his thoughts. She stepped inside first and then signaled him to enter.

As soon as they were inside the house, Rose pushed open the shutters, and a welcoming breeze helped clear the stale air in the room. Alex stood in front of the window and inhaled a couple of times before turning his attention to the interior of the cottage. The floors appeared to be waxed in the dim light coming from the moon. He watched as Rose lit a candle, placing it on a table in the foyer. A painter's apron lay on a nearby rocking chair, and pots with brushes of all sizes occupied the shelves on one wall. About seven large and at least ten small canvases were propped in the corners. Alex coughed when he leaned over the oils. He had always been allergic to them. After nights of constant debates, he had rented a studio for Sophia, so that she wouldn't have to paint in their apartment. He shook his head to chase away her memory and focused on the woman in front of him.

"You'll be safe here," Rose said.

"Safe from what?"

Rose peeked through the curtains, her back to him. The color of her hair coupled with the smell of the oils was familiar. Alex closed his eyes, and Sophia's image came to mind again. Sophia wouldn't be happy to know that he was so far from home and incapable of making sense of the entire situation.

"Didn't you hear me?" Alex asked, opening his eyes and staring at the curve of Rose's neck.

Rose continued to look out the window. "You came from the other side of the cave," she said. "You were such a marvel with those flickering lights and the bats around you."

Rose giggled, looking over her shoulder at him. Alex closed the distance between them, exhaling heavily.

"Is this funny to you?" he asked, suddenly tired. He paced about the room, rubbing his arms to keep them warm, and then untying his neck tie and opening a button from his shirt.

"Stay still," she said, furrowing her brows.

Rose resumed her previous task, watching for any sign of movement in the garden. Alex followed her lead. The wind played with the leaves in the nearby trees, a few flowers bent slightly in their flowerbeds, while the shrubs quivered gently. Alex breathed over her shoulder, noting her creamy skin and the gentle slope of her shoulder. He took a couple of steps back when the woman shifted toward him.

"What are you looking for?" he asked.

"I'm making sure no one followed us. It would be hard to explain your presence here."

"Why? Are you scared that I may put you in danger?"

Rose's head jerked back, and she crossed her arms, making herself as tall as she possibly could while she faced him. "You lack confidence." The fire in her eyes burned, her face a match for her red hair. Her breath reminded him of chocolate and mint. She had a strong voice, much like his late wife's, but her frame was smaller than it looked in the portrait. She looked like Sophia—the same height and tiny waist, same eyes and flowing red hair—and this thought disturbed him. Her cheeks were still touched with a hint of pink from their earlier exertion.

"I never introduced myself. I am Rose Estes. Countess Rose Estes," she said. "And you are…"

"Delighted, of course," Alex said, raising her hand to his lips and kissing her slender fingers. He held her hand in his own while studying her face.

"Would you fancy letting go of my hand?"

"Certainly, how rude of me," Alex said, beaming as he released her hand. "I'm Alessandro Santini."

Rose's face flushed, redness expanding over her chest and arms. Never in his life had Alex witnessed someone shifting between colors so quickly. He was afraid she would faint. The haughty way she looked down on him, with her pointy nose and dark green eyes, made her even more attractive.

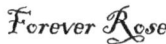

"What year is this?" he asked, rapidly.

"1737," she answered.

Alex groaned. He had landed from the twenty-first century into the eighteenth century by the mere passing through a tunnel and had met the woman from the painting. If he was correct, it was the end of the three hundred years of the House of Medici ruling over Florence. Sophia had always told him that Italy was the cradle of civilization and that it was his duty to pass down to his children their traditions, language, legends, and myths.

"Alessandro Santini," she whispered his name, "you're staring."

His eyes gleamed with amusement. "Pardon my rudeness," he said. "So, what town is this?"

"Welcome to Estes's estate. We are close to Florence, just a few hours by horseback over the hills." Rose circled him slowly, studying him intently. She fingered the buttons of his shirt and then jerked her hand away. "Pardon me. Your clothes have a strange cut."

"They are from a time much different than yours."

Alex frowned. Just a few short hours ago, he had passed through a swirling vortex into a different era than his own, but he wasn't in the Florence of his time, and the woman in front of him wasn't Sophia, but an Italian countess eerily similar to her. Of all the women in the world, he had to meet someone to remind him of his guilt. The image of Sophia lying dead against the back of the chair, blood springing from the wound down her dress, her mouth slightly open in surprise as she looked at him, made Alex shiver.

"I have to return. Can you show me the way back to the cave?"

"Not at this moment. Tell me more about your time," Rose said.

"What? I must go back. What do you know about the portal?"

Rose straightened her back, and her face flushed again. The portal had disappeared. She didn't have any idea what triggered its appearance in the first place or when and if it would happen again, and if he would be able to return to his time. She shook her head and leaned on the wall, looking at him with eyes that changed to a shade of green darker than the shrubs in the garden.

"Once, on a night much like this one, with a full moon that stretched over the entire sky, my dog, Mora, entered the same cave you came from. I followed her, thinking that it would take me to the other side of the garden. I remember passing between rolling belts of light. I covered my eyes for just a heartbeat. When I opened them up, I was in a room with a candle hanging from the ceiling. There was broken furniture where the fields should have been."

"You stepped into the twenty-first century," Alex said.

"I followed Mora up the stairs, and I saw strange things there. The night tinted the roads in gray, and the carriages had no horses or coachmen. I grabbed Mora and returned to the room where a man dressed just like you was talking into the palm of his hand."

Alex shook his head. "He was talking on a phone, not into his hand."

"A what?"

"Did he see you?" Alex widened his eyes while he waited for Rose to continue.

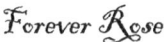

"I ran out the cave before he had time to spot me," she said.

"You are just like the painting."

"What painting?"

"I saw your portrait in my time."

"Impossible. It's not finished," Rose said. "The place you come from...what is it called?"

"It's the future."

If he told his best friend that he had traveled through a portal and ended up in the past with a woman resembling Sophia, Renaldo would think he had lost his mind again, just as he had when he woke up from the coma and discovered that his wife had died in the robbery. It took him three years of intense therapy to accept that her death wasn't his fault but a cruel twist of fate. He shook his head and stared at the woman next to him.

"So, Mr. Santini, what brought you here?"

"Please, call me Alex," he said.

"Mr. Santini, you're avoiding my question. What brought you here?"

"You brought me here. You're the reason I'm in this place," Alex said, blurting his words faster than he had intended.

"Me?" Rose pressed her hand over her heart, backing away.

Alex nodded, not knowing a better way of explaining his passing through the swirling vortex after he had admired her portrait in that dark storage room of the hotel basement.

"I'm not sure you will understand if I try to explain it."

"Why don't you make an effort?" Rose asked, her lips twitching.

"You are a determined young lady," Alex said, rolling his eyes.

Alex was ready to tell her about the myth of the supermoon opening portals to other worlds as the girl with freckles had told him in the hotel lobby, when the sound of barking dogs and shouts coming from outside stopped him. He ran toward the window in time to see greyhounds running around five carriages as they passed by the cottage.

"What is all the barking and shouting about?" he asked catching Rose's eye.

"My guests are coming, and I haven't yet dressed for the ball," Rose said, racing to the window.

"A ball? What kind of ball?"

"The one prepared for my twentieth birthday, of course. I must go back to the house." Her voice was shrieking.

"Calm yourself down and then go and get ready for your ball," Alex said, trying to conceal his irritation.

A soft breeze coming from the open window dried the sweat dotting his temples. He turned his attention to Rose, who was checking his attire.

"Will you fancy coming? I can borrow clothes from Papa, so you won't look so *different*."

"I'm in no mood for a birthday party. All I want is to go back to my apartment, and prepare for the important meeting for work I have in the morning," Alex said, raising his voice and pacing about the room again. He whacked his head. *Damn! I am going to miss the meeting if I don't get the heck out of here.*

Alex looked back at Rose. Time was slipping away. If the inscription on the frame was accurate, 1737 was the year of her death. The tightening in his chest made him blow out short breaths while he followed Rose through the room.

"I'm sorry for your misfortune, Mr. Santini, but it seems you're trapped in my world for a while. It'll be best if you adjust your attitude until we figure out what to do next," she said, politely.

"My attitude?"

"Yes, your sarcasm masks your natural charm." Rose closed the door behind her and disappeared between evergreens.

***

Rose picked up the hem of her dress as she ran toward the villa. Her curls were a mess, and her cheeks were on fire. She slipped through a dimly lit corridor leading straight to the dressing room where she shuffled through her father's clothes, touching vests made of velvet and silk. *The blue one would go well with his eyes,* Rose thought. She smiled as she assessed the outfit she had chosen for him. He had the olive coloring of her people and a full mouth that raised goosebumps on her skin. His clothes hung loosely on his body, probably from a lack of muscles. The oddity of the fabrics and their cut weren't something she had seen at the balls the Grand Duke of Tuscany held at his palace. The pants weren't tied at the legs as the fashion required, and the lack of stockings was another defect in his vestments, for which she had to find a solution and fast. She was hurrying down the stairs when her mother's sudden call startled her.

"Where do you think you're going? And what are you doing with your father's clothes?"

"Mother, I spilled ink on Father's clothes. I'm taking them to the washroom. Please, Mother, don't say a word."

They walked side by side, as they descended to the first level of the house. Knowing how her mother hated when she didn't wear shoes, Rose hid her dirty feet under her dress. One of her mother's sermons still rang in her ears—"Behave like a lady in any circumstance"—and Rose was anything but a lady.

"Our guests are already here and look at you. You haven't even dressed yet."

"I'll be ready in time. Don't worry! Tell Lucia to prepare my dress, will you?"

Her mother nodded and turned toward the hall where hundreds of candles in candelabras brightened the room. Aromatic bouquets of roses and jasmine with a pinch of citrus flowers filled the corners of the chamber. Rose stepped into a hallway connecting the ballroom and the kitchen and peeked inside. Lots of relatives and friends crowded the ballroom, and she smiled. She couldn't help but overhear the conversations going on in the ballroom.

"Good evening, Countess Estes. What an incredible gathering!"

"Good evening, Lady Perella. You look stunning, my dear," her mother said to the plump woman with a mole above her lip, who waved her feather fan as she scanned the ballroom. Countess Estes kissed the air around her friend's cheeks before she turned toward her companion. "Count Perella, what a pleasure to have you here."

"I can't believe how fast time flies. Just yesterday our Rose was playing with dolls," Count Perella said, kissing her mother's gloved hand.

"My daughters are my pride and joy. Make yourselves comfortable. Rose will join us soon," Countess Estes said before she turned toward Viscount Graziani, one of Rose's admirers, who had entered the ballroom from the terrace. Rose spotted the skeptical brow forming on her mother's forehead when she extended her hand to him.

"I'm glad you made it, Viscount. Rumors about your hunting accident and your misfortune reached us. I hope it's nothing too serious to stop you from dancing tonight," Rose heard her mother say.

Viscount Graziani kissed the tips of her mother's fingers. Rose pulled back, holding her breath when his gaze rested on the curtains where she hid.

"Nothing will stop me from dancing with our beautiful Rose. But where is she?"

His inquiry remained unanswered, for a group of loud young people approached. Their chatter and laughter consumed Countess Estes' full attention, and Viscount Graziani retired toward the dinner table. Rose looked around the ballroom and rested her gaze on her father who was talking with Count Asante. She shuffled behind the curtains until she was parallel with them.

"I'm thrilled you made it. We wondered if you'd honor us with your presence. Your affairs have kept you in Venice for the past months," her father said, approaching a tall man, who stood out from all of the men and women in the ballroom.

One evening, when they worked on the ledgers in the library, her father said that Count Asante would never understand her artistic qualities. In his opinion, with which Rose was in total agreement, he was the worst match for marriage.

Count Asante sipped his wine. "I'd never miss the chance to celebrate Rose's birthday, especially when I intend to win her heart tonight," he said with a presumptuousness that sent chills down her spine. "Did you consider my marriage proposal, Count?"

"Rose should be the one considering it, not me." Her father patted Count Asante's shoulder, resting his gaze on the curtains where she was still hiding. Rose stopped stirring, convinced that her father already knew she was there by the way he was clearing his throat.

"A girl shall listen to her father. It is the norm in our society. Women don't need too much independence. They indulge in senseless acts if they don't submit to a man's judgment," Count Asante said.

Count Estes frowned, and Rose did the same.

"Not for my daughter. Rose has been raised for greater things than marriage. Tell me, what news you bring from the capital?" he asked as he took a sip from his glass.

"We just received the new Grand Duke of Tuscany."

Rose left her spot from behind the curtains and slipped through the French doors into the garden where the bushes offered the perfect disguise. The cottage with its red roof came into view, and she stopped, trying to catch her breath. Then, she opened the door and searched for him.

CHAPTER 3

"Alessandro? Mr. Santini, where are you?" Rose asked as she closed the door.

The silence in the cottage amplified the tune of the crickets. Rose set the clothes on a chair and then followed the streak of moonlight on the floor. Alex stood in the heart of the room, gazing at her paintings. He had one hand on his hip and scratched the nape of his neck with the other. His shirt was too big for him, and his bones protruded through the fabric, but when he straightened his posture, he filled the entire room, sucking the air from it and leaving her breathless. She gulped when he extended his arm toward the cloth covering her latest creation, the one she was still painting.

"I wouldn't remove that if I were you," Rose said.

Their eyes locked when Alex turned around to face her.

"You're a good painter, Rose. Your focus is an interesting choice," Alex said in a low, husky tone that made her shiver.

"History is a daring avenue where one finds a supply of inspiration. Women of my time don't explore it because it's difficult," Rose said and turned away from him, passing her hand over the surface of the easel and refusing to look at him again.

"But not for you—"

"I decided to produce large-scale history paintings after my return from London."

Rose sucked air in short bursts as she looked at Alex. His oval face held the pleasant appearance of a gentle soul. His eyebrows were arched and thin, not the bushy black common to most men. Even the few wrinkles around the corners of his eyes made him dangerously attractive. Rose sighed. She should get away from him and fast because he would have to go back to his world one day. She should listen to all those bells in her brain telling her to leave, but she found that it was hard to move her feet. It was as if they had been pinned to the floor.

"They might fit you well," she said, pointing to the clothes she left on the chair. "It's time for me to head back. And don't get noticed if you decide to come."

"I'll do my best. We must talk about the portal, Rose. I must return. I don't belong here."

"Patience is a virtue, Mr. Santini," Rose said, taking a last look at him before she exited the cottage and vanished between the evergreens.

Alone in the cottage, Alex squeezed his fists. The full moon had opened a portal to another world as the girl in the hotel lobby had predicted, and it was just his luck that he had traveled to a time where he stumbled over Sophia's replica. The truth was he hadn't fallen in love with anyone since Sophia died three years ago.

***

"I couldn't save her. I killed Sophia," he cried, collapsing into his friend's arms and sobbing uncontrollably. Renaldo Bruno had been his best friend since high school, his best man at his wedding, and the one who had taken care of the funeral arrangements.

Every night, Alex returned to an empty apartment, and he found comfort in being surrounded by Sophia's clothes, her books, and her art collection while he listened to her favorite music—Bach. He played the robbery scenario countless times over in his mind. He stopped the car at a red light when the murderers approached them. One of them pointed a gun at Sophia and demanded money. When she said she had none, he shot her and snatched her gold necklace. Then, he shot Alex when he leaned over Sophia and shook her shoulder. That night, he wasn't lucky enough to die with her and their unborn child. Two weeks later, after he awoke from his coma, Renaldo told him that he had lost both.

Year after year, he marked her birthday with lilies and her favorite white chocolate cake. He stood in the dining room with the gifts between his seat and her picture. The first year, he bought a pin he thought she would like, with an emerald the color of her eyes, and a teddy bear for his daughter. Another time, he bought a first edition book he had discovered at an antique bookstore and a porcelain doll. Renaldo showed up without fail the day after her birthday and ate the delicious dessert, convincing him that Sophia would appreciate his gesture.

One day, Renaldo came to his apartment with boxes.

"It's time," he said, and Alex knew he was right. Sophia's dresses disappeared into the containers, and they took them to the church to give to the poor. He saved their wedding pictures on his cell phone, and wherever he went, Sophia traveled with him. He had nearly had a heart attack when he misplaced his phone.

He had spent two days in the ICU with Renaldo by his side. After Renaldo found it and brought it to him, Alex's face brightened while shameful tears drenched his hospital gown.

Seasons passed, and Alex buried himself in his work and attended the therapy sessions Renaldo recommended. From time to time, he allowed himself to visit the places he and Sophia frequented. Weeks became months, and months became years, and he forgot how to live. One day, he was putting apples in his basket in the marketplace when a woman with a child in a stroller stopped next to him. He patted the kid, who had curious eyes, and when he lifted his gaze, he gasped. The woman wore Sophia's pink silk pelisse. He took a step back and collapsed. The woman asked him if he was all right, but he didn't answer. He couldn't. That day he understood that pain didn't disappear, but became part of life.

***

Alex paced around the room a couple of times. When he spotted the clothes on the chair, fresh doubts about his circumstances replaced the earlier ones. He picked up the tight satin breeches, and a "Hell, no!" escaped his mouth. He had never seen anything more ridiculous than those pants he was expected to wear. Alex picked up the silk hose, and he checked the garters.

"No way am I wearing these," he said.

A sleeveless waistcoat topping the cotton shirt with a lace-edged jabot was the only garment that met with his approval. He left the cottage behind after he finished adjusting his attire, the light coming from the villa guiding him through the garden. Alex stopped in front of the cave, where darkness replaced the electrical limbs that had burned there a few hours ago. He searched the rough edges for a secret mechanism that would start the portal, and with luck, he could return to his time. His fingers slid along the stones, but he met with nothing but weeds and flowers in his search. He took a few steps and reached the other end of the cave. He sighed when he saw the shapes of trees and plants instead of the familiar sight of the stairs in the hotel basement.

Alex traced his steps back to the garden, the sounds coming from the villa catching his attention. He arrived at the terrace and halted. Women in sophisticated gowns and men in fancy outfits, similar to the one Rose had brought him, filled the ballroom. They looked outrageous by his standards, but fashionable in their time. Musicians played melodies belonging to Bach, and the soft tunes filled his heart with longing for his home. The image of his comfortable leather chair where he used to spend most of his evenings came to mind. He sighed.

Inside the ballroom, candles flickered, filling the hall with dashes of sparkling light. Couples and small groups talked in hushed, intimate voices. Women dressed in their ball gowns of silks and Indian muslins were laughing at the flirtatious men, their energy contagious as they played hide-and-seek with each other or engaged in small talk. The air smelled of perfume, powder, and candle wax.

Delicious aromas of cucumber sandwiches topped with cheese and salami reminded him of his hunger. Alex ate from the dozens of overflowing plates with meats, pungent cheeses, and garlic bread fresh from the oven, their sweet decadence pushing him to taste them all and to ignore the curious gazes of the girls who hid their faces behind elegant fans. He never stopped eating, perhaps from the nervousness he had felt since his arrival until the commotion on the dance floor pushed him away from the table. Everyone rushed to the heart of the ballroom where women and men parted, making a clear path between them. They stared toward the entrance, and Alex forgot about his hunger when Rose entered the ballroom. She waltzed between people, so gracious were her moves, and she didn't move a muscle when their eyes locked. The only acknowledgment he received was a slight bow of her head.

Rose took her place among the other ladies facing the men when the first dance of the evening started. Men and women held their hands in a flirtatious interlude with intricate steps and spatial patterns. They retreated to touch their right hands. Then, they changed quickly to touch their left hands before they fled again and returned to meet face to face and hold both hands. Alex recognized the dance as the minuet, a famous ballroom dance in the eighteen century, its blend of moves too complicated to follow.

Alex watched Rose as she danced in the arms of a man who captured her attention with his constant chatter. His breaths came coarser, faster, and he took a step forward when the man leaned toward Rose's left side and kissed her cheek. When she mouthed a faint "No," Alex clenched his teeth and pulled back, resting his back against a tall pillar and keeping an eye on the two of them. He couldn't help but listen to their conversation when they passed close to him.

"Miss Rose, would you do me the honor of accepting my proposal?" the man asked, and he dropped to one knee when the last notes of the song died.

Alex tilted his head and watched the expression on her face as she peeked from behind her fan. He tapped a foot while he waited for her answer.

"Count Asante, what are you doing?" Rose asked. "The matter requires careful consideration, and this is neither the time nor the place for a marriage proposal."

"When should I expect your answer, my lady?"

Never, you moron! Alex studied Rose intently, noting her perfect stance and uplifted chin. Rose wouldn't marry that windbag, not with her passion for life and adventurous spirit. Her mouth curled up in the right corner as she took two steps back.

"A girl has to consider all her options before making her selection. It's not something to decide on impulse," Rose said.

"Nothing would please me more than being the keeper of your heart," Count Asante said, kissing her hand and then playing with his bushy mustache.

Alex lifted an eyebrow. *The keeper of her heart?* He scratched his head while he assessed the man. By his clothes and the rings that glimmered on his fingers, Count Asante possessed varying forms of arrogance, from wealth and privilege to attractiveness and intelligence. But Alex couldn't stop the grin growing on his face.

"Enjoy this lovely evening, Count!" Rose dismissed herself as she pulled her hand from his grip, bowing and retreating toward a group of screaming girls. The stifled giggles shaking Alex's shoulders died when he met her sharp stare. There were a quiet confidence and an air of control about her that Alex admired.

Laughter and loud chatter filled the ballroom, the noise engulfing the guests until the sound of trumpets resonated throughout, capturing everyone's attention.

"The Count and Countess Estes," the butler announced.

A man dressed in a coat with golden buttons and tight pants bowed as he made his way across the room. Count Estes paused every so often, his moves gracious, in total contrast to the sharpness of his face. His broad shoulders and firm legs presented a man comfortable in his skin. He glanced at his wife, then back to the gathering. Countess Estes, a petite blonde with hair piled high atop her head, skin as pale as moonlight, and a bright smile. She leaned toward him and whispered something with which he seemed to agree. He raised a flute with a bubbling liquid, silencing the audience and the music. Rose flanked one side of her parents and another girl, who appeared to be another member of the family, the other side.

"We celebrate a fine time in our lives. Our Rose turns twenty, the perfect age for a young woman who has blossomed under our eyes and has become, as her name says a beautiful rose," Count Estes said. "Tonight, I bring you two messages. Annabella accepted Count Monti's marriage proposal. The wedding will take place after the required courting period." Count Estes paused and waited until the ovation and the shouts had died. "The second one is to announce Rose as heir of my estate."

Count Estes' words resonated throughout the ballroom and a hush fell over the hall. Annabella threw herself into a chair, crying softly. A tall man, as tall as Alex, with dark hair and a mole above his right brow, stepped forward and patted her hand. The girl looked at him and then at her father with tear-filled eyes.

"I need someone to carry forward my work and tend to my subjects with utmost care. You, Annabella, you think only of yourself, and everything is subject to your terrible jokes and amusement. How could you even imagine that I'd put in your irresponsible hands the handling of this household and my business?" Count Estes asked in a harsh tone.

"I am the rightful heir and, after the wedding, Fabio can carry on your job. You can't name Rose your heir. You can't possibly do this to me," Annabella said amid pitiful sobs.

"I've decided already. As for your future husband, Count Monti is busy enough with his own problems," Count Estes replied, crossing his arms over his chest as he shot piercing glances at the man by Annabella's side.

The man faked a smile. *Interesting*, Alex thought, looking from one member of the Estes family to the other.

"Mama, you can't let Papa do this. Don't ruin my life," Annabella cried, as she hugged her body and rested her forehead on her bended knees. A pile of golden curls brushed against the floor, and her skin turned red.

"Annabella, your dowry is set aside. Don't worry about your inheritance. When the time comes, you'll have your fair share," her mother said in a low voice as she stroked Annabella's hair.

Annabella looked at Rose, who had turned pale as she witnessed the whole uproar. Rose touched her father's shoulder, but he raised his hand, silencing her. She turned toward her mother who silenced her with a nod. Even the orchestra had a hard time concentrating on the next song. The women covered their faces behind their fans, and the men stared at Fabio, who stood close to Annabella, kissing her hand. Then, he lifted his gaze, fixing on a spot on the opposite wall. Alex looked toward the balcony too, then back at Fabio. Fabio nodded. It was but a flash, a movement that ended sooner than it started. The woman with black curls vanished, like a dream, and the curtains' movement became the only recollection of her presence at the ball.

In dire need of fresh air, Alex retreated to the terrace and hid in the shadow of a pillar. He smirked at some of the comments he heard through the open windows. The people in the eighteen century were no different from the ones in his time. They met at gatherings and gossiped about everything and everyone, without regard to who listened to their remarks.

"Poor Fabio, he chose the wrong daughter," one woman said.

"He did," another one agreed. "But why did Rose refuse his proposal?"

"It's a mystery. Weren't they childhood friends?"

"Rose stumbled onto something that made her push Fabio away."

"Count Monti, congratulations are in order," a man with a flute in his hand said. "With your wedding fixed, you can pay your debts now."

Surrounded by three men, Count Fabio Monti looked around. His cheeks flushed, and he breathed hard as if the men had sucked the entire supply of air from the great hall.

"Hell and damnation, gentlemen," Fabio blubbered. "Not here, please."

Alex peeked inside in time to see three pairs of eyes staring at Fabio. All men talked at once, creating a perfect cacophony where not a single word made sense.

"Have you no shame? You didn't make one payment. Should we bring in the collector or might you dare to explain what happened?" the first man asked.

"All I ask of you is that you wait a bit, and I will pay what I owe. Trust me on this," Fabio whispered, looking around.

"Your last chance, my lord. My patience is running low. All you'll see are the impressive sights of the local prison if you don't settle your debt," the second man said.

Fabio clenched his teeth and stormed onto the terrace. Alex retreated into the shadow of the pillar again. Fabio smashed the glass of Chianti by the marble stairs and descended into the garden.

"Rascal," Alex said and froze when Fabio kicked a chair that landed somewhere in the bushes. He was happy the waves of wisteria provided the perfect refuge.

"Fabio," a woman's voice pierced the night. She approached Fabio, and she cupped his face with her hands. Alex's eyes widened when Fabio pulled her toward him and kissed her until the only sounds in the night were her moans. Something familiar hit Alex when Fabio grabbed her hand and pushed her into a dark alley behind a bush.

Those voices, I heard them not too long ago, Alex thought.

"You didn't tell me you'd wed her so soon," the woman said.

"A temporary solution to a problem that threatens to become permanent," Fabio said.

"If you hadn't gambled away your inheritance, you wouldn't have to marry another woman. How foolish to think you could beat Lord Remington at cards. What were you thinking?"

"Now, now, don't be harsh. The end is near."

Fabio kissed the woman again, while their hands brushed over each other's bodies.

"Go back before they notice your disappearance," the woman said, pulling away from Fabio's embrace. She touched Alex with her gown when she passed by him, and the sweet scent of perfume marked her way. Fabio waited until she disappeared among the other guests, then he followed the same path.

Alex glanced at him, wondering what man would wed a woman for her money when his heart belonged to another. He couldn't intervene in these people's affairs. What if he, Alessandro Santini, did something wrong and he changed the future, as he knew it? What if the future was already changed while he roamed among sagas from faded times? He needed Rose. She must tell him how to open the portal.

CHAPTER 4

"Dance with me, Rose," her father said. "It's your night."

"You're gracious, Papa." Rose laced her arms around her father as they swirled around the dance floor.

"You are too. One, two, three," Count Estes counted, as they danced.

"Father, you've hurt Annabella by naming me the heir. It's her birthright, not mine."

"She's only a child charmed by her social position. She'll bring us to ruin if given a chance. And Fabio isn't to be trusted. Rumors about his gambling habits have reached my ears."

"You worry he's after Annabella's inheritance."

Rose stopped dancing and stared at her father, searching his face.

"Nothing is excluded," her father said.

As soon as the music stopped, Rose placed a kiss on her father's cheek. She leaned on his arm and bent to pick up the fan

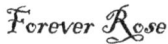

she had dropped on the floor. From the corner of her eye, she saw her father gasping, his cries filling the room.

"Rose!" Count Estes hollered before collapsing.

"Papa!" she cried, leaning over her father who was stretched out on the floor. Blood spilled from a wound in his shoulder where a dagger had hit. She put his head in her lap, stroking his hair.

"We need a physician!" Rose shouted while she reached for her father's hand. "Hurry!"

"Someone, go and fetch Dr. Guillermo!" a man shouted, looking toward the closest servant.

"On my way," a servant yelled back, his steps echoing in the ballroom.

"He will never make it in time," Rose said.

"Who could have done this?" Lady Perella asked the question on everyone's mind. "And why?"

"Count Estes and Rose were dancing when the swish of a knife passed by me. I yelled at him to duck, but I was too late," Count Asante said.

"This act has no precedent," another woman cried, clinging to a man's arm.

Rose looked at the woman who sobbed uncontrollably, unable to identify who she was. A man patted her hand, maybe her husband, by the way he held her close to him. Rose scanned the ballroom where she had been dancing and laughing with her friends only a few moments ago. The room was in complete chaos with servants and guests running in different directions.

"Did you see where the dagger came from?" Fabio asked a servant.

"I think from the balcony. I can't be sure," the servant answered, pointing to the upper tier. All followed the trajectory of the maid's arm. "I heard a noise, like a whisper, or a gust of wind, and turned my head."

"No one in here," another servant shouted from the balcony. "The intruder might have used the staircase leading to the garden."

"He might still be around," Rose suggested.

***

Alex was strolling through the backyard when he heard the shouts. He looked back toward the ballroom. People were screaming, ladies were fainting, and men were running out of the door when he entered the room. He stopped at the threshold, searching for Rose. *It couldn't have happened yet. Not yet!* His heart pounded in his chest, and a cold sweat covered his face when he reached the center of the ballroom. A sigh escaped from his mouth when he heard Rose asking for a doctor. He spotted the knife stuck in Count Estes's shoulder. A few more inches and the hit would have been successful, and the man just a memory. Count Estes's white shirt was soaked with blood while the color had completely left his cheeks.

"Let me pass. I'm a doctor!" Alex shouted, pushing aside the people gathered around the count. He kneeled beside him and checked his pulse. His heartbeat was weak. He opened the man's eyelids. *His eyes are blurry already. There isn't enough time to wait for the family physician to arrive.* Rose had instructed him to stay put and out of sight, but she wasn't a doctor. If the bleeding didn't stop fast, the man's life would be in danger. "Let's put him on a stable surface. Bring me alcohol and step away from the patient. He doesn't need more microbes and bacteria around his body," Alex said, as he waved his hands to push away the spectators. "And make sure to get me a needle and silk thread to sew the wound."

"I'll be right back," Countess Estes said, running out of the ballroom.

"Help him," Rose commanded the servants gathered around them.

Two servants picked up Count Estes and placed him on the nearest table. The count's cries grew strong, and the women covered their mouths. Guests hurried out of the door until only a few onlookers lingered in the ballroom. Alex ripped the count's shirt open and poured Chartreuse over the cut. He cleaned his hands with the rest of Chartreuse before he pulled the knife slowly out of his patient's shoulder. His moves were mechanical and skillful, his concentration on the patient's vital signs. He tore a tablecloth he pulled from one of the tables and pressed it over the cut.

"Where is the needle?" Alex asked, looking around the room.

"I'm coming, Doctor," Countess Estes cried as she ran with a basket in her arms. She pushed a woman out of her way and handed him the basket.

"Here, apply pressure to the wound," Alex instructed Rose. He opened the basket and pulled a needle from a pincushion. "Hold it to the candle flame," he said to a servant. "Where is the silk?"

"Allow me," Countess Estes said, searching among the clews. "Is this one good?"

"Give it to me," Alex said. He leaned over Count Estes and stitched the damaged vessels, closing the wound. Then, he dressed the injury with a bandage he prepared from the tablecloth. He wiped the sweat from his forehead, looking down at his hands covered with the count's blood.

"He needs to rest now," Alex said.

"Thank you, doctor," Countess Estes said, her voice shaking as she patted her husband's hand.

Count Estes swayed his head from side to side, while he kept his eyes closed and his lips slightly open. He ground his teeth as he tightened his grip on his wife's hand.

"I'm in your debt, doctor," he muttered. "Rose will take care of you."

"I'll tend to him, Papa," Rose whispered.

"Good," her father said before passing out.

"Papa!" Rose shouted, shaking his arm.

"He'll be all right," Alex said, and he pulled Rose into his arms.

She shook her head and wiped the tears staining her cheeks before she turned to face him.

"Follow me," Rose said.

"Give me a second," Alex said, wiping his hands with the rest of the tablecloth.

Rose grabbed a candlestick from a nearby table, walking ahead of him and out of the ballroom. She climbed the stairs to the first floor, and when they were out of everyone's sight, she said, "You must stay at the villa for the night. I'll take you to one of the guest rooms."

They walked in silence until she stopped in front of a massive oak door, the last on the second-floor hallway, and they stepped together into a room bigger than his apartment in Florence. The wall coverings were a mixture of red and gold, and he couldn't tell if they were silk or damask, but they felt soft to his touch. The thick curtains at the windows brushed against polished floors, and a poster bed occupied the heart of the room.

"What do you think you're doing by tending to Papa?" Rose placed the taper in a candleholder and then she rested her hands on her hips, chin pointed and back arching.

"I arrived at the right moment, don't you think?"

Rose fidgeted, switching her weight from one foot to the other.

"Yes, indeed, thank you for your help. But even if you saved Father's life, for which I will be forever grateful, how would you explain your intrusion?"

"Is this how you thank me?" Alex clenched his jaw, the sound of his own heartbeat thrashing in his ears.

"Have I not told you to remain unnoticed?"

Rose walked with slow, calculated movements, and he couldn't help but notice how different the woman was from his late wife. Sophia would have been terrified by the night's events, while Rose approached them with calm. Sophia had been a soft, delicate woman, who wouldn't hurt a fly. People who knew Sophia loved her because of her kindness. Rose was a warrior, beyond the women of her time. When she had applied pressure over her father's wound, not a muscle had moved on her face, and he couldn't stop admiring her confidence and poise.

"I'm talking to you, Alessandro Santini," Rose said when Alex didn't answer her question. "Father is too weak to ask who you are. I have enough on my plate without worrying about you too," she snapped.

Rose shook her head and took a deep breath, looking past Alex, out the window, and into the darkness.

"I must discover who orchestrated such an atrocity."

"How? You didn't see his face."

"And where were you?"

"In the garden," Alex said. "I ran to you as soon as I heard the screaming."

"Why?"

"I was afraid for you."

"You shouldn't be. I'm perfectly capable of protecting myself."

Alex sighed. He crossed his arms over his chest and said, "Of course you are. I wouldn't dare imply otherwise."

"Listen to me. If asked, you were traveling to Siena and stopped to request shelter. Your conscience dictated you to assist us when you saw what had happened."

"You're quite creative, Miss Rose. I hope you realize that without my help, your father would be dead by now," Alex said, arching his eyebrows. He touched her shoulder to stop her from trembling. His voice softened when he said, "You're the only one who knows who I am and how I can return to my time, Rose. Of course, I'll worry about you."

"Someone intended to kill my father, and what's scary is that the person might still be close by." Rose choked on her words.

What if the knife was intended for you? After all, this is the year of your death, Alex thought.

A gust of fresh air invaded the room through the wide-open window, and Alex looked down just in time to catch movement in the bushes.

"Put out the candle," he whispered. "Someone is outside."

Rose blew out the flame and tiptoed to the window. They stared at the gardens, the warmth of her body shocking him. It took all his willpower to pull himself two steps away from the woman. He cleared his throat a couple of times, trying to regain control.

"Can you spot anything?" she asked.

"Nothing," Alex answered.

"I'll go," she said, pressing her hands on his chest.

"By yourself? I can't believe this is happening." He imprisoned the woman between his arms, his mouth close to her ear. "You're staying here; you hear me?"

"You can't dictate what I do. I'm the one living here, remember?"

He sighed. "Then we're going together."

Rose pushed him out of her path. She went to the balcony and grabbed an iron ladder hidden beneath the climbing roses. She lifted her skirts, revealing half of the white stockings she wore, swung one leg over the rails, and descended into the garden while Alex stared.

"What are you waiting for?" Rose asked when she reached the ground level. "We don't have all night."

Indeed, for what am I waiting? If this woman has the guts to follow such an unpredictable route, so can I. Alex grabbed the ladder and was next to her in no time.

"I can't believe you did that," Alex muttered as he reached for her hand.

"Did what? You mean using the ladder? It's not the first time," Rose said, winking at him.

"You're managing yourself pretty well in that dress," he said, taking her hand in his, the frown on his face hidden by the shadows of the garden. A few crickets disturbed the quietness of the night, and the sound of her shoes kept them company.

"He'll hear us coming from miles away," Alex said, looking over his shoulder.

"Miles?"

"It's an expression. Take the shoes off."

"What?"

"You heard me. Take your shoes off. You didn't wear any a while ago, and it didn't bother you."

Rose removed her shoes and left them next to a bush, stepping barefoot onto the path. The pathway became rough. If they weren't in pursuit of a criminal, he would have carried her in his arms. *Damn that full moon and the portal.*

"Do you suppose he's still here?" Rose asked.

He scanned the garden, and every shadow of a tree or statue became a possible suspect.

"If he wants to finish the job he started," Alex whispered.

Rose cocked her head to one side, leaning toward him. "Oh, how I wish I could grab that rascal," she said, her voice taking a threatening note.

"We've lost him. We should go back," Alex said.

"Not until we find him."

"Are you going to grab him and beat him up?" Alex asked, studying her tiny physique.

"You don't always need muscles to win a fight. Brains are important too."

"Hmm, it will be rather interesting to see you thrashing him with your brains."

Alex tightened his grip on her hand. Rose was no match for characters with less than noble thoughts. The soothing sensation of her closeness to him, the strength of her will, and the tenderness of her touch added eeriness to the night's mystery.

"Even if he's still around, we would have no way of finding him," Rose complained. "I can't see a thing in this maze."

"Keep your voice down, just in case," Alex suggested, searching in every direction. "I don't recall passing the same spot twice in your gardens. He could be anywhere." He let go of her hand, and he walked ahead of her. They reached the center of the backyard and still found no sign of the intruder. A knot formed in his throat and his voice sounded harsh when he spoke. "How come you didn't scream when you first saw me? You weren't surprised at the vortex."

"The truth is I hoped one day someone would come from the other side and tell me what's there," Rose said, watching him.

"Really? Why?"

"Curiosity, I guess. I saw things, strange things on the other side, and I've always wondered what they were. There were flying coaches with no horses and coachmen, with lights, and loud noises."

"Cars," Alex admitted and laughed at her vivid description. "One day, I'll tell you about them."

Rose froze in her tracks at the leaves stirring nearby. She rested her hand on Alex's shoulder when she heard the footsteps of someone running in the opposite direction. Then, she grabbed Alex's hand and pulled him into the shadow of a tree. The rapid beating of his pulse along with his scent, a mixture of wind and salt, sent a tickling sensation down her spine.

"Stay here," Alex said, pushing her aside while he stepped in front of the man. "Halt!" he hollered.

"Or what?" the man asked, and he pushed Alex out of his way.

Alex grabbed the man's arms, throwing him to the ground. He tried to remove the man's mask when the man kicked him in his groin, his hands grabbing Alex's neck. They rolled a couple of times in the grass, and Rose gasped when traces of fresh blood appeared on Alex's shirt. Alex threw her a look, and the rogue pushed him aside with one shove and jumped over a fence. Alex ran after him, the unfamiliar terrain, branches, and bushes hindering his progress.

"He's gone!" Rose exclaimed, stopping next to him and looking toward the fence where the man disappeared.

"He can't be far. Let's search some more."

"Why did he hide behind a mask?" Rose asked, turning toward Alex. "I don't know who he can be."

Alex searched the ground. Rose followed the course of his gaze, and then they exchanged a look over the crumpled note that lay in the dirt road. She kneeled and gasped when she read the note. He brushed his hands on his pants to get rid of the blood and took the note from her hand. The letter bore no signature, but the words brought tears to her eyes. She wiped them away with the back of her hand and turned toward Alex, who put the note in his pocket.

"Someone else was the target and not Papa. The letter refers to a woman. But who from all the women present at the ball would be the target? It doesn't make sense at all," Rose said.

Alex kept his attention fixed on Rose. "One day it will," he assured her, cupping her face in his hands. They were warm, and his fingers were gentle. Rose wanted to touch the places where he had been injured but stopped herself.

"We shouldn't roam through the gardens at night. It's not safe. Let's go back in the house," Rose said, straightening her shoulders as she waited for Alex to follow her back to the villa.

Alex marveled at the air of authority Rose had so suddenly summoned, as if the anxiety of the preceding hours had been an inconvenient cloak she now shrugged off.

"Come with me to the cave. Maybe the portal will open again. The moon is still full," Alex said.

Rose took a deep breath, the stinging pain in her chest diminishing somewhat as she looked at him. A stranger in her time yet, at this moment, Alex was the only one on whom she could rely.

"I told you I didn't know how it worked. The first time it happened, it was a night like this one, with a bright, full moon. But the portal wasn't open the entire evening. Only for a while, and then nothing but darkness," Rose said.

Alex paused, shoving his fists into his pockets. "There must be a connection between the full moon and the portal."

"What type of connection?"

"Not sure yet. In my time, the news talked about a supermoon that was supposed to happen tonight. A young girl told me that the supermoon will open doors to other worlds or times."

"I've never heard of a supermoon."

"The supermoon forms when... " Alex started but stopped when he listened to a voice piercing the night.

"Miss Rose, where are you? Miss, your father, he needs you."

"My maid," Rose said, touching Alex's lips with her fingers. She straightened her dress and stepped into the light coming from candles that burned on each side of the path. "I'm here, Lucia. I'm coming." Then, Rose turned to Alex and pushed him onto the opposite path. "Go to the cottage and stay there until I send for you. You're not safe in the garden."

"What about you? What if your father needs me? I'm coming with you," Alex said.

Rose thought for a while and nodded. "Come." She strolled toward the villa, with the maid and Alex following close behind her.

"Her Ladyship would throw a fit if she knew you were alone with a man in the night," Lucia whispered, as she hopped from one side of the path to the other.

"Then she mustn't find out," Rose said. She didn't stop until they reached Count Estes's bedroom, and then she turned toward Alex, saying, "Give me the note."

Alex searched his pocket and gave her the note. Then, he rubbed his arms. The air had turned cold. It must have been close to midnight, and Alex still couldn't believe how much had happened in one day. Rose slammed open the door and entered the room. The few tapers that lit the bedchamber cast a pale light. It was quiet. Her father rested in his bed, his eyes half open, and her mother was holding his hand.

"Rose," Count Estes said, his voice weak.

"Papa, you have to rest. Please, don't talk." She leaned toward him and placed a kiss on his forehead.

"Oh, doctor, you're here. What a relief! I didn't thank you for saving my life," Count Estes whispered.

"You were lucky I was close by, Count," Alex said, as he approached the bed, stopping when he was just a few inches away. He bowed toward the Countess whose gown was stained with dried blood. Rose held her mother's shoulders and muttered something in her ear. The Countess nodded.

"Who would want to hurt my husband?" Countess Estes asked, looking at Alex.

"I'm sorry, but I don't know," Alex answered.

"They didn't intend to kill Papa. Here, this note says a woman was supposed to die tonight, and not him." Rose gave the letter to her mother who read it aloud, covering her mouth when she finished.

"Let me see," the count said, taking the note from his wife. "She dies tonight," he read. "Nothing in here provides a clue, and the writing is blurry. Oh, dear God, I'm so exhausted."

Count Estes closed his eyes and drifted off to sleep. Alex picked up his hand and did something, Rose couldn't tell for sure what, but he counted. His face was dull when he finished.

"Papa, wake up. Doctor Santini, do something," Rose said.

"Your father needs to sleep," Alex said. "I'll stay with him."

"You should rest too," Rose said, looking at her mother. "Why don't you go back to your quarters? There is no need for all of us to be here. The doctor knows what to do."

"I can't leave him alone," Countess Estes said, wiping the tears from her face.

"Miss Rose is right," Alex said. "There is no point for Your Excellency to be here. We'll send for you if anything changes in his condition."

Countess Estes sighed as she left the room, looking back one more time. Rose settled into one of the loveseats next to the window, resting her head on the cushion.

"Let me check your feet," Alex said. He raised her dress above the ankles, and when she protested, he silenced her with one stare. He cleaned the wounds that grazed the surface of her skin, and his touch was warm. No man had ever touched her body, and her toes curled up in delight. Scared by the effect he was having on her, Rose moved away from his touch, shoving her feet under her dress.

"I'll be all right," she said, cuddling between the pillows.

CHAPTER 5

Alex left Rose sleeping on the sofa as soon as the first rays peeked through a crack in the curtains and brightened the room. He retraced his steps from the previous night. When he reached the kitchen, he took into view the servants who were running back and forth between the stove and the storage room. The cook peeled potatoes, and then she cut them into small squares before dumping them into a pot where the chicken breast was boiling.

"What a scary experience!" the chubby woman with generous breasts said.

"Who would want the count's death?" Lucia asked while she dusted the slight traces of flour from the loaf of bread she pulled out of the hearth. She turned toward Alex as he stepped into the kitchen. "Here, Doctor, eat. You should put some meat on those bones."

Lucia placed in front of him a plate with a large slice of bread, cheese, and sausage from the last evening's feast. Alex slapped his belly when he heard the strange noises coming from his stomach.

"Thank you," he said. Since his wife's death, he had lost his appetite not only for food but also for life, his lean figure a testimony to his torment.

"Mr. Ciccio, aren't you hungry?" Lucia asked, turning to a middle-aged man with light brown hair who was reading a local magazine.

The man nodded as he looked around the kitchen, his gaze resting on Alex.

"Didn't you hear the story of Count Monti's ruin?" Mr. Ciccio chattered. "It was in the papers last week. Count Estes warned Miss Annabella about his financial state, but she didn't care. She said her money would be enough to pay off the creditors and bring Monti's estate to its former glory."

"Did he lose the entire fortune?" Lucia asked.

"He gambled his assets, and he's on a hunt for a wealthy wife," the cook filled in the details. "Lucia, the bread is burning!" she yelled.

"Young master is a troublemaker, I swear," Lucia said, pulling two scorched loaves out of the oven. "A poor choice of a husband."

"You're quite close to being a poor choice for a cook's help," the butler said.

"Indeed," the cook said, laughing and chopping onions as she sniffed her nose. "I don't blame Count Estes for his decision one bit."

"And Count Monti has to take care of his brother's widow, too. What a sorry state of affairs," Mr. Ciccio said.

The bell chimed, its echo traveling from one corner of the kitchen to the other. The Cook and Lucia looked toward Mr.

Ciccio, who pushed the last bit of food into his mouth and stormed out of the room.

"His Grace is calling," Mr. Ciccio cried on his way out. "Keep the food warm."

The cook nodded, and the room fell quiet after the butler left, the women concentrating on their tasks. Alex finished the last piece of bread and jumped when the door creaked, and a man entered. The newcomer stared at Alex, and then he hugged Lucia, his hair a wild combination of white and black.

"You scared the hell out of me, young man," the cook said, stirring the food.

"What's the matter? Did I miss anything?" The man picked a mug and filled it with cider, and something in his voice hit Alex. He searched the newcomer's face, as Lucia showed him a chair and placed a dish in front of him. She cut a slice of bread for him and broke off a piece of crust for herself.

"Didn't you hear? Someone tried to kill our Lord last night. He threw a knife at him, and if the doctor hadn't been there to help, God knows what might have happened," Lucia said.

"Don't say? Why would anyone want to hurt Count Estes? It doesn't make any sense at all," the man said, chewing his food while he waited for an answer.

The cook shrugged her shoulders and shook her head while the man emptied the plate. He rose from his seat, sweat forming on his forehead as Lucia opened the door to the garden. Alex left his spot too, for an invisible force urged him to follow the man. He remained a few steps behind them, close enough to hear what they were saying.

"Another hot day," the man said, as he wiped the sweat forming on his brow with the sleeve of his shirt.

"Stifling, indeed," Lucia agreed and searched the clear sky. "How is your family, Thomas? Are they still visiting relatives in Florence?"

"Yes, they'll stay there for the rest of the summer," Thomas whispered. "How is the count?"

"No way to say," Lucia answered. "The new doctor stayed with him through the night. Dr. Guillermo couldn't come."

"How is Miss Rose? Everyone knows she is close to her father."

"She slept in his room," Lucia said, "and the doctor too."

They stopped at a bush of yellow roses, and Thomas cut five of them. He cleaned the thorns and placed them in the basket that Lucia handed to him.

"Miss Rose loves them. I don't know why she wants fresh ones every morning."

"Word has it her mother loved them too. That's why she named her Rose. Our Miss puts them in a vase close to the portrait she keeps on her desk," Lucia said. "I've got to get going. Be safe, brother."

Lucia returned to the villa, and Thomas stood alone in the alley. He fell to his knees, cupping his head in the palm of his hands.

"What are you doing?" Alex asked.

Thomas jolted. He rose to his feet, and his stare was rigid.

"I'm pruning the roses. Miss Rose is fond of them," he said. "You're the doctor who saved our master last night."

"Yeah," Alex said, while he massaged his temples where a slight headache pressed. This world gave him the creeps. He peeked through the trees and caught sight of the cave. *I should check it again later in the night.* Slowly, he returned his gaze to the man who cleaned the dead leaves from the bushes and the weeds winding between the limbs of the plants.

"The maidens talked about what happened at the ball. Sad times, my lord."

"I can't shake the strange feeling we've met before," Alex said, and Thomas turned around.

"You might be mistaken. I've never seen you in my life. Good day, sir," he expressed in a low voice, and he took a turn at the first junction of paths. The thin fellow barely reached Alex's chin, and apart from a scar running from his left eye to the tip of his upper lip, he would have been considered a good-looking man.

"I see you've met our gardener." Rose startled him when she appeared unexpectedly from a side path. With sleep still in her eyes, she was out of breath when she reached Alex.

"Your gardener?" Alex asked, turning toward her.

"Yes, Thomas has tended to our gardens as long as I can remember. Is anything bothering you, Dr. Santini?" Rose asked.

He wasn't sure if the warmth in his body came from the sun or the woman, but one thing was clear: the brightness of her face in the morning was staggering. Rose was calm despite the fact that a criminal on the loose on her estate ruined her birthday party and almost killed her father.

"Your gardener resembles the one we met in the garden last night. The height is right, and the tone of his voice sounds familiar."

Alex frowned.

Rose laughed. "You can't be serious. Thomas?"

"Yes, your Thomas. I have a pretty good memory."

"Why would he want to hurt my father?"

"I have no clue. We should follow him," Alex suggested.

"Are you mad? Spying on my servants?"

"The place I come from has countless examples where servants killed their masters for a variety of reasons."

"You're scaring me, Doctor," Rose said.

"I've been scared since I arrived in your time."

Alex tore a rose from one of the bushes while they walked side by side toward the villa, and he placed it behind Rose's ear.

"What are you doing?" she asked.

"They are lovely, aren't they?" His voice trembled when he touched her skin. It had been a long time since a woman inspired any emotions, and his mouth became dry. "Just like you," Alex said, and he bit the inside of his cheek as soon as he spoke.

Her cheeks burned, and his heart threatened to break free from his ribcage when he kissed her cheek.

"Dr. Santini, you shouldn't act this way. Servants might see," she whispered, sounding alarmed.

"Your father didn't look well when I left his room. If I had antibiotics, I could guarantee his recovery," he said, ignoring the blush on her face.

"Antibiotics? What a strange name, Dr. Santini."

"Please, call me Alex. It'll make me feel welcome."

"We don't call one another by our first names unless we're family or close friends," Rose whispered.

"Then, think of me as your closest friend," Alex suggested, pinning his eyes on her. He ignored the tickling sensation in his veins, and he coughed a few times before he addressed her. "I've been thinking. Does your father know about the portal?"

"No one else knows. The gate to your world and the full moon are connected, and it will take a long time until the next one opens again."

"I had hoped I'd be able to return soon."

"Is my world such a despicable place for you, Dr. Santini?"

"Alex," he said. "You can't blame me for wanting to return to my time. My presence here is absurd," he mused. A tremor shook his body, and he turned his back to Rose. She circled her arms around him and pressed her face to his shoulders. When he tried to free himself from her embrace, she tightened her grasp.

"There's nothing I can do but keep you alive while you're here. If news about your coming from another time gets around, can you imagine what will happen?"

"Let's check on your father," he said. Alex freed himself from her embrace and walked ahead of her into the narrow path.

"Miss Rose, your bath is ready," Lucia hollered from across the main hall as soon as they stepped into the villa, and she pointed to Rose's curls scattered all over her face. The crumpled dress, a marvelous work of fashion once, was in pressing need of a thorough washing.

"Later," Rose protested. "Dr. Santini needs a bath."

Lucia frowned, and she shrugged her shoulders. "Follow me, Doctor," she said.

They crossed a hallway with warm sunlight where portraits of family members decorated the walls. Some men had somber faces, as others looked rather comical with their mustaches rounded up above the top lip. Dark, curly wigs flanked their faces. Only the women had loving, dreamy eyes, much like Rose.

They walked side by side until they reached a room on the back side of the villa. Alex gasped when he saw the porcelain bathtub with hot vapors afloat, and for the first time since his arrival in a different century, he relaxed.

***

On the other side of the villa, Rose met the penetrating stare of her parents. Her mother stood by the bed, holding her father's hand, her eyes on Rose when she entered the room. The bright, blue eyes looked like hollow spaces now, an image Rose wasn't accustomed to seeing. She ran to her mother and hugged her, and then she turned toward her father and kissed his forehead.

"Are you feeling better, Father?"

"If I could get rid of the numbness in my lower back, the pain would be tolerable." Her father moaned when he fidgeted in his spot between pillows. "We were fortunate to have the doctor at our festivity. Who is he?"

"I met him last night on my way back from the fields. He was going to Siena when thieves attacked his carriage. The coachman took off, leaving him alone on the dirt road. I assured him that we would help him get a new carriage," Rose blurted out and blushed. She didn't like lying, and she had done it for him twice. No way would she tell them about his passage through a magic portal in their garden. She had to protect the fool until he was able to return to his time.

"You can't go back on your promise. It's a miracle he escaped unharmed," her mother said. "What is his name?"

"Where are your thoughts today, Rose?" Count Estes asked in a pinched tone. His pale cheeks competed against the candles in his room. He had aged in one night, gray strands touching his temples.

"I'm sorry, Papa. I was thinking of the attack. It doesn't make sense for anyone to perform such an outrageous act."

"Many of my enemies would dance on my grave. Lord Remington would enjoy having control over the porcelain business in all of the Tuscany, for your suggestion to replace the flowers' designs with historical images frightened him."

"Because no one has tried it before," Rose said. "That's why he's scared."

"Exactly my thought," Count Estes said. He signaled her to approach while he leaned on one elbow, the struggle flushing his face. When he fell back on his pillows, a trace of fresh blood spread over his shift.

"You're bleeding, Giulio," Countess Estes gasped, her hand pointing to the spot steadily spreading over his garment.

"It's nothing. Don't worry, dear. Terrible times to be restrained in bed when I have problems to solve," he said.

Countess Estes wiped a tear from the corner of her eyes. She arranged two pillows behind his back and touched his forehead.

"What is it, Mother?"

"Your father is burning up. Where is the doctor?"

"Later," he whispered. "Come here, girl. There's something I need you to do."

"What is it?" Rose asked, holding his hands in her small palms.

"Go to Siena. Mr. Matteo is expecting you. I've sent word to harness the horses," Count Estes said, strengthening his grip on her hand.

"Anything for you, Father," Rose said, although it would be the first time when she went to Siena as her father's replacement and not for personal affairs. The Grand Duke's request to paint the Duchess's portrait before her departure to Vienna must wait. She would send an apology letter, convinced that the Duchess would understand the circumstances for the delay.

"Make sure to check the materials we've bought for the new production. We received orders from Florence, and our expansion depends on fulfilling their requests on time," he said, "and there's the theft issue." Count Estes patted her hands. "I'm sorry to put all of this on your shoulders, child. Elio agreed to help you. He'll know what to do."

"Yes, father," Rose whispered, and her voice cracked with emotion. The pounding in her head was loud. Rose rubbed her temples as her father continued.

"Check the ledgers, every entry, as I taught you. Last month I discovered a few suspicious logs. Don't tell a soul about your findings."

"I'll do as you ask," Rose said. "You suspect Mr. Matteo, don't you?"

"I wouldn't put the blame on him yet. If people have the opportunity, they will use it." Count Estes sighed, and he lowered his head to the pillow. "Don't worry, Rose, you'll do fine."

"Father, what about our guest?" Rose massaged her scalp until a feeling of lightness dispersed the aching sensation of thousands of nails hammering into her head.

"The doctor will tend to your father. Have you forgotten he's injured?" her mother asked, braiding her own hair. Last night's tears had carved fine lines on her face, and her eyes were bloodshot. "Are you sure you're doing the right thing by sending her to Siena, Giulio? She's nothing but a child."

Count Estes laughed, idly stroking his wife's cheek. "She will always be a child to you, Eleonora."

In her mother's view, Rose should stay at the villa and get married like her sister, instead of roaming around the property or doing the job of a man. If she could show her she was wrong, maybe her mother would stop insisting on accepting the marriage proposal Count Asante extended on her behalf, something she had no intention of doing.

"Papa is right. Someone has to keep an eye on the porcelain factory," Rose said, straightening her shoulders. "I'll ask Elio to look into the attack. He has the connections and the power to do so."

***

"Count Estes, Dr. Santini is here to see you." The butler announced Alex once he arrived at the count's sleeping quarters after he had finished his bath.

What a good laugh I would have in my time over this butler, Alex thought. If he hadn't accepted the invitation to present the laser pen at the press conference in Florence, he would have been in his home. The knot forming in his throat forbade him to swallow properly.

"Yes, yes, let him in." When the butler didn't move from the door, Count Estes deepened his tone. "Mr. Ciccio, you may let him come in."

With his back against pillows, pale, with dark circles around his eyes, breathing hard, as if the weight of the world pressed on his shoulders, Count Estes signaled him to approach. Countess Estes was wiping his forehead while Rose watched him from her spot by the window.

"Good morning," Alex said, and he marched toward the bed. "How do you feel this morning, Count?"

"The morning would have been good had I not been held hostage by this bed, doctor," Count Estes said, the note of sarcasm forming the illusion of a smile on his lips.

Alex checked his pulse and nodded. It didn't look good. "Let me check your wound," he said, pulling the blood-soaked bandages away from the cut. The region around the injury had blisters of yellowish discharge, and a rotten smell came from the wound. Alex washed the area, left it to air-dry, and touched the man's forehead. "Bring cold water and clean towels," he ordered. Nobody moved, and he turned to the butler. That man had a severe hearing problem. He waited, and the count's instruction sounded more like a whimper than demand.

"Do as he tells you, Mr. Ciccio."

"Yes, master," the butler answered and left the room.

Half an hour later, Mr. Ciccio returned with a girl, who was carrying a bucket of fresh water and towels. She was struggling under the weight that threatened to send her to the floor any moment. In two steps, Alex reached her, yanked the sheets from her hand and placed them on the bed. He took a towel, dipped it in water, and turned to the count.

"Your fever has to cool off fast."

Alex tore the count's shirt, replacing it with a wet towel. He did the same with the sleeves and wrapped cold towels around his arms, his eyes inspecting the wound.

"You need another surgery. The inflammation is not showing signs of retreat. We should keep the room as sterile as possible." Alex turned toward Mr. Ciccio and said, "Remove all these dirty carpets filled with bacteria and limit access to you and me. At least, until he shows signs of recovery."

"Gilda, do as the doctor says," Countess Estes said so fast that the girl tumbled over the carpet, landing on her belly. Alex thought that the entire situation would have been amusing if not brought forth by the gravity of the moment. Gilda jumped to her feet, and when she pulled the curtains down from their hooks, clouds of dust, like a storm in a desert, took over the room. Count Estes coughed, the dry, irritating cough choking him. Alex helped him drink from a glass of water while Mr. Ciccio signaled a footboy who was waiting in the hallway to enter the room.

"Take these away," Mr. Ciccio said.

Alex shook his head while he remembered the sterile medical instruments and the hygiene of the hospital where he used to work. To fix the count's shoulder would be child's play in his time, not a genuine challenge as it was in this century. His gaze followed Rose, who hadn't said much since he had stepped into the room. When she opened the windows, streaks of golden light invaded the room.

"Fresh air will do you well, Father," Rose whispered.

A gust of wind slapped across her locks. She stared at her father, her back resting against the edge of the window. Alex checked the count while he dozed. Cold sweat covered his body, and mild seizures shook him from time to time. He pressed two fingers to the count's neck and counted.

"Mr. Ciccio, I must open the wound and clean the infection to stop it from spreading to his internal organs. You can either help me or stay out of the way."

"What should I do?" Mr. Ciccio asked.

"Hold him down," Alex said, pressing his fingers over the blister. "If the fever keeps rising, it may be too late." He froze with his hand in midair when he remembered the briefcase, the one he carried with him when he passed through the portal. The laser pen would close the wound and leave only a tiny mark on the man's chest. "I'll be right back," Alex said as he went toward the door. "Mr. Ciccio, bring a sharp knife. Hurry!"

"Did you ask for a knife? Why? I can't follow such an outrageous command," the butler snapped. His gaze wandered from his master to the doctor, waiting.

"Mr. Ciccio, if the procedure doesn't happen, your master will die because of the inflammation. The bacteria will spread throughout his body. I must contain the infection before it's too late," Alex said, swallowing hard, his heart in his throat. *Of all the butlers in the world, I had to end up with the most irritable one.*

"Maybe we should consult another doctor."

"We don't have the luxury of waiting for another physician unless you want to go down in history as the butler who killed his master," Alex said. He opened the door and pushed Mr. Ciccio aside, running down the hallway. Behind him, Alex heard the butler running too. As soon as he reached the cottage, he slammed the door, grabbed the briefcase from the table where he left it upon his arrival and returned to the villa.

CHAPTER 6

"Hold it over the candlelight. Make sure to turn the blade on both sides," Alex said when the butler returned with a knife. He searched inside the briefcase, frowning.

"What are you looking for?" Rose asked as she peeked inside his briefcase too.

"I'm looking for this," Alex said, pulling out a shiny tool round at both edges and with a small button on one side.

"What's that?"

"The laser pen I'll use to burn the wound." Alex pressed the button, releasing a beam of blue light. "I'm glad that it's still working," he said, placing the pen on the nightstand after he had tried it a few times.

"Doctor, the knife is quite hot." Mr. Ciccio pointed to the blade in his hand, wiping the sweat from his forehead with the sleeve of his shirt.

"Give it to me," Alex said. He approached the count and signaled Mr. Ciccio to hold him by his shoulders. At the knife's contact with the skin, an odor of scorched meat spread through the room. The count's screams had echoed throughout the entire house before he fainted.

Alex pressed the sides of the wound to remove the infection, and then he cut the contaminated skin around the injury while Rose wiped the blood. After he had dried the skin, he picked up the laser pen and moved it slowly over the cut, the blue light closing the lesion and leaving a barely visible pink line on the count's shoulder.

"What is that thing?" the butler asked. "Witchcraft? Are you a witch doctor?"

Alex raised his brows and rolled his eyes. "Mr. Ciccio, there are no such things as witches. This instrument was used to burn wounds in the hospital where I worked."

Mr. Ciccio shrugged his shoulders. "Never saw one before."

"That's because you're not a doctor."

"How does it work, Dr. Santini?" Rose asked.

"The pen uses the sun to recharge and transforms the energy into the blue beam you saw. It's the cleanest method to close wounds. The healing process is faster than with ordinary ways," Alex said satisfied he had found a way to present a twenty-first-century invention to these people.

He had shaken his head before he opened the patient's pupils, which were blurry with fever.

"All we can do now is wait. Countess, keep his lips wet and give him two pills from this bottle every six hours. It will reduce the fever." Alex placed the container with his emergency aspirin into the woman's hand.

"I'll do as you say." Countess Estes blinked rapidly and tightened her fingers around the bottle. "Is it going to help him?"

Alex nodded. "I hope so."

"Where are you going?" Rose asked when Alex picked up his briefcase from the table.

"To sleep," Alex said and patted her shoulder.

"Why now?" Rose asked. "It's midday."

Alex turned around before leaving the room. "I haven't had one hour of sleep since I got here," he said.

He needed to get away from Rose and her father, and their inexplicable experience. Once he reached the cottage, Alex crawled into bed without bothering to strip off his clothes or to lock the door.

***

One, two, three knocks he had counted before he opened his eyes. *What the hell is this?* Alex grabbed his temples. He sucked in the cold air in the room, his lungs cramped with the effort, and he dragged his feet toward the door.

"Alex? Dr. Santini, are you in?"

He would recognize her voice anywhere. An immediate need invaded his groins, and he blushed at his body's unexpected reaction.

"May I come in or shall I wait here?" Rose asked from the other side of the door.

"Of course, come in, it's your home," Alex said with a strange note in his voice. His unbuttoned shirt hanging loosely over his pants, the ruffled hair, and sleepy eyes were a clear invitation to scandal. Rose looked visibly shaken when she met his penetrating stare, and he retreated a few steps, leaving her enough space to sneak into the house. "How's your father?"

"He's better now, thanks to you."

"Is he awake?" Alex asked.

"Yes, and he would like to see you."

"Have you been to Siena already? You had some business matters to attend to."

"I couldn't leave you all by yourself," Rose said. "I was worried about you."

"Why? I'm perfectly capable of taking care of myself," Alex said, as his eyes bored into hers.

Rose didn't answer, and her closeness was more than enough to wake up sensations he hadn't experienced since he lost his wife. The guilt of not being capable of protecting his wife and his unborn child didn't let him approach another woman, and the one standing a few feet away from him, with her hands on her hips, would be no exception.

"You still don't understand the gravity of your situation, Dr. Santini."

"There you go again with Dr. Santini. How many times have I asked you to call me Alex?"

"Things are going from bad to worse," Rose whispered. "Everyone is worried about you."

"Why?"

"They thought you left us."

Alex fell into a chair, massaging his temples, while his elbows rested on his knees. "And where did I go?"

Rose closed the door and stopped in front of him. She extended her arm and touched his shoulder. At the contact with the warmth of her hand, Alex jumped to his feet, pushing her hand away.

"Get away from me, all of you, with your plots, and crimes, and useless courtesy."

"I can't control nature. I wish I could open the portal and throw you back into your world, you, insensitive piece of wood."

"What did you call me?" Alex leaned toward Rose, his nose inches away from hers, his face on fire.

"Let's start all over."

"Let's do that," he said, sighing.

Her lower lip trembled, and she ground her teeth. "I brought you food. You may be hungry."

"Why don't you tell me about your trip while we eat?" Alex suggested while he tried calming down the heavy beating of his heart.

"I suppose I can do that much." Rose opened a basket and pulled out cheese, salami, and fresh bread. Then, she said, "Siena is beautiful. One day I will take you there."

"I know the city from my time, the new Siena."

"My time, your time, this discussion terrifies me. Alex, remember, no one knows you're from the future. Don't go around parading your knowledge and the new instruments you brought from your time. People will ask questions, and you're not ready to answer them."

They were sitting one foot away from each other and sharing a meal as if they had been friends all their lives. He arched his eyebrows and concentrated on the food in front of him, hard boiled eggs, cheese, olives, baked bread, and citrus fruits. Fresh coffee would have been better, but instead, he reconciled with the tea the woman had brought him.

"My aspiration is to become a history painter with subjects from classical history, mythology, and scripture," Rose said warmly.

"An unusual choice for a female artist," Alex said, chewing on his bread. "Where did you learn about creative arts?"

"I studied in Florence. My favorite artist was Leonardo Da Vinci."

"Complex, mind-blowing genius," Alex added with his mouth full.

"Fascinating man, especially his disappearance for two years," Rose said. "History says that he entered a cave, much like the one on my father's estate, on December 1476, and he returned in February 1478. No one knows where he had been for fourteen months."

"I've never heard of it, but then again, I'm not an artist. In med school, they taught us about the human body and how to treat illnesses." Alex paused, and he remembered the supermoon advertised on TV before his departure. He shook his head and asked, "Did you accomplish the tasks your father entrusted to you? You had to check ledgers and catch thieves."

"I didn't find any thieves, but I hired someone to look into it in my place. He has more experience in handling these matters."

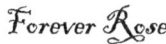

"Like a secret agent?"

"You're close. His name is Elio Marotto, the chief of the secret police and one of my father's best friends. Mysterious man—I wonder what his story is."

"What makes you think there is one?" Alex asked.

Her voice was soft when she spoke.

"His eyes tell a story even when his lips are sealed. Papa said that a long time ago he lost the woman he loved and buried himself in his work."

Just like me, Alex thought, pushing the chair back while he walked around the room.

"What about catching the man who tried to kill you or your father? I remember seeing a woman on the balcony, long black hair, and intent look. She pulled back when she realized I was watching her."

"That is a vague description of the woman you saw. Wait," Rose said. She went to her drawing room and returned with a sketchbook. She started to draw, and the lines made no sense, circles, then ovals, and more lines. Alex followed her hands as they flew over the page. She folded the page and started again, and the image took shape.

"I'm pretty sure she is the woman I saw on the balcony," Alex said.

"She's my friend, Viola, and she was a guest at my party." Rose sighed and leaned back in her chair. "I doubt we will find the rogue."

"The dagger is the key to its owner," Alex said. "Those carvings in the wood handle look exquisite."

Rose crossed her arms over her chest, her gaze fixed on an imaginary point on the wall. It was hard to say where her thoughts were. His own were navigating back and forth between telling her how much she reminded him of his late wife and his fear that she would die without him being capable of moving a finger to save her. He stretched his arm toward her and touched her hand. She jumped at the contact and rose from her chair. Alex circled the table, stopping in front of her.

"Am I making you nervous, Rose?" Alex asked, leaning toward her. Before giving her time to react, he claimed her mouth, his heart rapping against his ribcage, threatening to break free. She pushed him away, her strength no match for his own, while he moved his hands to the back of her neck, keeping her hostage in his embrace.

"Have you nothing to say?"

"I'm going to pretend you didn't kiss me, Alex. Probably, in your world, you're all savages used to taking women by force," she said.

He scoffed and released her from his grip. Then, he stepped away from her and lowered his gaze.

"I'm sorry. I don't know what happened. I should go and check the cave."

"We'll check it together. Come to the Villa," Rose said. "Father invited you to dinner, and he has something to ask you."

***

After Rose had left, Alex faced a genuine dilemma when he looked at the knee-length satin pants and those horrible stockings. If he removed the fluffy lace hanging loosely over his fingers, the shirt might fit.

"Silk buttons on the side," Alex huffed as he turned the shoes on each side. He decided to wear his own pants and shoes and cut the lace edges from the shirt's sleeves. A tunic with a golden border went on top and, after a few pirouettes in front of the mirror he left the cottage to meet Rose by the cave.

A fading sun sent a pale light over the garden, and the only sound came from his frantic breathing. In front of the cave, he paused, for he noticed a light coming from inside. He pushed aside the thick curtain of ivy and entered. There were flickering candles on the floor. A musty smell invaded his nostrils, tickling his nose and making him sneeze. Drawings covered the limestone. He watched as Rose passed her hand over them.

"They look like falling stars," she said. "Legend has it that every time a star falls from the sky someone is about to die. What if Father had died that night, Alex?"

What if you were the one who was killed? Alex stopped right behind her and followed the trajectory of her hand. "I should take you with me to my world," Alex suggested, biting his lower lip as Sophia's image came to mind. The authorities never caught her assassins, his wife's case going down in the archives as an unsolved mystery. He had lost sleep, weight, and the desire to live. He had immersed himself in his work to ignore the passage of time and the emptiness left by her death.

"My place is here, Alex, even if my life is in danger. I can't follow you," Rose said, leaving the cave and sitting on the grass. Alex mimicked her movements. He passed his fingers through the blades, and their touch was cold against the warmth of his palm.

"It doesn't look like I'm going anywhere myself," Alex whispered. "I hoped that if I stared long enough at this cave, the vortex would form again." He sighed, his head falling over his shoulders.

Rose pointed to the sky. "There is no supermoon, Alex," she said. Only two-thirds of the moon dominated the gray expanse where billions of stars gleamed. "Why don't you tell me about your world?"

"My world?"

"I saw bits of it when I visited," Rose said, flattening her dress. She leaned on one elbow, supporting her head, and the breeze scattered her hair. When a nearby bush caught a few of her locks, he freed them, playing with them for awhile.

"My world is beautiful, just like yours. People meet and fall in love every day, people die and suffer the same way as they do here."

"What's amazing in your time?"

"Amazing?" Alex chuckled. "There are many amazing things in my time. What would a beautiful girl like you enjoy?" He paused, shaking his head before he said, "Hmm, I think you'd love the cinema, or the cell phone, or maybe the car."

"Cinema, cell phone, and car," Rose repeated. "What are those things?"

"In a cinema, people watch movies. A huge screen, like a big canvas, is in the center of the room, and a projector, a type of machine, casts images of people and places. People perform roles, and they tell a story."

Rose clapped her hands and rolled on her belly, her head leaning on her fists. "Like the theater or the opera. I'd love to go to your cinema."

"You'd like it," Alex added and brushed a rebel loop from her eyes. "What else would you like to find out?"

"Cell phone sounds important. What is it used for?"

Alex told her that cell phones were a great way for the people to communicate with each other over vast distances. People of his time couldn't live without their cell phones. He still had his in the cottage. One day, he would show it to her.

"Can they use it if they belong to different times?"

Alex laughed. "No, they can't. They have to live in the same century to connect."

"How far away is your future from mine?"

"Three hundred years, Rose. You would be long gone by the time I'd be born."

He watched her as she pulled her knees under her chin. He pretended the grass held the secret of immortality and listened to her as she said, "That makes me three hundred years older than you, Alessandro Santini."

"You are not old, you are perfect, and from where I stand, I'm fifteen years older than you," he said, pulling her into his arms. Her body tensed, but she didn't pull away from him. She leaned against his chest and rested her hand over his heart. Now that he had found her, there was no way he would let her go. He would drag the woman by her hair if he must, but he would make sure Rose lived.

"The day you depart, don't look back," Rose said as a matter-of-factly.

Alex narrowed his eyes. "Why are you telling me this?"

"Just in case I didn't make it," she said with regret in her tone.

"You will live to be an old lady, Rose Estes. Look at me." Alex lifted her chin, forcing her to stare at him, and wished he could drown in the green waters of her eyes. "It's time to go and meet your father. He may wonder where we are, and I don't believe you're prepared to answer uncomfortable questions."

The weeds from her dress fell when she jumped to her feet. She arranged her curls back into the braid, hiding a smile behind her raised arm. The natural way he inquired about things, without regard to the etiquette imposed by her society, fascinated her. Perhaps, the years of evolution made people outgoing and blunt, very different from all those old norms her own people were forced to live by.

They walked side by side, listening to the garden's noises, and she shuddered when he took her hand.

"Here people don't hold hands. Our rules forbid personal contact in public. Only those who are engaged are allowed to walk as we do," Rose whispered.

"Does it bother you much?"

"No, not at all. I'm enjoying the time I'm spending with you." The beating of her heart grew loud, pounding in her ears. His proximity heated her body in ways she never thought possible. "Aren't you curious about my time? Is there anything you would like to find out?"

"Everything of interest is in front of me," Alex said.

Her pupils dilated, a shadow crossed her face, and she chased it away with a smile.

"I know," Rose whispered. "The cave won't go anywhere anytime soon."

"The cave?" Alex asked.

"See you at dinner," she said, leaving him staring after her.

CHAPTER 7

Rose smiled to herself, recalling the look of surprise on Alex's face. He needed help adjusting to her time, and without her assistance, she doubted he would make it past the end of the week.

"You seem distracted tonight, Rose, or shall I call you sister-in-law," Fabio said, startling her.

Chills crawled up her spine, and her palms became sweaty.

"Fabio, I didn't see you standing behind the bushes. One might think you're a thief by the way you hide, or even worse—an assassin."

"My dear, what wrong have I done to make you reach such a conclusion? I find your philosophy disturbing."

Fabio tore a bud from a nearby bush and played with it before he tucked it into a pocket of his vest. Rose turned around and checked for signs of Alex, who was supposed to be right behind her.

"I'm sure it will take more than a woman's small talk to offend someone like you," she said, flattening her dress and ignoring the smile on Fabio's face.

They entered the foyer together and stopped when they reached the dining area. Rose turned toward him and said, "I didn't congratulate you on your engagement. Annabella will make an excellent wife."

Fabio sighed.

"I wish it would have been you, Rose. I always assumed we'd marry once you came of age."

Rose touched Fabio's cheek where the beginning of a beard appeared and said, "You were only my best friend. Let's go inside. They are waiting for us."

She was the first one to enter the dining room, and then Fabio followed. Annabella's face brightened when he kissed her cheek.

"I thought you forgot about dinner. Fabio offered to come and rescue the doctor from your spell," Annabella said. "But where is he?"

"Dr. Santini is here," the butler announced after Rose occupied her place at the dinner table. The chatter stopped when he entered the room.

"Good evening," Alex said as he followed the butler, who showed him a seat across from the count, at the head of the table. Rose sat to his left and Annabella in front of her sister. Count Estes occupied the place on the other side of the table, looking much better than Alex remembered. His wife sat on his left side and Fabio on his right. A bit of red colored his face, and he seemed in good spirits.

"So, you are the great Dr. Santini," Fabio said.

"Have we met before?"

"I'm Count Fabio Monti. I'm in your debt for saving his Excellency's life."

"I only did what a doctor should do."

"Your work is remarkable, Doctor. The entire estate talks about the object you used to burn the wound. I've never heard about it. What is it?" Fabio asked.

"Dr. Santini isn't from around here," Count Estes said, and his brows arched above his dark eyes.

Annabella inspected him with a typical woman's curiosity. Alex knew that he looked out of place among the people around the dining table.

"I was on my way to Siena when the attack happened," Alex said.

"Your misfortune was our luck. You arrived at the right moment," Countess Estes said, and everyone nodded.

"I'm glad I could help," Alex said, staring at Rose, who knitted her brows. That night when they stumbled over the note, they decided to keep the letter's affair private. Rose took the note with her to Siena, and she gave it to Elio. Other than her parents and Alex, no one on the estate needed to know that the chief of the secret police was looking into the attack.

"You were lucky to escape unharmed from the thieves," Fabio said. "We live in turbulent times. It's best to keep your eyes open at all times."

"Do you think they followed the doctor here?" Annabella asked. "Were they the ones who attacked Papa?"

"The political situation in the entire area is blurry indeed," Count Estes said, as he signaled the butler to serve dinner. "Nothing is out of the question, especially with our new Duke."

"It's going to change when Francis becomes Holy Emperor," Alex said. "His wife will pull all the strings."

"Do tell," Count Estes said. "And she'll be the one to reign in his place?"

"Of course."

"How do you know such things, Dr. Santini?" Fabio asked.

"Dr. Santini is a visionary," Rose said, shaking her head. That man had to stop revealing facts from the future before anyone took notice. Rose kicked Alex under the table. His lips opened a little. He closed them without saying a word when she touched a finger to her lips, silencing him.

"Count Asante is expecting an answer to the marriage proposal by the end of the month," her mother said, turning toward Rose.

"Is he?" Rose and Alex asked in one voice. He clenched his fists, and she narrowed her eyes until they became two smooth lines on each side of a nose the size of a button.

"I'm not interested," Rose said, looking at Alex. "I have other plans."

"No, she isn't," Alex added, not taking his eyes off her. "Her plans are more important than marriage."

He became silent when they stared at him. The marriage proposal left him uncomfortable, although he had no reason at all to feel bothered by Rose's future. As soon as he figured out how to access the portal, he would return to his time and forget about her and her world. Alex emptied the glass of wine in front of him, and he signaled the butler for a refill.

"Rose, let's go to the studio," Count Estes said, offering her his arm. They talked about her visit to the factory, and she told him how Mr. Matteo walked her through the ledgers, and that he was very helpful during the salary negotiations. Then, Count Estes steered the discussion toward Dr. Santini and his arrival at Luce Del Sol just in time to save his life. He suggested that Rose should ask Dr. Santini to travel with her to Siena and tend to the workers for a generous wage.

Rose dropped her bottom lip at her father's suggestion, although the idea of spending every day in the doctor's company wasn't entirely unpleasant. That way, it would be easy for her to keep an eye on the doctor and to protect him, even from himself if she must. She encouraged her father to return to the dining room, assuring him that she would be right behind him after she straightened the ledgers on his desk. With one gulp, she swallowed a mouthful of Amaretto, the bitter taste of delicious chocolate reminding her of the first time when she sneaked inside her father's studio and took a sip directly from the bottle. Her father didn't scold her then, but he sent her straight to her room and forbade her to leave until she took a good nap. Rose dropped the glass when she heard Fabio whispering in her ear.

"Stealing from papa's drinks, are you?"

"You shouldn't be here," Rose said. "Annabella will come looking for you."

Fabio leaned toward Rose. "She is helping her mother with refreshments," he said. "So, what's new in Siena? Is everything in order at the factory?"

"Yes, everything is how it is supposed to be, Fabio," Rose answered, his fixed stare making her uneasy.

"Annabella mentioned theft. Is that right?"

"She should mind her own business and you too."

Rose turned toward the door when Fabio grabbed her wrist. A rush of adrenaline spiked through her veins at his rough touch.

"Everything happening in the factory and the estate is my problem too. We're family," Fabio said, tightening his grip. "Do you think Asante is a better fit than me to handle the affairs?"

"What are you afraid of? That he will be a better son-in-law than you?"

Fabio seized her arm, twisting it to her back. Chills went up and down her spine when his breath brushed against her skin.

"Never," he whispered. "I still picture you as my wife, Rose. There's enough time to change your mind. You'll be happy with me."

"You'll always be my friend, Fabio. You're someone else's love now. It's not healthy for you to entertain romantic feelings for me."

"If I can't have you, then I'll make sure no one will."

"Stop, Fabio, you're hurting me!" Rose shouted as she fought to escape from his hold.

"You should listen to the lady!" Alex hollered and, with a strength he didn't realize he possessed, he grabbed Fabio, pushing him onto a nearby sofa. Although the men were of similar height, Fabio was more muscular than Alex was. He could have easily knocked him off his feet if he wanted. A vein throbbed on the side of Fabio's neck when Alex lowered his tone. "Your fiancé is looking for you."

Fabio brushed off his clothes and jumped from the sofa. He frowned and cursed to himself.

"Doctor, what do you think of this?" Fabio asked, and he pulled a rectangular object from his pocket.

Alex gasped at the sight of his cell phone in Fabio's hands.

"I never saw anything like it before," Alex said.

Fabio played with the phone for a while, and Alex prayed he wouldn't learn how to turn it on. The man made his blood boil, and Alex tried grabbing the phone from his hand. Fabio took two steps back, tucking it into his pocket. His face seemed even darker than his eyes.

"We'll meet again, Doctor," Fabio said, closing the door behind him.

"Of course," Alex muttered, checking the bruise on Rose's skin. "Are you hurt?"

"Not badly. What was that?"

"My cell phone. I hid it at the bottom of my briefcase. How did he find it?" Alex didn't tell her that if by chance Fabio turned the cell phone on, all would be lost. His wedding picture was on the screen. "I need the phone back. In his hands it's a destructive weapon, Rose," he said, his voice choked with emotion.

"We should follow him. His estate is over the hill," Rose suggested, as she buttoned Alex's vest. "Aristocrats are proud men, Alex, pay close attention to your attire."

"Since we're here, let's take a look at the dagger," he said, pushing her away from him.

Rose lifted the knife from a drawer in her father's desk. Close to the top, a monogram looking like a crown was imprinted in the handle. It had gildings with golden leaves on both sides, and a blade as sharp as the winter's wind. Alex passed his finger over the edge, and a line of blood appeared.

"You're bleeding," Rose cried, covering his finger with a handkerchief. "You shouldn't go around telling everyone things from the future."

Alex lifted her chin. "You're right. My mother told me to think first, and then talk, but somehow I always mix up the order." He threw the dagger into the air and caught it with the other hand. "Where would you buy an encrusted dagger around here?"

"There's a merchant in Siena. He imports merchandise from the West Indies. He should recognize the dagger and tell us who bought it," Rose answered.

"It's a start."

Rose rose up on her toes when she said, "Meet me in front of the cave, later tonight. Then, we'll go to Fabio's estate."

"You can bet on it."

***

They rode together until they reached Fabio's estate close to midnight. Everyone and everything slept. Rose tied the harness to a tree, and they stopped at the front door.

"It's locked," Rose said. "Follow me."

She grabbed her skirts and tied them around her waist, exposing her white stockings. Rose threw her shoes into the grass and began climbing the iron ladder she pulled from under the wisteria that covered the façade of the house. Ascending took all her strength, and Rose was quiet when she reached the balcony.

She rested her hand on Alex's shoulder as she gasped at the sight of Fabio's naked body.

"Who do you think the woman is?" Alex asked as he peeked through the window inside the room.

"One of the maids, for sure," Rose said.

The woman's mouth followed the line of Fabio's neck, sliding over his chest in small circles. Rose couldn't tear herself away from the window. Her cheeks were burning, her legs were shaking, and beads of sweat soaked the back of her dress. She covered her mouth as she stared at the woman with waves of dark hair and skin without fault. She closed her eyes, taking deep breaths, her mind traveling to the romance novels she read. After a few breaths of fresh air, Rose turned around in time to see the woman wrapping a robe around herself. Her steps were subtle, her pace steady. She closed the door to Fabio's room and left him alone on the bed they had just ravished.

"Only a couple of hours has passed since Fabio hugged Annabella and he is already with another. I'll kill him with my bare hands and his slut with him!" Rose shrieked, teeth hitting against teeth, her tone as sharp as a razor blade. She clenched her fists as if ready to fight. Alex grabbed her shoulders, pressing her against his chest. He circled her body, and the pounding of her heart against his chest was strong.

"His clothes are all over the floor. Once he's asleep, we'll grab your cell phone, and then we're out of there," Rose said, ducking when Fabio approached the window.

It had started to rain. Branches swung back and forth in the nearby trees. Raindrops pounded over the land slowly at first, their tap intensifying by the minute. With his hands on his hips, Fabio stood naked in front of the window, and Rose swallowed hard. Alex covered her eyes.

"Stop staring," he whispered.

"I can't," she said, pushing his hand aside. "He is gorgeous."

Alex sighed. This woman was a little devil in disguise. Alex pulled Rose next to him, his head touching hers. They waited until they heard Fabio snoring, then they sneaked into the room through the window. Alex gave Rose a cape he picked up from the floor, keeping his eyes on Fabio, who was still sound asleep in his bed. He lifted Fabio's vest and checked the pockets. He turned toward Rose and prepared to tell her that he couldn't find the cell phone when she shushed him. He lifted his shoulders, arching his brows. She pointed to the table, next to an old armchair, and he followed the direction of her finger. He grabbed the phone and gasped when he saw his wedding picture on the screen.

"What's wrong?" Rose asked when Alex pushed her onto the balcony, closing the window behind them.

"Fabio knows I'm not from here. He managed to unlock the phone."

Rose tried to catch a glimpse of the phone that Alex hid behind his back. "What was on the phone?"

"Pictures from my wedding," he said.

"You're married?" Rose asked loudly.

Alex pressed his hand over her mouth. First, she opened her eyes wide, and then she narrowed them, biting his hand before she descended into the garden. The rain was heavy, the air chilly, but Rose's silence was by far more frigid than the cold night. Not once did she look at him as they rode back to the villa.

CHAPTER 8

Weeks passed, and Alex spent his time tending to the servants' superficial wounds, pulling a few teeth and enjoying Rose and Annabella's company. He stopped at the cave on the nights when the moon was full, waiting for the portal to open, and he returned to the cottage at sunrise. One morning, he was lying in bed when he smelled her perfume.

"I think you have quite a habit of staring at naked bodies."

Rose blushed at being caught staring at his half naked body, and he couldn't remember meeting anyone looking as delicious as she was with her hair loose over bare shoulders.

"What an outrageous thing to say, Mr. Santini," Rose said. "You forgot to lock the door last night, but I knocked."

"And here I thought you showed up with wicked thoughts in mind."

Alex leaned on his side, not making the tiniest gesture to cover his bare chest. Rose turned around, marching toward the door when he threw the covers off.

"I'm here to gather the colors and canvases for our trip. Servants will load the chest at midday," Rose said.

She left the bedroom and busied herself in the next room, avoiding eye contact with him. Alex pulled his pants on as soon as she left the room. He followed her, leaning in the doorframe and watching her as she sorted colors and brushes.

"Siena is going to be a nice change of scenery. You'll like it," Rose said.

"When do we leave?"

"As soon as you're appropriately dressed," Rose said, locking a wooden chest and sitting on the lid. She rested her hands on her knees and searched around the room before turning her attention to him.

"So, are you a famous painter in your time?" Alex asked, buttoning his shirt.

"Not yet. I'm still working my way up through the ranks of all the masters. Colors give me a sense of peace, and history provides the perfect stories. I painted portraits of each member of the royal family while I studied in London. They asked me to stay at the palace as an instructor for their children, but my father told me to return because his health wasn't good. I had to postpone my dreams for awhile," Rose said, sighing.

"You should paint my portrait sometime. It would be nice to have something from you."

"To take to your world when you leave?"

"Something along those lines," Alex said. "One day, I will leave, Rose. It may take months or years, but one day, I will go back to my time."

"The portal won't open again for months, Alex. You have a choice. Stick by me or try to make it on your own."

He met her gaze halfway, an aching silence falling over them. Was it disappointment he read in her eyes? Did she want him to stay? She had no idea his career as a surgeon would be in jeopardy if he decided to remain. Alex looked toward the door when he heard a woman humming on the porch.

"Your maid is here," he said.

Rose looked just in time to see Lucia coming through the door. The girl stopped in the doorframe, staring at them, her hands resting on her knees. "Miss Rose, your father is looking for you. He sent me to fetch you, and he expects the doctor too."

"Is he not well?" Rose asked. "Is Father all right?"

She hurried outside, stomping toward the villa. Alex and the maid followed, trying to keep up with her. *This woman is fast,* he thought. They reached the house in no time, and Rose climbed the stairs, two at the time.

"Your father is waiting for you, Miss Rose," Mr. Ciccio said. He turned toward Alex, pointing the way toward the other side of the hall. "Doctor, you must come too."

Mr. Ciccio walked ahead of them and cracked open the door to the library, announcing their presence. A pale light filtered into the room where fabrics in soft browns covered the sofas, and silk pillows were thrown on chairs.

"Dr. Santini, I hope you are finding your stay at my house agreeable."

"Of course, Count, I couldn't ask for more than a roof over my head and a bed to rest my bones," Alex said.

"Your help over the past weeks hasn't gone unnoticed. Everyone talks about the doctor who tends to the wounded without charging a fee. You're quite a sensation."

"You've been gracious to offer me shelter. It was the least I could do for your servants."

Rose kissed her father's cheek. "What is it, Papa? Why did you call for us?" she asked.

"Doctor, I entrust the safety of my daughter into your hands." The count paused, and a hush settled over the room. "Not too long ago, we agreed that I wasn't the target of that knife. I was dancing with Rose at the ball, then the music stopped, and she bent to pick up her fan when the dagger hit me."

"Let's not forget the note," Alex added.

"So, I was the intended victim." Rose gasped, and she covered her mouth. She grabbed the back of a chair to steady herself.

Count Estes nodded.

"You're leaving before anyone gets wind of it. Rose, be cautious."

"But, Papa, I didn't have time to pack anything but the painting tools."

"Everything you need is on its way to Siena," the count said, pressing Rose's hand into Alex's hand. He held both their hands for a while, and when he released his grip, he turned around to hide the trembling of his lips.

"I'll take care of her," Alex said, his voice gaining strength he didn't remember having.

Count Estes embraced his daughter and escorted them to the door where Annabella and her mother waited next to the carriage.

"You'll miss all the wedding preparations." Annabella sobbed, hugging Rose.

"I'll be back in no time," Rose said.

"Lucia will leave at sunrise and take your trunks with her to Siena," Countess Estes said, embracing her.

Alex grabbed Rose's hand and helped her into the carriage. She waved to her parents until the villa disappeared from view, and then she frowned. The coachman drove the two horses hard, leaving a trail of dust that covered a sky pink with sunset. The rhythmic movement of the wheels on the dirt road made the carriage shake, every hole and every soft swell in the road's floor sending them up from their seats.

"What might be so funny?" Rose asked when Alex laughed.

"I've never traveled in a carriage before. It's quite an experience," Alex whispered. He wanted to share with Rose what it was like to travel in his car with air conditioning and music going full blast. He was convinced she would enjoy it if she would agree to come with him in his time.

"Why not? Are there no coaches in your time?"

"They are still used in the country, but most people ride in cars."

"I'm intrigued about your time, Alex, and about you. You have the knowledge of how the world is going to change, and about what will happen to our country."

Her curiosity took him aback. Even the few freckles on her nose became dangerously attractive to Alex. He looked out the window. The sun made it to the other side of the rolling hills and night was upon them.

"Italy will become the Roman Republic governed by consuls, forty-two years from now, and your new Duke will be at the helm, as the Holy Roman Emperor," Alex said.

"Don't tell," Rose gasped. "You shall come with me to the Palazzo Pubblico where the royal family stays."

"I won't reveal anything from history. I have no intention of changing the course of events," he said, although meeting great characters from the history books was more than he had ever expected.

"I wouldn't advise you to do so. It would put you in danger."

"One thing I remember for sure. Your Duke will die of a heart attack," Alex said.

Rose jerked, and she covered her mouth with her fan. She took a deep breath and said, "You can save him. You're a doctor." After she had laid her fan back on the empty seat next to her, she asked him, "Why did you become a doctor?"

"I wanted to cure people's illnesses. I'm a heart surgeon in my time."

"It's a noble profession."

"Yes, it is," Alex said, and he followed her gaze as she looked out the window. Alex wished he knew what she was thinking just then. After the weeks they had spent together, Rose hadn't disclosed her plans for the future, other than her desire to become famous through her paintings.

"Why did you lie to your family about my identity? You could have told them the truth when you had the chance."

"Yes, I could have, but I wasn't prepared to share the portal's existence with anyone yet. I didn't want everybody finding out about the place you came from."

Rose fidgeted in her seat, the color of her eyes darkened as she stared at him, and her bottom lip trembled. The breeze scattered the falling curls over her shoulders, and he couldn't resist the temptation to catch one lock and roll it around his finger. Rose paused, searching for words.

"Your wife might be worried about you," she said.

"Sophia is dead."

Rose gasped.

"Tell me about her."

Alex sighed, as he pulled the cell phone from his pocket and moved next to her. He was showing her Sophia's picture when the battery died. Rose shivered when he told her that Sophia had been his best friend since high school, and they had married when both were in college. She studied art design, and he studied medicine. In her spare time, she taught painting to children with special needs. She was four months pregnant when she was killed.

Rose remained silent, and Alex would have given anything to hear her thoughts. She braced herself, sitting as still as a marble statue. Finally, she said, "Is my resemblance to your dead wife the reason you're here with me, trying to protect me?"

"It may be the only way to redeem myself." Alex shivered, and he moved back to the seat across from hers, only the sounds of the forest disturbing the quiet of the evening. "Why was Fabio angry with you?"

"When?"

"That night when he grabbed your hand."

"I refused his marriage proposal."

"I don't follow you. I thought Fabio was into your sister."

"It's a long story," Rose said. "We grew up together. Annabella, Fabio, his brother, and I were practically inseparable. Fabio hoped I'd share his romantic feelings. I pity his fate. When his brother died in a hunting accident last summer, he became his widow's custodian."

Alex studied her as she talked. The woman was intriguing. She was firm in her position, daring, ahead of the women of her time who would have run or fainted if ever in her situation. He remembered the way she had checked out Fabio's naked body, and her curiosity made her charming. Her only soft spot was her vocation, which she had put on hold to fulfill her father's desires.

"Is Asante the man who stole your heart?"

"Not in a thousand years. The world is big, and I long to explore it, not to get restrained inside marital vows," Rose said.

A knot grew in Alex's throat.

"So, you don't want to marry nor have children. What are you planning to do with your life?"

"I want to become the best history painter of my time."

"What about the factory? Aren't you the heiress?"

"My last visit gave me many ideas. I intend to make changes, before expanding to Florence," she said, her eyes sliding from his face to the road ahead. "I can't fulfill someone else's dream and abandon mine. But now is not the right time to bother my father."

Aged trees with squeaking branches stretched toward the carriage, their limbs rustling when the first raindrops hit their leaves. The horses whinnied, the rhythmical beating of their hooves mingling with the crying of the forest. Alex couldn't stop the sensation that they were being tracked.

"I am adopted," Rose began. "My mother, the only daughter of the Estes family, fell in love with someone below her social status and, to add to the total shame, she got pregnant. I was the outcome. They never told me who my real father was, and I didn't dare ask. I don't want to be an heir, for it is Annabella's birthright, but I can't go against their will either."

"Your father trusts you to carry on his work. He is proud of you," Alex said, patting her hand.

The warmth of his skin left her hungry for more, and the image of the naked woman, screaming under Fabio's weight, came to her mind. Her body began to slowly awake, and she blushed at her visions. She searched Alex's face as he stared at the blank screen of his phone. That woman, Sophia, was without a doubt her twin, and she was the reason he stood by her at that moment. He must pity her for her fate. She wouldn't cry, not in front of him, and not then. Rose sighed and closed her eyes, emptying her mind of all thoughts.

The last traces of light looked like freckles on the plum sky. Rain brought fresh air, and it cooled the carriage. As the coach followed the meandering road, Rose drifted off to sleep, her head banging against the wood frame. The count's request to look after Rose rang in Alex's ears, his deepest fears erupting. First, they should stop at the merchant's shop. The merchant must have a record of who wanted the emblem encrusted in the dagger's handle. As he thought of how to approach the storekeeper and inquire about the knife, he jumped when he heard the gallop of another horse.

"What's happening, coachman?" Alex asked.

"A rider is approaching. He seems in a hurry. A hunter for sure, young master," the coachman yelled from his seat.

"What is it?" Rose asked, awakened by the sudden change in the carriage's speed.

"I don't know," Alex answered, looking back at the road.

The rider was one with the horse, his body plastered to the animal's body. He pulled an arrow from a bag hanging over his shoulder. Alex shivered and pulled Rose closer to him. The first arrow landed in the back of the carriage.

"Alex?" Rose screamed when he shoved her to the carriage's floor.

"Lie down," he roared. "Go faster, coachman! Whoever is after us is not our friend."

The coachman twiddled his whip, urging his horses to run faster. Two more arrows hissed as they passed by Alex's ears. Thunder rumbled somewhere close by, lightning struck in the forest, and then all was quiet. The pounding of hooves was in unison with his heartbeat.

"Abandon the coach!" the coachman yelled, as his whip whistled. The horses neighed as they raced on a road filled with remnants of branches. One of the arrows grazed Alex's cheek, the other one nicked one of the horses.

"What about you?" Rose screamed to the coachman from the carriage's floor.

"The horses are trained runners, my lady. I'll be fine," the coachman cried back. "Go now."

"Look at me," Alex ordered as he forced Rose up from the floor. "If we want to make it out of this alive, we have to jump."

"I can't jump from a moving carriage. It's madness!" Rose yelled. "We should stop and talk to him, make him reason with us."

"If he wanted to talk he wouldn't have used arrows. We jump together, Rose. I won't let go. We'll be okay," Alex said and, for the first time in years, he was afraid that history would repeat itself.

A broken tree fell behind them, blocking the road and slowing the hunter. Alex gripped Rose's hand. At the first curl in the road, they jumped, dropping onto the grass, lying still near some bushes. He pulled her into his arms and covered her body with his. The carriage drove on with the coachman still urging the horses, and seconds later, they heard the rider passing them.

"Will the coachman be safe?" she asked.

"Yes, he'll be safe."

"I'd never forgive myself if any harm would befall him," Rose said. She tidied her dress filthy with mud and leaves. She wiped the thin line of blood on Alex's forehead and inspected the rest of his body.

"We must move. By now, the rider might have caught up with the carriage and discovered our disappearance," Alex whispered close to her ear, and his warmth felt reassuring to her.

"We should look for shelter. It's dark already and, in this weather, I doubt we'll reach the city," Rose said.

She fretted as she scanned the forest around them. They were steps away from the main road, surrounded by wet bushes and grass. Her hair was damp, and so were her clothes.

"How far are we from Siena?" Alex asked.

"I'm not sure. I've never traveled on foot."

"We're in the heart of nowhere."

"There is a cabin somewhere close," Rose said. "My father used it when he was hunting. I only hope I can find my way in this storm."

Rose wiped the mud from her face. They followed the faint path draped by the broken tree limbs and didn't look back.

"He's back already. The rider discovered we went missing, and he's returning to finish what he started. We have no time, Rose. Run!"

Alex tightened his grip on her hand, and they raced through the woods. The gentle stirrings of the woods joined with the distant sounds of hooves hitting the forest's floor. The hunter was getting closer. Branches whipped and stung them while they ripped through, but they kept running. A pearly mist troubled their advance. Trees swayed, leaves rushed, and the twilight faded. They got lost in the canopy of trees, their steps muffled by a thick blanket of grass and leaves. Not a single light shone from above to guide their way. The rain poured, and the whipping wind slapped across their wet bodies. They ran deep into the woods until the main road was nowhere in sight, their hearts thundering while their lungs cramped with the effort.

"I can't run any longer," Rose said, and she sucked in the cool evening air. "We must stop."

Rose pulled her hand from Alex's clutch and dropped to the ground, embracing her legs. With her head on top of shaking knees, she breathed deeply. After he had lowered himself beside Rose, Alex propped his back up against a tree and stretched out his legs, his instincts alert to the sounds of the forest. His eyes were accustomed to the darkness by now, and he encircled Rose's body, holding it close to his. He couldn't help but notice how soaked she was, and how she was trembling. He cast a sidelong glance at Rose, and then he shook his head.

"We can't stay here. You'll catch a cold in this weather," Alex said.

"Let me rest a while," Rose gasped, laying her head on his shoulder.

He strengthened his grip, blowing warm air over her clamped fists. He massaged her arms, thinking how weird everything was. A small opening appeared in the curtain of clouds above, big enough for a faint light to penetrate. The cabin they were looking for was no more than thirty feet away from them.

"Look, the cabin! Do you see it? Come with me," Alex said, crashing through the bushes and pulling her with him. They stopped at the cabin's entrance, peeking around and listening for any hint of activity.

"Do you think anyone is here?"

"Not sure, but we're out of options."

CHAPTER 9

"There should be some candles here somewhere," Rose said, knocking over a chair in her way when they entered the cabin.

Alex had caught her right before she fell. "Did you hurt yourself?"

"A little," she muttered, rubbing her leg.

The night became cold, and a mist settled in. Alex locked the door behind them, took his vest off, and dropped it on the table by the window.

"A fire would do us both good," Rose suggested. "Strike the flint edge against the steel and burn the papers in the fireplace. There are always dry logs next to it."

Alex did as Rose instructed, and when the fire came to life, they sat on the floor in front of the aged fireplace. As he looked around the room, Alex found a lone bed, some linen up on shelves, a wooden table, and three chairs, and pots and pans. A comfortable sensation filled his body, and he noticed Rose's head falling to one side. The attempt to hold her eyes open failed and, although dirty from head to toe, she carried herself in the dignified manner of her ancestors.

"You should sleep," Alex suggested. "You're exhausted."

Rose dragged her feet toward the only bed in the room. "I'll rest for just a little," she said.

"I'll protect you, don't worry. He won't find us," Alex whispered. He made his fist so tight that his fingers turned white from tension.

"How will you do that when you can barely protect yourself?" Rose asked softly.

The fire warmed the room, filling it with the fragrance of burned wood. He looked at Rose, stirring and twisting a lot, fighting demons in her sleep, but tiredness took control in the end. After he had pulled the thin blanket over her, he turned toward the fireplace. He searched through the ashes and threw on another log, the flicker of the flames capturing his gaze. He was drowning in worry. There was no escape and no one to turn to for help. The events of the last hours had left him shaken, and he grasped his head, massaging his temples. His drenched clothes began to dry, their smell reminiscent of moist soil.

Alex turned toward Rose when her moans grew steady. He rose to his feet and came close to the bed. There was sweat dripping down her neck, and her lips were dry. He looked around the room for water. *Of course, there is no water.* Alex grunted and snatched the empty bucket from the table. He opened the door, listening to the sounds of the forest, and then he left the house. The beating of his heart intensified the further away he got from Rose. Alex walked through the woods, and the stream he remembered passing on their way to the cabin still didn't show up. Finally, he heard the sound of trickling water against stones. He ran toward the spring and dipped the bucket in the stream, the water shimmering in the moonlight. The rain had stopped, and the clouds began to disperse, allowing the half crescent moon to take control of the sky. Holding the bucket in one hand and shoving branches away with the other, he came to an abrupt stop. He jolted at the snort of a nearby animal. Alex sneaked a quick look between scrubs and caught sight of a silhouette patting the back of a mare.

A branch snapped close to his location, by the stream. Unable to move, Alex searched the ground for a stone or a branch to use if he must. At the sound of birds fluttering nearby, the rider halted, just three steps away from Alex. The man coughed, pulled a knife from his sheath as he pushed the bushes aside, and searched the ground. Alex held his breath and closed his eyes when the man passed by him and didn't dare breathe again until the man mounted his horse with a white diamond on his forehead and departed. Alex ran in the opposite direction, still holding the bucket in one hand and the stick in the other, and didn't stop until he reached the cabin where he had left Rose asleep.

He locked the door behind him, stopping next to the bed where Rose lay fighting her chills. She rolled in her sleep and uttered strange words. Alex wiped the sweat off her face and arms, his heart aching with worry for her. Her traveling clothes were still damp. He threw the muslin skirt on the floor and then removed the bodice. He put a wet rag on her chest, her nipples hardening under his fingers. Alex pulled his hands away from her body, giving in to his exhaustion. He kneeled and rested his head on the side of the bed, dozing off to sleep.

It was morning when Rose opened her eyes. A few rays of sun sneaked inside the room through a crack in the shades. She looked at her ruined dress in a heap on the floor and removed the rags that covered her chest and her forehead. She staggered to her feet, swaying a little, and she shook Alex's shoulder. She waited, and when she got no response, Rose shook him a little harder.

"What? Where?" Alex asked, jumping to his feet.

"What is the meaning of this?" Rose asked, pointing at her ravaged dress.

"It's not what you're thinking. It's not as bad as it looks," Alex answered.

"Do you care to enlighten me? What exactly am I thinking?"

Rose furrowed her brows as she waited for Alex's reply.

"Don't worry! I didn't take advantage of you in your condition. You were fighting a fever. I tried to wake you up, but you didn't respond to any of my attempts, so I did what any doctor would do for his patient. I freed you from your wet clothes."

"Dr. Santini, I appreciate your concern for my health. But don't rip apart a woman's dress next time, especially in a situation when she has no other change of clothes at her disposal. How exactly do you expect me to walk through the forest and show my face in Siena looking like a bum?"

Her posture, with hands resting on hips, her hair a pile of burning fire, was rather outrageous. Laughing would be the least appropriate thing to do in these circumstances. She looked delicious as she searched the shelves for some clothes. Without intending to do so, Alex registered every detail of her body, her curvy legs, slim waist and small, round breasts dancing with every step she took in the room, and the realization she was naked under the thin chemise left him paralyzed.

"Will you cover yourself?" he asked. "Your backside is showing from under the shift you're wearing."

"That's what I'm trying to do. Can you reach those garments on the top shelf?"

Rose pointed to the clothes on the upper ledge, and a pile of dust filled the room when he pulled them off the shelf. They both started to cough and waved their hands, scattering the dust. If he thought women in his time were sensual and attractive, this woman was the hottest he had ever encountered. Alex caught a slight glimpse of her thighs and gasped for air as he handed her a pair of pants too large for her slender figure and a cotton shirt two sizes too big. Rose tied back her hair and ditched the dress in the fireplace, watching as the flames turned it to ashes in a matter of minutes.

"No time to waste," she said, storming out the door into the crisp air of the early morning.

***

"With my disguise, it may be safer to return to the main road than to wander through the woods. This forest is not particularly well known for being safe. Papa said that just last week a carriage was attacked by thieves who raped the women and killed the men," Rose said.

"Interesting times! I don't think the one who's after you intended to rape you, but I'm sure he'll kill you on sight if he gets the chance. And, he is here, somewhere. I saw him last night when I went to fetch water from the stream."

Rose stopped and turned toward him while she put her hands on her hips. She swallowed hard, and when she spoke again, her voice had a high pitch.

"Why didn't you wake me up?"

"I tried, but you never moved a muscle," he said, shrugging his shoulders. "My only concern was to lower your temperature, Rose. I'm a doctor, not a warrior."

Rose's voice trembled, but her features remained calm.

"I realize what you're not, and that is why I'm scared. Papa asked you to protect me, but you can barely defend yourself, Alex."

"That's why you shall come with me, to my time. We can stay in front of the portal until it opens again. Forget about the factory and the enemies you've made here. No one will harm you in my time," Alex said with a note of excitement in his voice.

"Thirteen months is a long time."

"We don't know for sure that it'll take that long."

"Suit yourself in believing whatever you want. I know better," Rose said. "I'll discover the rogue behind all of these attacks with or without your help."

Her words shook him, and he understood his medical skills would not be enough to save her. They didn't save Sophia either. If he intended to guard Rose, he would need more than luck: he'd need wisdom and strength. He would force her to stay in front of the portal, tie her down if necessary, and wait for the next supermoon.

"Hurry," Alex said. He linked his fingers with hers, and their shoulders touched. A smile crept back on his face. He wouldn't fail Rose as he had Sophia. "We must return."

He dragged her by her hand. His strides were long, and Rose had to run to keep up with him.

"Return? Are you crazy?" Rose yelled, snatching her hand from his.

Alex grabbed her, heaving her over his shoulder as if she were a bag of potatoes. She kicked him and pounded his back with her fists until he lowered her to the ground.

"Stop, you fool! We can't go back. I'm needed in Siena."

"Fine, we'll do it your way. We'll continue our conversation when we reach Siena," Alex said, and he walked ahead of her through the forest.

They didn't talk until they reached the main road where the wrecked carriage came into view. Rose gasped. The rear wheels were broken, and the carriage rested on one side. The two horses whinnied when they saw them, and they shook their manes. *No sight of the coachman must be a sign he made it to safety*, Alex thought.

"Maybe he escaped," Rose whispered, patting the animals.

A loud cry escaped from her mouth when a hand covered in blood, with ants crawling over the fingers and flies hovering over it, protruded from beneath the carriage. A putrid smell filled the area around the wreckage, and Alex turned Rose away from the scene.

"Stay by the horses. It's not a pretty sight."

Rose remained in the heart of the road as Alex kneeled next to the corpse, checking for a pulse. He raised the wheel enough to pull out the body. Then, he studied the injuries, as he had done countless times in med school when he had to treat assigned patients based on his analysis of their wounds. The coachman had a knife stuck in his throat, and the shock of what had happened to him was mirrored in his opened eyes.

"We should bury him," Alex said. "We can't leave the man here for the wild animals to feast on him. Did he have any family?"

Rose shook her head, unable to talk as she shuddered from head to toe. The black horse licked her cheek, and she patted his muzzle.

"People can't die because of me. It isn't fair!"

Rose collapsed in Alex's arms, crying softly. He kissed her damp hair, and he rocked her as if she were a little girl. His hands stroked her spine, and he whispered in her ear.

"Many things are not reasonable in life, Rose. One day, you'll learn to accept it and live with it." *Just as I learned to live with my guilt.* He pulled her close to him, tightening his fists.

"He didn't have anyone in this world but us," Rose said between sobs. "He worked for the family since he was a boy. Papa brought him to the estate after he found him wandering through the woods during one of his hunting trips. I remember how dirty and hungry he was."

"Let's go back to the cave, Rose."

"We can't leave him here. If we can't give him a proper burial, at least, we should cover his body," Rose insisted, and she began to gather stones and thick branches for his grave. Alex had no choice but to help her cover the dead coachman's body. Only the horses' neighs disturbed the grimness of the moment.

Rose looked both ways, and then she unhitched the horses from the carriage, fixing the bridles on them. She turned toward Alex.

"We better go. The horses are acting as if something is wrong. Follow me," Rose said as she climbed on the black horse.

"Ah, Rose, we have a small problem."

"What is it?"

"I never learned to ride a horse, let alone to ride without a saddle."

"I don't believe it. You mean to say they didn't train you with the necessary survival skills in your med school?"

"You're welcome to laugh if you want, but somehow you must teach me to ride that... animal." Alex gasped, pointing to the horse. "Is it laughing at me?"

"The horse?" she asked, raising her eyebrows. "All right, Dr. Santini," Rose said with a chuckle. She dismounted her horse and approached Alex and the mare. "First, grab the horse's mane. Then, jump up and throw your body onto the horse's back. Next, swing your leg over the other side of the horse and push yourself up until you rest comfortably on its back."

Alex swallowed hard, and his eyes widened as he stared at the horse.

"Are they normally this big?"

The horse watched him with watery eyes and shook its head, scattering long strands of hair in every direction.

"You make it sound very easy," Alex muttered, following her instructions.

"You got it, Alex. Now, hold the bridle firmly and use your heels to let the horse know you want to go."

"Easier said than done," Alex said.

He touched the horse's belly with his feet, held his shoulders straight, his buttocks glued to the animal's back. He slid to one side, and he tightened his hold of the mane, pulling himself up and regaining his balance.

"You did it. It's not as hard as it looks." Rose praised his efforts, hiding her amusement by looking in the other direction.

They followed the winding road, barely noticing the beauty around them. Alex studied Rose's rigid posture as she rode her horse. Her hands, clenched around the reins, turned purple from the pressure she put on her fingers. Determination governed her figure, her eyes fixing on an imaginary point ahead of her. She didn't seem to remember Alex until he rode up next to her and shook her shoulder.

"I'm riding this horse, you see," he laughed.

Rose glanced at his stance. "Indeed, you are, and you've gotten quite good at it," she said. "I don't know what I'd do without you."

"You'd do what you do best: survive. You'd fight for your life and try to separate the foes from the friends."

"I never realized I had enemies." Rose paused, shook her head, and turned toward him. "I'm not giving up without a fight. I have a factory to run and people to manage. If worse comes to worst, I'll let fate decide the course of my life."

"I think we can control our own destiny, but if I must stay here, then you should teach me how to live in this world," Alex said.

"You have a long way to go. But with patience, I think you can pass as one of us."

"What does patience have to do with anything?"

"Oh, Alex, you'll need it more than you think."

"Look, we're in the city."

Alex pointed to the stone pillars arching above the city's gates in the distance. Rose spurred her horse until they were at full gallop. Her hair escaped from the loop she had managed to create before leaving the cabin in the forest, and the wind played with the flames in her curls. She stopped right before the gates and waited for him to catch up before they entered the city and rode through the main street.

"We must cross the entire city since our house is on the other side of town. An excellent excuse for admiring Siena," she said.

"It's going to be my home for some time," Alex said, already a captive of the historical sites. Although he was aware that the city was the same one he knew from his time, he couldn't help but stare at the agitated merchants, the animals pulling wagons with fresh fruits and vegetables, and the old stores lined along winding streets.

"Siena is a city of winding alleyways and steep steps. Piazza Del Campo stands at its heart, and Duomo is its cultural landmark."

Rose pointed out each structure they passed and paused when she noticed Alex's gaze lingering on one building or another. Blankets hanging over simple wrought iron balconies overloaded with pots of flowers stood out against the yellow color of the walls.

"Santa Maria Della Scala is our hospital. One day, I shall take you there for a visit," she continued.

"Impressive," Alex said as he stared at the ancient cobblestone streets. They looked the same as the ones from his time, and he was amazed at how well preserved they still were after hundreds of years. The animal odor combined with human sweat and food aromas was a mixture that made Alex turn up his nose.

On their way through the city, they passed numerous patrician villas with ceramic roof tiles in rustic red and fabulous gardens with rows of citrus and cypress trees. As they neared the heart of the city, the cobblestone streets resonated with the sounds of a new day. People hurried by, wearing their worries on their faces, governesses pushed children in strollers for another

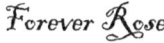
visit into town, and merchants shouted after beggars caught stealing from their counters.

"We should stop at the shop and inquire about the mark on the dagger," Rose said, as she dismounted in front of a store. Alex mimicked her actions.

They entered a shop filled with ornaments of silver and gold, silks from the Indies, and Persian carpets. They met with the owner, a short round man, half Alex's size, with thin hair, a thick mustache, and olive skin. They explained that they were searching for the owner of the dagger, and the merchant agreed to search in his ledgers for the price of fifty scudi that Rose agreed to pay at the delivery of his findings.

CHAPTER 10

After they had left the store, Rose and Alex walked side by side, leading their horses.

"We're getting close to the house," Rose said, clearing a path through the conglomeration of people and animals on the road.

Men in white robes marched across the street, heading toward the Duomo, and twelve nuns sang as they walked behind them, their eyes pinned to the cobblestones. As soon as Rose and Alex traversed the center of the city, a three-story house appeared in the middle of a garden that stretched from the main road all the way to the hills behind the property. Tall oak trees in pale shades of brown shaded the path toward the house. Dozens of bees attracted by the unusually warm November day gathered around them, and when they started to swarm over his head, Alex waved his hands.

"Don't do that," Rose whispered, "or they'll attack you. Stay calm!"

"Yes, your majesty," Alex said.

A stone fountain in the center of a cobblestone driveway splashed tongues of clear water. In the heart of the basin, Alex noticed a statue that looked like Venus. Red bricks covered the U-shaped villa, and ivy crawled all the way to the top floor. A man in a dark uniform opened the front door and signaled a footboy that appeared out of nowhere to tend to their horses. Short, with the same olive complexion and dark hair, the butler reminded Alex of Mr. Ciccio, the butler from Villa Luce Del Sol.

"Miss Rose, I didn't recognize you at first. What happened? We expected you last night," the butler said.

"As you can see, Mr. Benito, we were delayed," Rose said, pushing the butler out of her way and entering the house.

Two young women and a boy, house servants, covered their mouths as they examined her clothes. She was dusty from head to toe, and her hair was a mess. The old garments she was wearing needed much work to make them fit her frame.

"Thieves attacked and killed the coachman. Save for Dr. Santini, who is going to stay with us for the time being, I'd have been prey to the wild animals and the treacherous human beings." Rose turned to the man named Benito, and she told him, "Show Dr. Santini to his quarters."

"As you wish, my lady," Mr. Benito said, bowing.

The house was elegant, with a warm feeling. Alex ignored the curious stares from the servants whispering in each other's ears as he checked out the arched doorways and the huge windows. He lifted his gaze and looked at the ceilings with whimsical images depicting deities revered in ancient Rome.

"Dr. Santini, follow me," Mr. Benito said, and he advanced through a maze of corridors and rooms. "To your left is the kitchen, but unless you need something or there is an emergency, you won't go there. A footboy will deliver your meals to your room if your presence isn't required at the dining room table. Behind the kitchen is the storage room. We bring fresh fruits and vegetables from the market every day."

The butler limped along the dark corridor, pointing out each room as they advanced.

"The washroom is in the back of the house," the butler said lastly. "You may want to pay that room a visit later."

"Ah, a bathroom," Alex said when Mr. Benito announced the only room that he found useful. In pressing need of fresh garments, he stayed one step behind the man in a uniform buttoned up to his neck. As soon as they reached the stairs, the butler blew out the flame of the candle he was carrying and set the candlestick near the stairway.

"The guest rooms are on the third floor. Family members occupy the second floor. All come to the first level to eat or entertain their guests. The library is also on the first floor if you need access to books or writing materials. Miss Rose's studio is on the same level as your room. She likes the serenity of the place and the view of the city from her room," the butler explained. He puffed as he climbed the spiral staircase with Alex following close behind.

The noises from the rest of the house faded when they reached the third floor.

"This is your room, sir. Count Estes instructed us to fill your wardrobe with new clothes. Your bath will be ready within the hour," Mr. Benito said, his tone neutral.

"Thank you," Alex responded, taking into view the spacious chamber. It was no different from all of the other rooms from Villa Luce Del Sol. The walls were covered with silk, the windows stretched from floor to ceiling, and he had access to a balcony.

Mr. Benito flashed a smile at last and closed the door behind him. With the butler gone, Alex stepped toward the windows, and he gasped when he saw the cathedral's towers with their elegant style and refinement. Finally, a view he was accustomed to seeing in his time. Coming from a religious family, Alex had attended services regularly until Sophia had died. After her death, he stopped going to the cathedral and praying altogether. Alex blamed God for allowing her death. He blamed himself for stopping at the red light, and he blamed the police for never catching the criminals. He pushed his friends out of his life, estranged Sophia's family, and he only talked to Renaldo.

"What in the name of...," Alex said, looking down from the balcony when the horses began to grunt.

His gaze followed a man with a brown shirt and a hat that covered his face. There was something familiar about him. Alex couldn't remember where he had met the fellow, but he was convinced it had happened after his arrival through the vortex. The stranger had looked at the windows before he disappeared toward the back of the villa, and Alex swore the man had a scar on his face. He stormed from his room, racing down the stairs and pushing maids and footmen out of his way, and he stepped into the soft light of the new day. But the man had vanished by the time he reached in the garden. Alex went to the stables, where four horses were eating fresh grass in their stalls. They shook their heads and swished their tails when Alex approached.

"Perhaps I'm dreaming," he told himself and patted the animals on their backs.

The noise at the entrance to the stables made him turn around in time to catch a glimpse of Mr. Benito. He was panting, and he bent his head to his knees, taking shallow breaths.

"Dr. Santini, come quickly. Miss Rose fainted in her room," he said.

"Is she hurt?"

"We don't know for sure. We lay her on the bed, and I came looking for you."

Alex ran from the stables, throwing open the door in his way. The door flew off the hinges, and it fell to the ground, light dust rising around them. Benito sneezed a couple of times and covered his nose with his sleeve. In his rush to reach Rose, Alex took the lead. He turned around, waving toward the butler.

"The second floor, Dr. Santini," the butler yelled from the bottom of the staircase.

Alex climbed the stairs two at the time, and he opened every door until he reached hers. Rose rested on a massive bed in the heart of a room painted in a light purple. One maid was rubbing eucalyptus oil on her chest while the other was wiping the sweat from her body. Alex pressed two fingers on a vein under her chin and counted her heartbeats. They were too fast. He touched her forehead. *An infection!*

"She might have caught a cold in the rain last night. What a misfortune," the first maid said.

"Did you see what she wore?" the second maid asked.

"Dirty and dusty, poor soul, she went through a lot," the first maid answered.

Rose started to cough, and her coughs sounded to Alex like a complicated case of the flu. She hadn't trembled all morning, but she shook from head to toe now. Maybe a bug had bitten her while they ran through the forest. He checked her arms and then her neck for marks.

"She was reading this when she fell," the first maid said as she handed Alex a note. "The merchant said it was important."

"Check her body for bite marks," Alex instructed the maid.

He took the note and read it. It stated that a woman had bought the dagger as a gift for her lover. She had asked the merchant to mark the knife with the initial of her lover's name and to make it look like a crown.

Alex stayed with Rose until darkness fell over Siena. Then, he returned to his room, leaving word to be informed of any change in Rose's condition. As soon as he crashed into the fresh sheets, he drifted into a deep sleep and, in his dream, the crown took the shape of an M.

***

The first glimpse of daylight peeked inside her chamber, sunbeams playing on her face. Her eyes throbbed a little. Rose found the strength to open them, and the light blinded her. She lifted the covers, and when she rose to her feet, five roses fell next to her toes. Rose picked them up and touched the petals. *He is sweet, and the roses are perfect.* She grabbed the back of a nearby chair and stopped by the window, staring into the new day. Shades of lilac and pastel pink tinged the sky. Last night, she had collapsed after reading the contents of a note. She covered her chest with her right hand. It couldn't be him. Mr. Matteo was not a killer. Her father said to watch him close because of the missing entries in the ledgers, but she wouldn't believe him to be the one behind such a scheme. He wouldn't hurt a fly, let alone her father or her.

She turned to the door when it opened, and a smile spread across her face.

"You're up already," Alex said, shutting the door behind him. "You should still be in bed."

Alex reached her in two steps. His warm breath on her skin left her trembling.

"Mr. Matteo is waiting for me at the factory," Rose said.

"You're barely standing."

"The note? Have you read it?"

"Yes," Alex said, nodding, and he took her hands in his palms. "Let's sit. Your maid told me you fainted after reading the note. Why? Look at me."

Rose lowered her head.

"The note said a woman bought the dagger as a gift for her lover. But who is the woman and who is the lover?"

Alex shook his head as he sat on the bed.

"Let's start with the people around you and your family. That is how we do it in my time. I'm afraid Fabio knows I am not from around here. He's a smart fellow, and he's still deeply in love with you."

"How do you know?"

"By the light in his eyes when he looks at you, silly," Alex said, cupping her hands.

"I don't have such feelings for him," Rose said, "and I told him so. Fabio is nothing but a friend, or at least I used to think of him as one."

"What if he discovers the portal?"

"Then my entire family will be in danger," Rose said.

"What is it, Rose?" Alex asked when her breathing accelerated. "Are you hurting somewhere?"

"Only in my heart. Monti starts with an M, the letter looking like a crown. Matteo begins with an M too. So, which is it? Count Monti or Matteo? Lord, help me decide."

Alex rose to his feet and took her hands into his. Rose needed to stop looking at him with those misty eyes if she expected him to behave around her. Her breath brushed against the skin of his neck and, for a split second, he wondered if her lips tasted like honey.

He shook his head and murmured, "Isn't it obvious? We must return to the cave."

"To do what? The portal won't open for another thirteen months if our calculations are right."

There was no way out, and the feeling of being incapacitated made him stomp around the room. Alex had the strong feeling that he wasn't meant to go back to his life without saving this woman first. He rolled his eyes as he said, "I'll keep an eye on you. I'll be your shadow. Wherever you go, I'll go."

"The roses are lovely," she whispered. "I didn't picture you as a romantic poet, Mr. Santini."

"What roses?" Alex asked.

"These—"

The door opened without giving Rose enough time to answer his question.

"Your bath is ready, my lady," Lucia said, sticking her head through the half-open door.

"When did you get here?" Alex asked.

"Yesterday morning, per His Excellency's orders," Lucia answered. "Come with me, child, before the water gets cold."

"I'll be close if you need me," Alex said, leaving Rose with her maid and hurrying toward the gardens.

***

For the next three weeks, while Rose recovered from her illness, Alex walked around her gardens with flaming red and orange leaves and velvety roses protruding from scattered bushes and, from time to time, he went into the city with Mr. Benito. He learned how to reach the Piazza Publico by himself, and he studied the architecture of the buildings.

One day, Alex decided that it was time to brush up on his knowledge of horseback riding.

"What was it that you wanted, Doctor?" Mr. Benito asked when Alex stepped in front of him. "You came looking for me."

"Mr. Benito, bring me a horse," Alex demanded.

"Right away," Mr. Benito said, and he signaled a footboy. "Do as the doctor says!"

The boy ran to the stables, and he brought him the horse he had ridden when he came to Siena with Rose. Although his newly acquired skills hadn't had time to cement, Alex was determined to continue his riding lessons and improve on them. If he was to live in this time, then he must learn how to survive.

"Let's go. I have much to learn and time is scarce," Alex told the footboy, who became his companion per Rose's request.

They rode every day in the nearby fields. Alex learned how to give the horse signals with his legs and how to become one with the animal. The time he spent outdoors brought color to his cheeks and new light into his eyes. His slim figure began to change, and his atrophied muscles started to improve. The staff in the house, especially the young maids, giggled when he passed by with sweat on his body and smelling like leather. Even Rose, whose health had started to show signs of improvement, studied him every so often.

One morning, Alex went to one of the servants and said, "Ride with me, boy."

The footboy looked at the butler, waiting for his approval.

"Go with Dr. Santini," Mr. Benito instructed.

If Alex told Mr. Benito his plan, for sure, he would run to Rose. She would stop him, saying it was craziness. He touched the pocket where he hid the dagger and the note from the merchant. He had already spent two months in Siena doing nothing but riding the horse, making plans, and waiting for Rose to recover. The more he thought about the entire affair, the more he was convinced that Fabio was the owner of the dagger and not Mr. Matteo. Didn't he see Fabio making love to a woman when he went to retrieve his cell phone from his residence? Perhaps, the woman was the lover who gave Fabio the dagger as a present. The people in that time had an odd sense of humor.

Today, Alex rode ahead, and the boy followed. When Siena became a small point on the horizon, the boy advanced, and they rode side by side. He didn't seem to be much older than sixteen.

"What's your name, boy?"

"Antonio but my friends call me Toni," the boy answered. "Where are we going, young master?"

"To Count Monti's residence," Alex said. "That man needs a lesson in manners."

"Master, Count Monti is known for his short temper. Last week, he killed a man in a duel, and the previous one, he wounded another. He is the best swordsman in Siena, and the fastest man with a gun," the boy said as he bounced up and down in his saddle.

"Don't worry about me, boy," Alex said.

They rode for a few hours on the same path he had followed with Rose, and when they arrived at the crossroad, they chose the road going to their right, toward Fabio's estate. The air smelled like grass and wildflowers, and Alex broke a twig from a tree and chewed on it. The bitter taste invaded his mouth, and he wrinkled his nose, spitting on the grass.

The estate came into view after they had reached the top of the hill. Alex got off his horse, and the boy did the same, standing with the horses while Alex climbed the steps to the front door. Fabio's residence was a three-story villa covered with ivy on the sides. Alex counted over twenty windows on one level.

"Going somewhere, Count Monti?" Alex shouted when the door opened before he even knocked.

Fabio stepped over the threshold. He scoffed.

"What are you doing here?" he asked with a grin on his face while he took a step toward Alex. "Shouldn't you be saving lives?"

Alex bit his bottom lip until the salty taste of his blood invaded his mouth. He sucked on it, and his eyes never left Fabio's.

"Let's go, master," Toni said, tugging at his sleeve.

Alex ignored his request.

"Do you recognize this dagger? The merchant said it belonged to you," Alex said as he waved the knife in front of him. Fabio didn't blink, only sneered, and he touched his gun. "You're not using arrows this time, but a gun?"

"Careful with your accusations, doctor," Fabio warned. "They can go both ways."

"What are you talking about?" Alex asked.

"What have you to say about the silver case with images? The woman looked like our Rose, but her clothes were strange. Who are you?"

"I'm a doctor," Alex said, advancing toward Fabio until the two men were two feet away from each other.

"Rose is a naive woman, but I'm not a credulous man. Maybe I'll invoke the High Council or take you in front of the Grand Duke for deception?"

"What are you talking about, Count Monti?"

"They'll damask you for what you are, a charlatan, an imposter pretending to be a doctor," Fabio said.

A dry itch coursed through Alex's throat, but he'd be damned if he would let Fabio win. On the other hand, if his identity were made public, Rose and her family would suffer too.

"Don't change the subject. I'll demonstrate that you are the one who hurt Rose's father."

"Why would I? He is my future father-in-law," Fabio said, not a muscle moving when he spoke.

"I will fight you, Fabio Monti," Alex said.

"Fight me? How? With thread and a needle, or maybe with the infamous tool you used to burn Count Estes's wound?" Fabio laughed. "One month from today, at dawn, in the Piazza, Dr. Santini, you'll meet your fate by my pistol," Fabio said.

Fabio slammed the door so hard that a few windows shattered into dozens of pieces, shards of glass hitting the ground. Alex jumped to one side, pulling the boy with him.

"And don't send her roses!" Alex shouted. "Stay away from her."

Alex lifted his gaze and stared at the house, a slight movement at one of the windows catching his attention and keeping him in front of the villa for some time. The slim brunette he had first noticed in the balcony at the ball was looking down at him.

"Who is she?" he asked the boy.

"She is Countess Viola, his sister-in-law. She remained on the estate after her husband's death. Count Monti provides for her as long as he lives. Rumors say that she doesn't have any relatives left, and without a dowry, it'll be hard for her to find another companion."

"How do you know all of this, boy?"

"Servants talk, sir," the boy added, lowering his gaze. "And they whisper more."

"More?"

"Like she's influenced Count Monti, and that she's more than a sister-in-law to him. The count hasn't been acting like himself since his brother's demise. Servants say that the hunting accident wasn't in fact a mishap."

"Did she have anything to do with it?"

"No one knows for sure. But she keeps a keen eye on her brother-in-law's affairs."

"She isn't his lover, is she?"

"I'm afraid she is, my lord," the boy added, spurring the horse.

A strange sensation accompanied him all the way to Siena. He had barely spent two months in the past, and yet he had managed to anger a master in duels. With every fiber in his body, Alex had a feeling that Fabio was the offender behind all the attacks on the Estes family. His instinct was telling him that Fabio was in the garden the day Alex had arrived, and he had been talking to a woman about doing whatever it took to put his affairs in order. If only the damn portal would still be open, he could drag Rose away from these rogues and keep her safe. Then they could do whatever they wanted with their wealth, the factory, and their drama.

***

"You did what?" Rose cried. "A duel with Fabio? Are you crazy?"

"Yes, I am crazy from worrying about you getting killed. I'll do whatever it takes to prevent it!" Alex yelled, and then his voice cracked. "I'm not losing you too."

"Like Sophia, you mean."

"Yes, like her," he said, emphasizing every word.

"Even if it means getting yourself hurt or possibly dying?"

Rose trembled. Alex was still in love with his late wife, and he was searching for a way to redeem himself by protecting her now. He would never see her as anything but Sophia's replacement, and she found that thought disturbing.

"I'm not afraid of dying," Alex said.

"How can you say such a thing? Don't you know how hard it is for the ones left behind?" Rose searched the dirt on the ground, and he knew she was avoiding looking at him. "You don't know how to use a gun or a sword. You can't win."

Alex cupped her face between his palms, his touch soft and warm.

"You'll have to teach me," Alex said, laughing.

"You're a mule. Mr. Matteo is waiting for us," Rose said, pulling herself away from Alex's embrace and entering the carriage that waited for them in the alley.

The pounding of horseshoes against the cobblestones resonated between the stone buildings with their brightly painted windows and garlands hanging over the windowsills, while pedestrians hurried about their chores for the day, swarming on the streets. Other carriages cruised back and forth on the main road. When they stopped before an iron gate, a man in his fifties, bald and with a round belly, analyzed Alex from head to toe as soon as he descended from the carriage.

"The new doctor, I reckon," the man said.

"Mr. Matteo, this is Dr. Alessandro Santini," Rose said.

"Count Estes informed us of your arrival. We are ready for you."

"Have we received the new materials yet?" Rose asked.

"We got them at dawn," Mr. Matteo said, turning toward Alex. "We've prepared a room for you. Would you care to see it?"

"Meet me at the cathedral in three hours," Rose said, walking toward her office.

"See you then," Alex said. "After you, Mr. Matteo."

Alex followed the administrator, who led him toward the end of a lengthy corridor with old floors that creaked with every step they took. Workers flanked each side as they passed and their faces were shiny with sweat. Alex peeked through the windows inside the manufactory where men baked porcelain at high temperatures until they achieved the transparency required to add historical scenes. It was what had made the Estes' porcelain famous across the entire continent. Rose mentioned they received orders from as far as London and Paris, even the Grand Duke of Tuscany, for whom Rose painted the family portraits, expected a new set by the summer's end. She had mentioned a private meeting with the Duchess and had asked Alex to accompany her. Alex was excited to meet such a prestigious woman, and all of the sudden, his coming into the eighteen century wasn't as bad as he had feared.

The medical room had shelves, and drawers, and a wooden table. Two large windows overlooking the backyard allowed the light to shine in. Rectangular bricks paved the courtyard, a few of them cracked on the sides, leaving enough space for the weeds to claim their freedom. Alex pushed open the door to the courtyard, and after a few steps, he turned toward an alley between two buildings covered with a mosaic of gray stones.

Alex followed the shouts coming from one of the storage rooms where three men were having trouble lowering a wooden box. One of the men pointed to a busted strap. The weight of the trunk hung dangerously above the man's head. Alex lifted his hands, getting a grip on the vulnerable side of the chest.

"Thank ye,' mate, I thought I'd break my neck," the man said, massaging the back of his shoulders. "The trunk must leave today. We can't afford any delays."

"Luckily, the pieces are intact," the second man said after he had inspected the contents of the trunk.

"Mr. Matteo would have a fit. Let alone Miss Rose, who's here today," the third man added.

"I heard she's the heir now, and that she'll talk to all of us later in the week. Mr. Matteo mentioned something the other day," the first man said.

As he listened to their chatter, Alex caught sight of a gray cape in the back of the room. He sprinted toward it, disregarding the workers who loaded the trunk into a wagon. Alex raised the cloak and grabbed the bow and the arrows that hung from a quiver.

"Whose are these?" he asked, staring at the men across from him.

"Oh, they belong to my cousin. He stored them here until his return. The man likes to hunt in the forest, near the city limits, and to sell the game at the market. He'll be back soon," the third man said while he wiped the sweat from his palms onto his pants.

Alex turned the brown leather bag over on every side, and it was then that he spotted the drops of dry blood. Thoughts crept into his mind. He turned around, preparing to leave, and he stopped dead in his tracks. The same black horse with a white diamond on his forehead, which had been in the forest, was drinking water from a wooden bucket. Alex looked around the storage room, a chill running up his spine. The man who killed the coach driver was close. Alex waved to the three men, and as soon as he disappeared from their view, he sneaked back into the storage room, looking for a place to hide. He covered himself with a rug and waited.

CHAPTER 11

"Elio Marotto is here," Mr. Matteo said, opening the door for a man with green eyes. His hair was tinged with gray, and he had a hat in his hand. Elio had joined Dragoni di Sardegna corps in 1730 as a volunteer, and then he accepted a position with the police. Rose's father used to joke, saying that Elio's taste for adventure hadn't altered with the passing years.

The room seemed to shrink when Elio stepped into Rose's office. He looked at the stack of leather ledgers scattered in front of her and waited for Rose to finish her last entry.

"You remind me of someone," Elio said, teasing her.

"I hope in a good way," Rose said, rising from her chair. "Any news?"

Elio shook his head, and he paced a couple of times through her office, with his hands laced at his back.

"Nothing. What about you?" He stopped in front of her and lifted her chin. "Rose Estes, don't lie. I know that look."

Her voice trembled a little when she spoke.

"I stopped at the shop that sold the dagger and asked the merchant if he remembered the buyer. I paid fifty scudi to make him search through his archives. He sent a note saying a woman had bought it, and that she wanted a mark on the handle, a letter looking like a crown. Only an M met her request. But I refuse to think Mr. Matteo arranged the whole scheme," Rose said, and her brows met above the bridge of her nose.

"Absurd," Elio said. "For what motive?"

Rose shrugged her shoulders and flattened her skirt.

"That's why I called you. Maybe it wouldn't be a bad idea for you to follow him for a while."

"As you wish," Elio said, nodding. "You can't imagine what people will do if something's at stake."

Elio checked Rose's face and said, "You resemble your mother." Then he played with the gold locket protruding from his unbuttoned coat.

Rose couldn't take her eyes off it. "It is precious to you," she said, pointing to the necklace.

"It belonged to my wife. You reminded me of her when she was your age," Elio added, a smile curling his lips.

Rose's father said that Elio's wife had been a kind and gentle woman who died in childbirth, just like her mother, along with their child. Rose looked Elio in the eye, and she found confidence, an arrogant determination to uncover the truth. If anyone were able to discover the mystery surrounding recent events, it would be Elio. He was perfectly suited for the job. He was the chief of the secret police, and the best in Tuscany, according to her father.

"Keep the matter private. Enough rumors are going around," Rose whispered.

"Count on me. I'll inform your father of my findings," Elio said, shoving his hat over his head before disappearing into the corridor.

After Elio had left, Rose peeked through the window at the rain falling over the city. The streets were deserted, and everyone was tucked away in front of a fire where she longed to be. Maybe if she had listened to Alex to remain in bed, her sickness would pass. She locked the door when she left the factory, then she climbed into the waiting carriage, sinking into a seat and resting her head against the seat back. When she closed her eyes, Alex's face came alive, filling her body with a desire she had never felt before. A warm surge came over her heart, and her heartbeats intensified.

The carriage came to a stop, and the coachman helped her out. She lifted her gaze and caught a few drops of rain on her tongue. It tasted like honey. The moments when the first droplets stroked her body were her favorite part of a storm. Thunderstorms scared her out, rain calmed her down and inspired her. Many of her paintings used rain as the background, for history was like rain, events pouring down, shaping the fate of the world.

"Miss Rose, come in from this rain, or you'll catch a cold," Donna De Luca, her tailor, said from the threshold. "Your dress is ready for fitting."

The masquerade ball the Grand Duke of Tuscany held at the palace attracted the high circles of Siena's nobility. Although Alex suggested she should stay home, she had no choice in the matter. She had promised her father to look over the factory, and she had every intention to keep her word. With her life at risk, Rose lacked the energy and the desire for social entertainment, but everyone, including the Duchess, would be present. She touched her forehead. It was burning, and the headache Rose had had for the past weeks intensified. She turned around, looking toward the door when laughter erupted from the next room. It sounded familiar, and Rose wondered if she imagined things because of the fever.

"The lady is here for the same reason as you, my lady: the ball," the seamstress said, sewing tinsel around Rose's cape.

***

Alex remained quiet until the noises faded in the storage room. The three workers left the door open, their voices weakening as they walked through the alleys. Only the horses offered him their company. A few claps of thunder shook the entire structure while silver bullets of rain shot the ground. Strings of fine dust tickled Alex's nostrils. The terrible itch inside his nose turned unbearable. He sneezed, and then he scratched his arms and his thighs, examining the marks he left on his body. Alex jolted at a nearby cough, and he stopped his fidgeting, his mouth growing dry. Someone had entered the storage room, his shadow projected on the opposite wall, his silent, mechanical steps muffled by the straw on the floor.

The man advanced toward the back of the room where he had left his belongings. Alex didn't breathe. The mantle covering his body had enough holes to allow him to see. If only the man would turn around, so he could get a glimpse of his face. After the man had looked around the storage room, he opened a letter. He moved next to a small crack in the wall for some light, folded the paper after he read it, and put it into his mouth. He chewed, and then swallowed, coughing a few times afterward.

"I'm not going to lose it again," Alex heard the man say. The stranger picked up his cape, and the bow and arrows, the money in his pocket jingling as he walked. After another look around, he grabbed a harness and led his horse out of the storage room, locking the door behind him when he left.

"Great," Alex said, tossing his cover away and brushing the dust from his clothes. He jumped from his spot and landed right in the heart of the room. Alex turned to the door and tried the knob. "Damn handle," he cursed. "Now, how do I get out of here?" He checked the distance between the floor and the window pane, considering the odds of him being intact if he climbed out of the window and jumped outside. "All I need is a ladder," he whispered. "If only I can find what I'm looking for in this mess."

After a few minutes of searching, Alex stopped, crossing his hands on the top of his head. His face lightened up at the sight of a rope hanging over some wooden boxes. The workers had left it in their hurry to leave the storage room, and Alex was happy that they had done so. He grabbed it and swung it over his head as he had seen cowboys do in the western movies he used to watch. The rope hissed a couple of times, and after a few unsuccessful attempts, it finally caught a bolt by the window. Alex climbed up the rope, the effort straining his muscles.

"Somebody help me. I'm in here!" Alex shouted from the window, and the wind carried his words, only for them to die in the rain. Beads of cold sweat formed on his face, as he caught a glimpse of the back of the man who locked him inside the storage room, riding into town.

Alex realized that if he wanted to catch up with that man, he had no other solution but to jump from the window, a task easier said than done. The window was on the second floor of the building, and, if by sheer luck, Alex managed to land on the ground, his knees wouldn't withstand the effort and would give up under his weight. He continued screaming and hoping that one of the workers would pass by and help him out.

Half an hour had passed before a worker came running down the alley toward the storage room.

"Dr. Santini, what happened? We searched for you everywhere," he said, pulling the latch from the door.

"Someone locked the door and left. I hoped somebody would remember me," Alex said, sliding down the rope. The palms of his hands burned, and he ran toward the bucket of water the horse had drunk from not too long ago and dipped them inside while he breathed a sigh of relief.

"Miss Rose is waiting for you at the cathedral," the man continued.

"The cathedral?" Alex asked.

"Do you need help to get there?"

"I'll find my way," Alex shouted, sprinting toward the Piazza Publico and leaving the worker behind him.

Pedestrians nudged one another, yelling at Alex to be careful while he continued his race. After a good twenty minutes of running, he stopped at the cathedral and noticed that the horse with the white diamond on his forehead was in front of the church. Alex halted, resting his hands on his knees. He was drenched to the skin. Thunder rumbled close by, the sound resonating between the stone walls.

The cathedral's doors were wide open, and people were going in and out from mass. Alex stepped inside and looked around. The few people inside the church prayed, some on their knees and some on benches. An organ echoed in the vast nave. Alex glanced at the religious paintings and the sophisticated architecture. Nothing had changed, except the faces inside the cathedral. The last vestiges of light penetrated through the round stained-glass windows from where angels watched over the crowds. Marble mosaic tiles depicting scriptural images covered the entire floor and icons lined all the walls.

Alex searched the church until he spotted a man who looked out of place in the sanctity of the site. His mantle covered his face, and his steps resonated when they pounded against the floors. The man headed toward the first row of benches. Alex stopped one row behind him, bowed and then he jerked when he heard other steps approaching. He lowered one knee, and then the other until his forehead touched the back of the chair in front of him. With his face on the ground, he caught a few exchanges between them.

"I found a way, my Lord," the man, whom Alex had followed, said.

"I want the matter settled. Don't forget your family depends on you," the second man said.

"Please, Lord, don't hurt them. I'll finish the task. I promise. Let me see them," the first man begged, his voice breaking up.

"After you've finished your task, not before."

The second man's voice sounded familiar, although his tone was harsh, and the more Alex thought about it, the more he was convinced he had talked to him recently.

"Son, are you ill?" one nun asked him, touching his shoulder.

"No, sister, I was asking for wisdom," Alex said, rising from the floor at the same moment when the two men turned around.

Recognizing Fabio as one of the two men speaking, Alex opened his eyes, hid his face in the sleeve of his shirt, and increased his speed toward the street doors. Shades of purple streaked the sky when he left the church. At a fork in the road, Alex turned around in time to see the men walking in opposite directions. He leaned against the building behind him, looking both ways and deciding to follow Fabio and to let the man with the cape and the arrows go on his way. Alex hid behind an arched door when Fabio turned around. With no weapons at his disposal, alone in a strange time, Alex didn't know whether to laugh or to be scared. *Adventure in a new place*! Alex chuckled, remembering Renaldo's suggestion after one of his therapy sessions.

The crowds on the streets thinned out, leaving Fabio and him alone on the street. Alex remained on the opposite side of the road when Fabio stopped in front of Three Lilies Inn. Alex waited for a few minutes and then crossed the street too. He was ready to enter the tavern and ask for a hot meal when he heard a carriage stopping a few feet away from him. He turned around and sighed when he recognized Rose's coachman.

"What are you doing here? I thought that we were supposed to meet at the cathedral," Rose said, as Alex pushed her back inside the carriage. "I was there minutes ago, and to my surprise, you weren't. A flower girl pointed to a crazy man running like he had seen ghosts. It didn't take long to realize who that was," Rose teased as she looked toward the inn. "I've never been here before. Is there anything special about this place?"

"Rose, Fabio is here, at this inn," Alex said.

"He might be here for a fitting. The masquerade ball attracts everyone in the city," Rose said. "Come in quickly from this rain, or you'll catch a cold."

Alex was soaked to the bone. Rain dripped from his clothes when he entered the carriage. He closed the door, and Rose signaled the coachman to leave.

"A masquerade ball," Alex said, pressing his temples with small, circular movements. *But why did he meet with the hunter that wanted to kill them while they traveled to Siena?* He shook his head and took a deep breath.

"It's quite a sensation among the aristocrats," Rose continued.

"How can you think of another ball when killers are after you? I forbid you to go."

"You can't forbid me to do anything, Alex. This city is my home. You're the guest. Instead of playing the offended party, hone your knowledge of this century."

"Have you forgotten about my duel with Fabio? I need to practice my shooting, not learn about your time. There is nothing that interests me here, except staying alive."

"You should have thought about staying alive before you annoyed Fabio. Even if Mr. Benito assists you, there's not enough time. Why don't you back off on your provocation?"

Alex scoffed."I would rather die trying than give him the satisfaction."

"Fool," Rose whispered. "You don't understand that you can't behave the way you do in your time. Swallow your pride and apologize!"

"Never," Alex said.

For the rest of the trip, Rose looked out the window, and the wheels rattling on the pavement pierced the night. A dog barked nearby. An owl cried, the night carrying its lonely tune across the sleeping town. Rose realized that she didn't feel as lost since she had discovered she was adopted. It had happened to overhear a discussion between her father and her grandmother after Annabella had been born. Rose's grandmother had requested her father to name Annabella heir to the estate, but her father had decided to wait until both girls would come of age to make his decision. Her mother's love story was never brought to light, and her adoptive parents had never discussed it. In their eyes, Rose was their first born and the rightful heir to the estate. Rocked by the carriage and soothed by the falling rain, Rose fell asleep.

Alex studied her face as she slept, and he wished he could interpret her frowns. What was she dreaming about? He touched her cheek, and a smile crept onto the corners of her mouth. He leaned back into the cushion of his seat and his thoughts went back to Fabio and the meeting with the mysterious man at the cathedral. Perhaps he should pay him a visit in the morning and confront him with his findings. He would use all his persuasive powers to make Fabio talk and maybe, with some luck, he would discover the archer's identity.

"We've arrived," the coachman announced, interrupting the questions on Alex's mind.

Alex placed his finger over his lips, and the coachman nodded. Alex picked Rose up, her head resting on his shoulders, her arms hanging loosely. Her breath on his neck sent hot tingles, and he couldn't take his eyes off the pink of her cheeks. Mr. Benito opened the door, illuminating the way. The candle cast a pale light over the house, and their shadows grew on the walls.

"Is Miss Rose all right?" Mr. Benito asked.

"She had a long day," Alex whispered. "I'll take her to her room."

Mr. Benito nodded, leaving the candle at the foot of the staircase as he retired to his own quarters. Alex hugged her as he climbed the stairs toward the second floor. There was a fire burning in the fireplace that spread tongues of warmth across her entire chamber. Lucia rose to her feet as soon as he opened the door.

"Here, doctor," Lucia said. "I'll tend to her now."

Lucia took the shoes off her feet and covered Rose with a quilt.

Alex patted Lucia on the shoulder and said, "I need a bath. Fresh clothes would help too."

"Follow me, doctor," Lucia said, blowing out the candle and closing the door after she had thrown a last look at Rose.

Lucia led him toward the washroom, where a fire was burning.

"You have everything you need in here," Lucia said before she closed the door.

Alex stripped his clothes off and submerged himself in the warm water. He rested his arms on the sides of the bathtub and gazed at a half-moon hiding inside the clouds. Alex had followed the lunar cycle for months and marked the passage of time by cutting the fourteen moons he had drawn in a notebook. He had already cut six moons, and he had eight more left if his calculations were right. Along with tending to the factory workers and learning to ride horseback, Alex had brushed up on his knowledge of literature and science, and he and Rose had extended discussions in the evenings. Sometimes it was hard to remember that she wasn't Sophia, but lately, he discovered it didn't matter too much.

Alex gazed out the window. The rain had stopped, and the clouds began to dissolve. Perhaps, if given a chance, he could grow fond of this time.

CHAPTER 12

"It's time, Doctor," Mr. Benito said in the morning after Alex finished eating the last scone on the breakfast plate.

"For what?" Alex asked, getting up from the chair and wiping the crumbs off his chin as he followed Mr. Benito to the garden.

"For your shooting lesson. You won't be ready for your duel, but at least you'll die a hero."

Alex opened his eyes wide. *Damn, this times and this people!* Alex stomped behind Mr. Benito as they followed the gravel path to the garden, pushing away limbs from the citrus trees that brushed against them. The butler removed his jacket and rolled up his sleeves when they reached a clearing in the back of the garden. He picked out a gun from the case he carried and signaled Alex to grab the other one. Then he pointed to ten pots with flowers arranged at equal distances on a stone fence.

"These are your targets. Shoot as many as you can," Mr. Benito instructed after he showed Alex how to hold the gun and remove the safety pin. "Stand with one foot ahead of you, and one behind. Put your weight on the back leg and bend your knee slightly. Turn your body toward me, and consider that your gun is an extension of your arm. You're one with your pistol. It's part of your body. Now aim at your rival!"

Although Alex did as instructed, the pots were still intact when he finished shooting. Aside from a few birds crying in the nearby trees, which Alex had disturbed with his clumsiness, not a leaf had moved from its place.

"Impressive," Mr. Benito said. "Try again!"

It looks easy in the movies. They aim, shoot, and the enemy falls. Alex shook his head as he put the powder in his gun, as Mr. Benito had shown him, then the bullet, and he aimed at the target once again.

"You'd be dead by the time you remembered the stance," Mr. Benito said. "While you aimed at your enemy, he would have already blown off your head. He'd live, and you'd be honored for stupidity."

Alex swallowed, and he tried again, his shots echoing across the property. It was late in the afternoon when Mr. Benito declared the exercise finished. They returned to the house, and Alex massaged his arm, which was hurting from the strain. He thanked Mr. Benito and promised to meet him again in the evening. He hadn't been that physically exhausted since he had gone to the gym with Sophia. Alex rotated his shoulders and pulled his arms over his head to stretch before he entered his room. He fell asleep the instant his head hit the pillow.

Days passed and Alex's shooting skills improved with Mr. Benito's help. They weren't excellent, but he managed to shoot five pots after twenty days. He went with Rose to the factory, tended to minor injuries, and grew restless as the day of the duel approached. He was inside his office when he saw Mr. Matteo leaving the factory. Alex decided to follow him. He snatched a cape and closed the door to his office. If Rose should inquire about his whereabouts, he instructed a footboy to tell her that he had to check the piazza where Fabio had suggested meeting at the break of dawn. The Inn was close by, and it wouldn't hurt to check on Fabio's whereabouts too. Alex lifted his gaze. *It'll rain again; a passing shower in the spring.* It was May already, and he had spent seven months in the past. He had to survive seven more, a task which seemed impossible with his upcoming duel and the growing feelings of affection he had developed for Rose. The work of discovering who was behind the attack on Rose's father and who was behind their terrifying experience with the arrows on the road was still unfinished. Not even Elio with all the police resources at his disposal was able to shed light on the attacks.

The first drops came down fast, hitting his face. Alex fastened his mantle. A few steps ahead of him, Mr. Matteo, who limped on his left side, leaned on his cane. The knock of the cane resonated on the cobblestones, and Mr. Matteo never turned back. Alex kept his distance, his steps muffled by the falling rain. He remained outside the inn, keeping his eyes on the wood door. Rose's words about the administrator being behind the attack on her father rang in his ears. No one left, and no one arrived after Mr. Matteo entered the inn. The aroma of baked sausage and bread gave rise to the gurgling in Alex's stomach. He leaned on a stone arch across the street from the inn and cracked open the sunflower seeds he found in his pocket. Soon, dozens of empty shells mixed with the fallen leaves and the dirty water on the ground. It wasn't long before the door opened again, and Mr. Matteo left.

"Signor Matteo, you forgot your cane!" the innkeeper yelled through the rain. Mr. Matteo didn't look back. He advanced between stinging droplets, fat with cold water. Alex prepared to leave too, when a heartbeat later, another person emerged from the tavern and entered inside a carriage stationed a foot away from the inn. Alex ran after the carriage, following the wet, empty road, never letting the carriage out of his sight. The coach turned on the first crossroad, and it stopped in front of a tailor's shop. Alex wished he were close enough to the carriage to steal a glance at the passengers. He ducked behind a tree when the coachman held the door open, and a woman descended from the carriage, her face hidden by the hood of her cape. As soon as she entered the shop, Alex approached the carriage and peeked inside through a small opening in the back. He managed to see Mr. Matteo's cane resting on the front seat next to a silhouette draped in gray before everything went black.

***

"Mr. Matteo? Is that you?" Rose asked from her desk when she heard the squeak of the front door.

"Miss Rose, are you still here?" Mr. Matteo asked from across the hallway.

A sliver of light made its way through the cracked door. Rose was looking out the window when the administrator entered her office. The cold rain knocked at the window as the wind hummed through the night. It was late already, and Alex still hadn't returned. She gazed back at the papers in front of her and held her breath for five beats of her heart. *How things changed in just a matter of hours. It had been sunny most of the day and then turned stormy as the night settled the town.*

"Mr. Matteo, a ledger is missing, the one with entries from last month," Rose said, looking at the administrator.

Mr. Matteo wiped his forehead with the back of his sleeve. His face flushed, and he opened a window. "Some fresh air would do us good. I have had a long day."

Rain washed the windowsills, and an unexpected gust of wind scattered the pile of papers on the desk all over the room.

"Mr. Matteo, close the window. The rain will ruin Father's office."

"Yes, my lady," Mr. Matteo said.

"How about the ledger?"

"The ledger? I left it at my house, though I was sure I'd shoved it in my briefcase this morning. I took it with me to catch up on my work. I'll bring it tomorrow, Miss Rose."

Rose put the papers back on her desk. The deep aching inside her body hadn't left her since she had arrived in Siena, back in February. Seven months had passed since she first met Alex. Other than adding some color to his cheeks and learning how to ride and shoot, he hadn't changed much. He kept to himself most of the time, and she knew he was restless to leave her world behind and return to his time. Her father went to Florence often to supervise the opening of their second factory, and Annabella was preoccupied with the wedding. Rose was left to deal with the factory's problems alone, and no one knew that she had to watch over Alex too.

"We'll settle the matter tomorrow, after the meeting with the laborers. It's late, and I have errands to run. Tell the coachman to ready the carriage," Rose said.

"Right away, Miss Rose," Mr. Matteo said before he disappeared into the hallway.

Rose locked her office and left the factory.

"Take me to the gunsmith," Rose ordered the coachman, as she leaned into the seat.

Mr. Matteo had worked for the family since before she was born. Her father trusted him with their finances and the factory. The more she thought about what had happened, the more she realized that he couldn't orchestrate such an atrocity, like trying to kill her father or her. The passage of time had softened his face, and thin lines furrowed his skin. He had dark circles under his eyes now and a slight tremor in his hand. Mr. Matteo was anything but a criminal. He had never married or had a life of his own because his work always prevailed over such trivial issues. He came from a family of ten from the outskirts of Siena. He was the oldest son and was responsible for feeding his brothers and sisters after their parents had died from the plague that swept through all of Europe at the dawn of the century. There was no way that she would ever believe him to be a criminal.

After half an hour, the carriage stopped at the only gunsmith in the city, not too far from the factory. Along with the other three men in the shop, Rose browsed through the pistols on display as the shopkeeper watched her intently. Rose didn't pay attention to them, nor did she care for the way they were nudging each other. She searched for a flintlock, fast and durable, and when she discovered the brass furniture pistol, she signaled the merchant to approach.

"One hundred scudi," the man said.

Rose opened her purse and paid him, and then she took the gun from his hand and shoved it into the back of her purse. Then, she asked the coachman to ride home. She would give it to Alex before his duel. That stubborn man would be the death of her. Worrying about him parading all those things he brought from his time around as if they were nothing would kill her one day. The cell phone had died because, as Alex said, it couldn't be *charged* in her century. People in the eighteen century lacked the *electricity* needed for his phone to return to life and bring back all those images of his late wife that he cherished so much. Only the laser pen was still functional because of the sun. Rose tried to understand how the sun charged the laser pen with energy, but she still found his explanations confusing. She remembered that one evening she had told Alex that he should get rid of the watch he was wearing around his right wrist, and he agreed to shove it in the back of the briefcase he kept in his room. Rose had managed to keep him safe for the past seven months, but the portal wouldn't open for at least seven more.

***

Someone shook him.

"Wake up, mister," Elio said.

Alex felt a burning sensation in the back of his neck where he had been struck, his body trembled with spasms, and an excruciating pain flooded through his head.

"My head," Alex moaned, holding his head between his palms. He looked at the man with green eyes and grabbed the hand that he had extended.

"You aren't from around here," he said. "I'm Elio Marotto, chief of the secret police."

"I've heard about you. I'm Alex Santini. Pleased to meet you."

Elio studied him, and his eyes narrowed under thick brows. "I wish I could return your enthusiasm, son."

"What happened to the carriage?" Alex asked.

"I didn't have enough time to track it. A man hit you in the back of the head and disposed of you under this tree. By the time I woke you up both had disappeared from my view."

Alex thought for a minute, searching the man in front of him.

"Why were you here?"

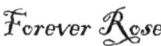

"Miss Rose hired me to track Mr. Matteo, and I saw you doing the same thing. I followed you."

"She thinks he's the culprit, but my gut tells me otherwise."

"I better take you home, Doctor, before this weather gets the best of you," Elio said, throwing Alex's arm around his neck and helping him walk.

***

The night was as dark as Rose's thoughts. The sight of her villa at the end of the alley made her take a long, deep breath. The falling droplets smashed against the pavement. Rose hugged the purse where she had tucked the pistol she intended to give to Alex when the butler emerged from the house.

"Miss Rose, the Doctor is hurt," Mr. Benito said as soon as she passed over the threshold.

Rose sighed and asked, "Where is he?"

"In the library, with Mr. Marotto," Mr. Benito added.

Her stomping on the marble floors resonated throughout the foyer. Rose opened the door to the library where a fire was burning, taking in the entire scene. Alex lay on the sofa, with a rag on his head, his clothes wet and caked with water and mud, while Elio sat next to him. When she entered the room, Elio jumped to his feet.

"What did you do?" Rose asked.

Alex shrugged his shoulders. "Nothing."

"I found him lying next to Madam De Luca's shop," Elio answered for him. He pushed Rose away from Alex and poured her a glass of sherry. "You look like you could use a drink, my dear."

"What happened?" Rose took a sip from her glass.

"After I left your office, I decided to stick around. When Mr. Matteo left, I tracked him to the Three Lilies Inn," Elio said, sitting again on a chair by the fireplace where a fire was burning.

"My head," Alex moaned.

"So far, I don't see anything unusual in what you're telling me," Rose said, searching Alex, who moved his head from one side to the other.

"I know. That's what I thought too. But you see, Mr. Matteo entered the tavern with a cane, and he left without it. I found this to be interesting," Elio said.

"Maybe he forgot the cane," Rose suggested.

"No, he didn't. Another person left the inn with Mr. Matteo's cane," Elio added.

"That's why I chased after the carriage. I thought Fabio was inside," Alex said, joining their conversation. "Someone left the inn in the carriage, and I followed. The coachman stopped at a tailor's shop around six or seven."

"So, what happened next?" Rose asked.

"A woman entered the shop. Alex tried peeking inside the carriage. It happened fast. Someone appeared out of nowhere and hit him in the back of his head. He blacked out," Elio said, fidgeting in his chair.

"Oh, Elio, what a terrible thing! Alex could have lost his life."

Rose crossed her arms over her chest, while she looked at Alex.

"One thing is sure. Somehow Matteo, Fabio, and the mysterious woman are connected," Alex said. "I'll be meeting with Fabio soon. Maybe I can drag the answer out of him."

"You?" Rose and Elio asked at the same time, the skepticism in their voices not escaping Alex.

Elio left his spot next to the fireplace, and he put one hand on Rose's shoulder.

"Does anyone care to explain this meeting that will happen soon? And what is it that you have in your hand?"

Rose had pulled the pistol from her purse. It shone in the light.

"For you," Rose said, dropping the pistol in Alex's lap. "You need it since you provoked Fabio to a duel."

"A duel?" Elio asked. "You're out of your mind if you think you can beat Fabio."

Rose told Elio about Alex's determination to protect her from Fabio, who in Alex's opinion, wanted to kill her and get her inheritance. As Elio listened, not a muscle moved on his face. Alex threw the wet rag from his forehead, set the pistol on the bed and rose to his feet.

"Rose thinks Mr. Matteo is the one who plotted against her family. I totally disagree," Alex said.

"So, I should follow Mr. Matteo while Alex fights with Fabio," Elio spelled it out for all of them.

"Correct," Alex and Rose said in unison.

Rose cupped her face with her hands and remained silent for several minutes. *Mr. Matteo, the man her father trusted deeply, involved in such an atrocity?* A tear threatened to spill, and she lifted her chin, pursing her lips.

"You want me to believe that a man and a woman are involved in this scheme and that Mr. Matteo is their accomplice? And who is the archer who followed us on the road to Siena?" Rose shook her head. "No, it can't be him. We're missing something," she said. "Indeed, Mr. Matteo lied about the ledger. He said he had left it at his house. Father said he had discovered entries without justification in the books. I wonder about what other things he's lying about. He's acting suspiciously." Rose took Elio's hands into hers. "You may be right, Elio. Keep an eye on him."

"He could lead us to the real conspirators," Elio suggested. "We'll get to the bottom of this, Rose, I promise."

"Will he be all right?" Rose asked.

Elio looked at Alex, who had returned to the sofa, his head resting on a pillow and his shirt unbuttoned.

"He'll have a headache in the morning," Elio whispered. "I must retire, my lady. The hour is late."

"Don't let him face Fabio all alone. Go with him. It'll make me feel better knowing you're with him."

CHAPTER 13

From his window, Alex watched as Rose left the villa at dawn. He leaned on the windowsill, thinking of the past day's events. Whom did Mr. Matteo meet at the inn and who was the woman who went into Donna De Luca's shop? The connection between the two was a mystery indeed, but the identity of the figure draped in gray, who was now in possession of the cane was even more puzzling. And why did that person have Mr. Matteo's cane?

Alex didn't hear the butler entering his bedchamber. His voice startled him when Mr. Benito said, "Dr. Alex, Miss Rose left already."

"I know, Mr. Benito. Can you bring me a horse?"

The butler sized him up, nodded, and then he shouted to Antonio, who stood at the main entrance.

"Dr. Santini requires a horse. Make sure to saddle the black one."

Hearing his name, Antonio looked up, shading his eyes from the sun, and nodded.

After he had given the order, Mr. Benito turned to face Alex. "Do you need him to ride with you into town?"

"No need, Mr. Benito. I can find my way," Alex said.

Alex exited the house and mounted the horse that stood waiting for him by the front door. He held the reins in his hands firmly, just like Rose had taught him, and headed into the city. The air was crisp, and there were only a few people on streets. A stray dog barked, splitting the silence of the dawn. Alex stopped in front of the Three Lilies Inn where Mr. Matteo had entered the day before. It was quiet inside, except for the noise coming from the kitchen. The host, a fat man, almost bald, with a short black beard and a huge smile, greeted him.

"Good morning, sir. I'm Carlo, and she is my wife, Corina. How can we 'elp you?"

The man appeared to be in his late forties, and his wife, not more than thirty. Alex looked at them fascinated by the frozen smiles on their faces, which made them look like they belonged on a stamp. He flashed a smile.

"I'm searching for a friend of mine. I wonder if I may have a word with him," Alex said.

"A friend, you say? You know, senor, we don't reveal the names of our guests, the inn's policy, unless we're instructed to do otherwise. We 'old their identities confidential."

"I understand, Mr. Carlo. Maybe these," Alex said, placing ten scudi in his hand, "will help you remember if Count Monti is still a guest at your inn."

"Would you like some wine while I check to see if your friend is still 'ere, my lord?" the landlord asked, not losing sight of him.

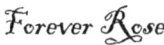

"Bring me a red one," Alex said, "and some food. I'm starving. I hoped to eat with the Count."

"My wife is an excellent cook. She used to work for the late Duke of Tuscany before 'e got married and his wife 'ired a French cook. I offered 'er a job in my tavern and ended up marrying 'er three months later. She'll take care of you," Mr. Carlo said, smacking his wife's buttocks.

Corina, the innkeeper's wife, placed a glass of wine in front of Alex and returned to the kitchen to whisk eggs. After she had finished beating the eggs, she threw them in a pan on the stove, stirring them from time to time with a wooden spoon. The fragrance of baked bread blended with the aroma of salami and olive oil. It wasn't long before she returned with a full plate and placed it on the table.

"Madam, you have my compliments. I haven't eaten anything this delicious in a very long time," Alex said, licking his fingers after the first bite and leaving the payment of three scudi on the table.

"Thank you, young man," Corina answered before she put the money in her pocket. "My husband will bring you news of your friend if he hasn't left us already."

"I surely hope so. I wish to have a word or two with him, concerning his estate," Alex said as he shoved the last morsel into his mouth.

"The Count left early this morning and didn't say when 'e will be back," the landlord said when he returned to the tavern, carrying the guest register.

"That is unfortunate news," Alex said. He rose from the chair and pushed away from the table. "Thank you for the food. I shall come here more often."

"Farewell, my lord, and please, do so. We are 'appy to feed a 'ungry stomach," Corina said.

As soon as she finished her sentence an arrow flew through the air, and it stopped right above Alex's ear, sticking in the wood pillar behind him. They ducked, backs against the walls while a scream escaped from the woman's mouth.

"Keep quiet. Is there another exit other than the front door?" Alex asked.

The landlord pointed to a door in the back. He crawled to his wife, grabbing her shoulders and holding her tight. Alex rolled on the floor, hardly making a sound, and he crawled until he reached a semi-obscure hallway filled with boxes. He stopped at the door leading to the back, cracked it open and peeked at the building across the street from where the arrow had come. The shooter was on his knees on the roof, with the bow pointed at the inn's front door.

Alex ran across the street when the archer happened to look to his side, distracted by the sound of flying birds, and he grabbed a ladder that was leaning on the side of the building where the attacker was. His body was covered with sweat when he reached the roof. The grinding of the stones under Alex's feet made the man straighten up. Alex's heart was drumming in his ears, and his blood was boiling. He jumped on the man, smashing him under his weight. In the flash of a moment, Alex managed to free one of his arms, and he punched the man in his left cheek.

"Who are you?" Alex asked.

The attacker threw Alex over his back and punched him in the stomach. Alex landed hard, struggling to push him away, while the stones pierced his shirt, bruising his back. The blade in the attacker's hand shone in the sun, sending chills up his spine. After one more altercation, they rose at the same moment, facing each other.

"Wait a minute. I know who you are."

The attacker threw the knife in Alex's direction before he turned around and ran among the colorful chimneys. Alex ducked, the knife missing him completely, before he descended from the roof, his hands shaking badly by the time he reached the ground. He would have recognized that scar anywhere—it belonged to none other than Thomas, Lucia's brother.

**

"Mr. Matteo, two coaches are leaving in less than an hour. Here, send the documents with the trunks. The addresses are clearly marked, so the carrier shouldn't have any problems," Rose said.

"I'll let him know," Mr. Matteo said.

"And don't forget to ask the owners to sign the receiving slips after they inspect the products."

Mr. Matteo hurried out of the door just when Alex squeezed in. He locked the door behind him and took a few steps before collapsing into one of the chairs facing Rose's desk.

"What happened to you?" Rose asked, searching his clothes splashed with blood.

Alex grabbed her hand, motioning her to sit in a chair next to him. "I discovered who wants to get rid of you," Alex said.

"Did you?" Rose asked. "Who is he? Tell me his name."

"Fabio," Alex answered in one breath.

Rose pursed her lips and burst into laughter. Alex rose from his chair and leaned over her, shaking her shoulders. Rose freed herself from his grip and indicated with a look in her eyes that he should sit again. Her voice was soft when she spoke.

"You can't be serious. Fabio is going to wed my sister and become part of the family. Why would he commit such an atrocity?"

"He's using Lucia's brother, Rose. You have to believe me. Is he even in love with your sister?"

"I'm not sure," Rose said. "She loves him dearly. I hope, for her sake, his feelings are real."

"I doubt it," Alex whispered and stared at her as she played with a curl, "but I intend to find out tomorrow."

"Me too, if you come out alive from your duel," Rose said.

***

Alex was already dressed when Mr. Benito knocked five times on his door early in the morning. His rattling of the doorknob went unnoticed; everyone else was still asleep in the villa.

"It is time, Doctor," Mr. Benito said, handing Alex his gun and following him down the stairs. "God be with you!"

"Mr. Benito, God has better things to do than watch over pitiful men like us," Alex said, as he sneaked out of the house. He mounted the black horse that the footboy brought from the stable and left the property while the fog concealed both the rider and his mare. As soon as he reached the main street, another horse breathed close by, and Alex turned his head to his right in time to see Elio. His coat was buttoned up to his neck, his pistol protruded from its sheath, and his hands held the reins tightly.

"Ready, Doctor?" Elio asked.

"As ready as I'll ever be," Alex answered.

"You're brave to summon Count Monti when people run away from him."

"My heart tells me he's on the verge of hurting anyone who stands in his path," Alex said. He clenched his jaw and ground his teeth.

"Don't panic, Doctor. Hold your gun firmly and aim at your target."

The streets were deserted at sunrise, and the first rays of sun made the last traces of rain sparkle. It was a crisp day, the air spicy with the scent of leaves and citrus. Alex bit his bottom lip until he tasted blood, sweet and warm, and he closed his eyes for a moment, calming his heart and emptying his mind. He was fighting for a woman's life. He would be defeated. He was convinced he would lose because he wasn't good enough to protect any of the people important to him. He was no match for people who shot others for the fun of it or as a way of conveying their importance. Confronted with the perspective of joining his dead wife and child, Alex breathed a sigh of relief. He would pay his debt. He would avenge Sophia's death by saving another woman's life.

"We're here," Elio said. "Fabio and his servant are waiting." Elio pointed at Fabio, who waited next to his companion.

Fabio wore a white shirt, and he had his sleeves rolled up to his elbows. His hair was hanging loosely over his back, and his eyes were icy as he followed Alex and Elio as they approached the Piazza Publico. Alex dismounted from his horse when he got about five feet from Fabio and set the horse free. Elio jumped from his mount too.

"Count Monti, you know the rules," Elio said.

"Doesn't everyone?" Fabio asked, and his eyes never left Alex. "Shall I explain the rules to you, Doctor? The place you come from might have different ones."

"What place is he talking about?" Elio asked, looking at Alex and waiting for an answer.

"Not now," Alex whispered. He would have loved to grab the villain by his throat and make him count the rocks on the road, but he cracked his knuckles instead. Alex extended his arm. His hold was firm on the pistol, his eyes were narrowed, and his mouth set in a firm line. Fabio took his stance and waited for the signal. A crow circled over their heads, its desperate cry disturbing the silence. Alex lifted his gaze toward the sky, following the circular motion of the bird's soaring. *You are free of rules! How I envy your freedom.* He chuckled, calculating the distance between him and Fabio. They were about twenty feet apart. Alex had serious doubts that he would come away alive from the duel.

"On the count of three, fire," Elio said. "One shot, gentlemen, and no cheating."

"No one would dare cheat," Fabio said.

Fabio's servant covered his eyes. Elio stood by their horses while Alex cocked his pistol. He remembered every rule that Mr. Benito had taught him in the past few weeks: back straight, feet apart, aim at the target and shoot without hesitation.

"You're brave, Doctor," Fabio said. "It'll be a shame to kill you."

"How gracious of you, my lord," Alex said.

"One, two, three," Elio counted, his voice piercing the silence of the square. Two shots echoed in the empty piazza, the odor of burning powder tainting the air.

The throb in his shoulder made Alex bite his lip. He studied the wound. Judging by the size of the growing spot on his shirt and the pain in his muscle, he had been severely injured. The bullet had never exited his body, and the longer he waited to receive medical treatment, the harder his recovery would be. He had to get back to the villa while he was still conscious because there was no way he would go to a hospital and answer uncomfortable questions about him.

Alex fell to his knees.

"Next time, it'll be the end of you, Doctor. I'll send you back to where you came from," Fabio said, his face as rigid as the marble statue behind him. He mounted his horse and raced straight out of the piazza. Alex sighed as he looked at Elio, who shook his head while he helped Alex mount his horse.

"It seems it's my fate to rescue you, son," Elio said.

"He's an excellent marksman," Alex said. "I should thank him for sparing me the embarrassment of dying."

"You need medical attention, and fast. You're losing too much blood."

"I hate hospitals. Take me to the villa instead."

Alex leaned on the horse as they raced along the street where a few men, attracted by the sound of gunshots, began to gather. Blood dripped from his shoulder, down his arm, and over the horse's back. He knew that he didn't have much time until he entered into hypovolemic shock. Alex tore his sleeve and tied it around the wound. For Rose's sake and her family's, he had to make it inside the house before everyone started to inquire about the identity of the mysterious man who dared to provoke Count Monti, the illustrious marksman of Tuscany, to a duel. Alex spurred his horse, and Elio followed him.

***

"The ledgers are in your office," Mr. Matteo said as soon as Rose stood on the threshold. She couldn't stop Alex from dueling with Fabio. She would never forgive herself if Alex died in the duel because of her. The thought of it left her feeling empty.

Rose hurried along the corridor with the administrator following close behind her.

"Let's take a look," Rose said. Leaning over the thick ledgers on her desk, Rose scrolled down each page and studied every entry until a nagging pain between her shoulder blades made her call off the meeting. She was ready to close the last journal. "And this?" she asked, pointing to the final dates in the ledger. "Why the difference in the payments?"

Rose stared at Mr. Matteo. Although the previous day's storm had chilled the air, and the early sun wasn't high enough to heat the room, she couldn't help but notice how hot it was in the chamber. Her heart started to beat fast, a slight dizziness making her feel sick.

"Are you all right, Miss Rose? A cup of water, perhaps?" Mr. Matteo ran to the door, and she heard him yell. "Someone, bring water fast!"

"I'm all right, Mr. Matteo, don't worry," Rose whispered.

"Hurry up, boy!" Mr. Matteo shouted from the threshold. "Do you want me to call the doctor?"

"Don't bother. It'll pass. This awful cold is more stubborn than me." Rose straightened her posture, back against the chair, hands resting on her desk, eyes slowly rising from the book. "Mr. Matteo, what should I make of the missing entries?" A skeptical brow hardened her features.

"I thought you wanted to keep the payment for Mr. Marotto's investigation out of the books. Who knows how high his expenses will become?"

"The affair slipped my mind," Rose said.

Mr. Matteo was right. She forgot about hiring Elio not only to find the assassin but also to help her recover the lost contracts for the opening of the factory in Florence. Her father decided to expand their trade to Florence. He had spent the last month's meeting with construction companies and looking over architectural plans for a new facility from where he intended to manage the porcelain business. He had left the contracts he had signed with the builders in Rose's care, but they had mysteriously disappeared, and her father was afraid his competitors would find out and take advantage of the situation. Elio's job was to discover what happened before anyone else did.

Rose, Elio, and Count Estes decided it was in their best interest to keep matters private, so they didn't tell Mr. Matteo about the contracts. No one had to get wind of the suspicion hanging over the administrator's head. Elio suggested checking Mr. Matteo's acquaintances and his finances. Alex said that Fabio should be under observation too. Divided between her conscience and her heart, Rose agreed that both Fabio and Mr. Matteo had a connection with the mysterious woman and the archer and that Elio's agents should follow them. Perhaps, in due time, they would be able to come up with the answers.

"Enter," Rose said when she heard a knock on her door.

"My lady," Elio Marotto said, holding his hat.

"Elio," Rose said. "Mr. Matteo, return to your tasks," she commanded and waited until the administrator had left the office. "What news do you bring me?"

"Not good news," Elio said.

"How's Alex?"

"Fabio didn't kill him." Elio took a seat close to her, his eyes looking troubled. "Fabio blew a hole in his shoulder. He insisted on treating his injury himself. He refused to go to the hospital. Very strange," Elio said, shaking his head. "When I left him, he was in a lot of pain."

Rose covered her mouth.

"What is the place from where the doctor comes? Fabio kept saying he should return to his home," Elio said, looking at Rose.

Rose's cheeks burned, but she couldn't tell him about Alex.

"Not now, Elio, time is slipping away," she said, storming out the door and leaving Elio inside her office.

Rose ran down the hallway, passing Mr. Matteo on her way out, and she mounted her horse. She reached the villa and ran up the stairs to his room. She found him resting on the bed. His bloody shirt was on the floor, and Mr. Benito stood with him. The butler put his fingers to his lips, and Rose remained quiet. Rose leaned over Alex, studying him. He was pale, a bandage covered his shoulder, and his arms hung limply.

"I had to give him five full spoons of laudanum before he slept," Mr. Benito said. "The doctor is a sturdy fellow. He pulled the bullet out by himself, using a knife, and then he used this instrument," he said, pointing to the laser pen next to him, on the bed.

"It's a new medical device they use to close wounds, Mr. Benito," Rose whispered, soaking Alex's lips with a wet washcloth. "I'll stay with him. You may return to your duties."

"As you wish, my lady," Mr. Benito said. "He needs to stay warm."

"Start a fire," she said, "and, Mr. Benito, discretion."

After the butler had left, Rose covered Alex with a quilt and prepared another tonic, forcing him to drink. She spent the afternoon and evening there and decided to sleep in a chair next to his bed. She jumped to her feet every time he moaned throughout the night. In the morning, when he opened his eyes, Rose asked him if he wanted to eat.

"No," Alex said and slept through most of the day.

Rose didn't leave his side, save for the moments when Mr. Benito changed his bandages.

The next day, Mr. Benito brought him a bowl of soup, and Rose said she would feed it to him. When he burned his tongue on the soup, Alex pushed the bowl away and fell back on pillows. Rose didn't say a word. She helped the maid clean the mess, and she left his room only after he fell asleep.

Days passed, and Rose, Lucia, and Mr. Benito took turns watching Alex. Both servants complained about his disposition and refused to stay with him under the pretext of having chores to finish. Rose read to him from books she thought he'd enjoy, and they counted the months left until the portal would open. Rose didn't blame Alex a bit for wanting to return to his time. She couldn't imagine herself being trapped in a strange time and having to survive for so long. Alex was the bravest man Rose had ever met, and she had grown fond of him in the past months. The more time she spent with him, the more she came to understand his behavior. It wasn't that he was an angry fellow, not at all. He was only frustrated with the entire situation. Rose would have been too if the situation was reversed and she had found herself trapped in his time.

The days when she wasn't caring for Alex, Rose signed documents that Mr. Matteo had brought from the factory, released papers for orders or materials, or she painted in her studio. It was always a pleasant surprise when Alex inquired about the nature of her work.

"I just remembered a detail about the supermoon," Alex said one evening after they had finished eating a delicious cake filled with apricots that the cook had prepared in his honor. It was his thirty-fifth birthday. Alex was fifteen years older than Rose was, and he felt that he owed her his life. He knew he wouldn't even be there had Rose not stumbled upon him in her garden that first night and taken him to her cottage to conceal his identity. Alex didn't know how he would ever repay her kindness, and he vowed that, as long as he remained in Siena, he would protect Rose.

"What is that?" Rose asked.

"The moon has to be full, and the sun, the earth, and the moon have to align in a straight line."

"Sounds complicated," Rose said, gazing through the window at the gardens below. "How will you know if they align in a straight line?"

"The portal to my time will open again. It's what the supermoon does," Alex said weakly.

He had been confined to the villa for two months, and Rose had spent every day caring for him. One day, she went to the door, and Alex hollered after her.

"Where do you think you're going?"

"I'll be right back," Rose said, closing the door behind her.

Since she couldn't go to the factory and leave Alex by himself all day, Rose decided to move her easel and brushes into Alex's room. Day after day, his health improved, and his mood seemed to change. If she left him alone, Alex began to shout, and his manners terrified all the maids in the house. He was at peace only when Rose was in the same room with him, and Mr. Benito recommended that she should stay with him, for all the staff's sake.

Exhausted from tending to Alex, Rose withdrew from the world and devoted her time to painting. The Duke of Tuscany had asked her to paint the signing of the Peace Treaty in Vienna when Tuscany was officially handed to him, and she dedicated her time to that historical moment. Rose spent an entire month running between Alex's room and the Duke's palace. Thoughts of Alex consumed her nights, and she tossed in her bed unable to sleep until dawn when she would return to painting. Her strokes became elaborate, her paintings in high demand not only in Italy but also in Austria and Poland. More requests came from the Duke of Tuscany, and Rose fulfilled them all. After weeks of hard work, one day, Rose took a step away from the easel, and she was pleased with what she saw.

Rose made sure that his outbursts didn't anger her staff. She thought of the morning when she had discovered Alex at the mouth of the cave, and it seemed like it had happened a very long time ago. She knew he didn't belong to her because he was a time traveler, and that one day, he would go back to his world. Rose wanted him to stay but lacked the courage to tell him how she felt about him. After his departure, she would go to Florence and paint. She would make her father proud by becoming the first historical painter in Tuscany. Rose didn't tell Alex about her decision to join the Art Department at the University of Florence. She already knew how proud he would be of her decision to take charge of her life. He always said that her passion showed in her paintings.

She was on her way to his room one day when Alex's wails resonated throughout his bedchamber. She cracked open the door and stepped inside his room.

"How much time does it take to go to your studio, grab your colors and return? And why didn't you ask your maid to just bring them to you?" he asked.

Rose had gone to pick up a color she had forgotten in her studio and then had spent two hours arranging her canvases on the studio's walls.

"They were busy with their chores," Rose said calmly.

"Why are you painting when you can talk to me?"

"I'm afraid painting is all I am good right now."

"I find that hard to believe. I'm sure you're good at many things," Alex said, closing the book he was reading.

"Painting is my escape from the world, Alex. It helps me to relax. And your company's awful."

Alex jumped from the bed and walked toward her. Rose took one step back, and he took another one toward her. He circled his arms around her shoulders, and she rested her forehead against his chest.

"I'm sorry. I hate being helpless," Alex said, touching her forehead. "You're burning up!"

"It's nothing. It'll pass."

Alex kissed her hair as he held her, and he was happy she didn't pull away from him. He realized he had been unkind to her, but he couldn't help it. Like most doctors, he had always been a terrible patient. The compassion in her eyes when she tended to him, her closeness, and the smell of her skin, all awoke dormant sensations, urgent needs. He yearned for her, and the realization scared him. He wouldn't allow himself to fall in love with her when he knew there was no future for them. Soon, he would leave to return to his time, and she would marry some wealthy aristocrat if she survived. All of a sudden, the months left until his departure seemed a very short period. Back in his time, he would wonder what had happened to her, and he hoped that history would keep detailed records of her life. Alex sighed, for today at

least, they were together, and Rose was safe. And he was safe too. Only his heart was exposed.

"Can you dance?" Rose asked, pulling herself from his embrace.

"Dance?"

"The ball is just around the corner. Remember?"

"Only you could think of dancing at a time like this," Alex said.

The truth was that he had two left feet. Sophia had tried teaching him, but she had abandoned her lessons after he kept stepping on her toes. She called him a hopeless klutz, a lost cause. Now Rose wanted to do the same. What was it with every woman trying to change him into something he wasn't?

"I don't know how to dance either. I thought you could teach me. Father used to count the steps for me when we danced. So far, I have only managed the waltz and the minuet," Rose said.

Alex started to laugh, and Rose joined him.

"We're quite a couple."

He extended his arm. Rose approached him. She put her hand on his shoulder while he encircled her waist. They moved forward a few steps, and Alex stepped on her toes. She grinned and started to count.

"One, two, three, one, two, three," Rose said, as he hummed a song he remembered from his time, the Blue Danube. They were close, the heat between them palpable. She parted her lips, and he swallowed. Her breathing accelerated, and he leaned toward her until he brushed his lips against hers. He kissed her while they waltzed around the room.

"When you look into my eyes, as you do now, I hold my breath for fear of losing the moment," Alex said when they stopped.

Rose held her breath before running out the door. Alex fell onto the bed. He couldn't deny his feelings for her any longer, and the thought scared him. He looked out the window and saw her running toward the garden.

Rose fell on her knees. She covered her chest with one hand while she touched her lips with the other. She shook her head, and minutes passed before she returned to the villa. Shocked by the attraction she felt toward Alex, Rose knew that she had to keep him at a distance. He didn't love her. She knew she was right about that. He only saw Sophia in her. Alex told her that he didn't approach other women after Sophia's death. She was a fool to love a man who couldn't belong to her. The right thing to do was to stay away from him and try to keep him alive for the rest of his stay.

Rose entered Alex's room. She touched his face and went back to her easel. Neither said a word about the kiss. Alex picked up the book he had left on his bed and tried to read. He studied her face as she concentrated on her canvas. When she lifted her gaze, he pretended to focus on the book.

"I believe we will manage a dance or two," Rose said.

"If you'll save me one," Alex added.

"May I ask you something?"

"Go ahead."

"What if, when the portal opens, you end up at a time other than yours? What will you do?"

Alex scratched his head. He hadn't thought of that possibility. "That would be very wrong. I'd be caught in a different time for the next fourteen months," he said. *And you wouldn't be around to make my stay enjoyable.*

"Have you ever considered staying?" Rose asked, and she stopped painting while she waited for his answer.

"To do what? I can't be a nuisance to you all your life. We'll discover who wants you dead and bring them to justice before my departure. Then, you'll get married and have children."

"I can't marry. No one will understand my desire to paint," Rose said.

"The right man will," Alex added. "Did you give up on love?"

"Love has nothing to do with being human. I loved once, and it was enough."

"What happened to your love?"

"He couldn't stay," Rose said, wishing Alex would change his mind. His ideas were too modern for her people, his skills, and knowledge way beyond this day and time. Eventually, the people of her time would uncover the truth about Alex, and she couldn't bear to see him hurt. Tomorrow, in her meeting with Elio, she would ask him to hurry with his search.

CHAPTER 14

The next day, Rose returned to the factory. She needed time apart from Alex, and the business would occupy her thoughts. She was in her office when Elio came, and he told her that he still didn't have news about the contracts that had disappeared. Rose was frantic because the date for her father's upcoming meeting with the builders was approaching.

"You must find them, Elio! You know father's interest in them."

"I'll do as you wish, my lady," Elio said.

As he prepared to leave the office, a knock on the door startled them.

"Viola, my dear, what a surprise," Rose said, embracing her friend. "What are you doing in Siena?"

"The same thing as you, my dear, I'm here for the masquerade ball. I can't miss the event of the season."

"Countess Monti, your beauty precedes you," Elio said, kissing the woman's gloved hand.

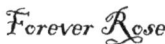

"You mean the gossip you've heard, Mr. Marotto. The pleasure is all mine," Viola added.

"You shall not pay attention to rumors, my lady. They die with grace, new ones replacing the old. Good day, Miss Rose, and I'll keep you informed."

"Farewell, Mr. Marotto," Rose said, and she turned to her friend. "Tell me about my sister. Is she well?"

"Annabella is fussing with the wedding preparations, and she refuses to attend the ball. I think it's the first one she will miss."

"I wonder if she'll finish in time," Rose said, stopping by the window. "Would you care for a cup of tea or maybe some water?" Rose asked. "What's the matter with you? You seem preoccupied."

"You're a darling, but no, thank you. I was on my way to the tailor and decided to drop in to see you. I was scared for your doctor when I heard he had fought with Fabio," Viola said. "The man was brave to accept a duel he knew he would lose."

"Men and their big egos," Rose answered. "Are you sure you are not hiding something from me? Are you ill?"

The color drained from Viola's face, and as she braced herself, Rose knew something was definitely bothering her friend. Since she had lost her husband, she locked herself in the villa, and she rarely attended social functions. Rose had to force her to go riding with her after her return from London, and Viola was inclined to refuse the invitation to her birthday party.

"Time to go," Viola said when the clock chimed twelve. "I must stop at Dr. Guillermo's, too. Don't give me that look! It's nothing but a routine examination."

"Why don't you come to dinner tonight? Then, you can tell me what you think about Alex."

"Alex," Viola repeated the name of the doctor while she pulled her gloves up to her arms and lifted a brow. For just a fraction of a second, Rose swore Viola was fuming. She cupped her fist with the other hand, and her chin trembled.

"In fact, his name is Alessandro, and I'm dying for you to meet him," Rose said. "I need your opinion."

"Rose Estes, is that mischief I'm reading in your eyes? You're not falling for him. Your family won't ever permit an unsuitable alliance," Viola said. "You're quite a catch now that your father named you an heir of his estate."

"Viola," Rose scolded. "You know what I want."

"To paint?"

Rose embraced her friend, and whispered, "To paint, yes, of course."

Viola rose from her chair, arranging the creases of her dress. "Your Alex must be quite a man."

"I've things to finish! Go now!"

Rose gestured to the door and pushed her friend out. "Around six will be great," Rose yelled from across the hallway.

***

It was a cloudy morning, and the sky had spun a moody hue across the city. Alex was waiting on the other side of the road from the factory when he noticed a thin brunette entering inside. Anticipation rose in the depths of his brain. He leaned against a tree, and cracked sunflower seeds between his teeth, spitting the shells on the ground. He couldn't help but notice how beautiful and gracious the woman was. He recognized Viola Monti, Fabio's sister-in-law, and Rose's best friend. Rose told him that her husband had died in a hunting accident, leaving her a widow in Fabio's care. She didn't spend much time inside the factory, and when she left, she climbed into a carriage parked in front of the office. Not long after her departure, the door opened again, and Mr. Matteo walked out. He limped toward the center of the city, and Alex followed him until he entered the cathedral. The hair on Alex's hair stood up when the door to the confession booth closed. Alex's cheeks flushed, and after he had looked around the church, he sneaked into a nearby booth and listened. He played with his tongue on the roof of his mouth. His breath echoed against the wood of the cabin.

"What's all this about?" Mr. Matteo asked as he dropped onto a kneeler, rustling a piece of paper he pulled from his pants' pocket. "I got your message. At four, at the Cathedral, one thousand scudi should be delivered or else."

"Did you bring the money?" Viola asked.

"I just paid you," Mr. Matteo cried.

Alex wiped the cold sweat from his forehead with the back of his sleeve. He felt a terrible headache coming on. He closed his eyes and pressed on his temples, and the circular motions seemed to ease the tension gathered under the skin of his skull. His ears perked up when Viola raised her voice.

"Did you bring them?" she asked.

"I'll never give you another scudo, let alone one thousand. You got what you wanted. Go right ahead with your threat and see if I care!" the administrator shouted.

"Are you willing to destroy your reputation and that of your lovely Rafael? So be it," Viola said.

"Do what you want to me, but leave Rafael out of it," Mr. Matteo warned, and he punched the wall that separated them. "I can squeeze the life out of you right here, right now," Mr. Matteo said. He surged forward, and Alex heard the woman yelling.

"Let go of me."

Alex's skin crawled, and a wave of heat splashed over his body. The sudden nervous energy that had been building in his innards for the past months demanded he did something. Alex stood a little straighter and bit down hard on his cheek. A door opened and closed in his vicinity. The pounding of running feet on the marble floor made Alex open the door of his booth. He stared at the woman's back until she exited from the cathedral and he followed her. Alex knew he had no other choice but to tell Rose. Perhaps Viola was the missing link, and Rose could be killed at any time, no matter how vigilant he was.

***

After Viola had left, Rose checked the clock. In one hour, she would meet the Duchess of Tuscany, Maria Theresa, the woman who had asked her to paint the war for the Polish Succession. Reds, blues, and browns combined into the battle of Bitonto when the Spanish forces defeated the Austrian troops in the Kingdom of Naples. During that time, Naples and Sicily fell under Spanish occupation, and Francis Stephen, the Duchess's husband, was given the Duchy of Tuscany as compensation for the loss of the Duchy of Lorraine. The painting was a gift from the Duchess to her husband.

Rose couldn't refuse the request since she had a love affair with history. Every night, after she returned from the factory, Rose locked herself in with her paints and worked on her masterpiece. She had paint on her hands and her cheeks, books lay on the floor, and when her painting took shape, she couldn't hide her delight. Rose touched the frame with great pride, for it represented the permit to gain the Duchess's favor. She would make her father the independent porcelain distributor over Tuscany, and for the first time since the attack in the forest, Rose relaxed. Elio was still searching for her father's attacker and the archer, but so far, everything had led to a dead end.

"Are you going somewhere?" Alex asked when Rose exited the office.

"To meet the Duchess," Rose said. "Would you care to join me?"

"Let's go," he said, following her.

Alex climbed into the carriage, and he grabbed her hands. They were hot and soft, and he tightened his grip on them.

"I must tell you something," he started. "It's important."

"Not now, Alex, I'm not feeling too great."

"Are you hurt? Where? Tell me!"

Rose pulled her hands from his, and she touched her chest. Then, she sighed, and Alex fell quiet. The carriage came to a stop in front of the palace, and the chaperone announced their arrival. Alex picked up the frame, and they entered the Great Hall where an army of servants ran back and forth. They waited in the foyer until a lady-in-waiting invited Rose into the drawing room where two girls played a game of chess, and one was reading poems.

"Wait for me here," Rose told Alex before the door closed behind the lady-in-waiting.

"I prefer to wait for you at home," Alex said.

Rose nodded and watched him as he left the palace. She had learned to trust Alex in the months they had spent together, and she knew that he would make it back to the villa intact. Alex had changed since she had found him in front of the cave, and Rose smiled at the recollection of his image with the bats flying above his head.

"Come with me, Miss Estes," the chaperone said.

Rose turned and followed the woman down a hall with a white and black marble floor and windows overlooking an interior garden. She bowed to the Duchess when she entered a stylish room with golden wallpaper and velvet curtains. A gust of wind filled the room with the aroma of lilac.

"Your Excellency, it has been a long time since I saw you," Rose said.

The Duchess raised her brows, a smile stretching across her porcelain face. She wore a dress from blue silk, and her wig gave her the appearance of a goddess. An aura of power emanated from the most powerful woman in Tuscany, and Rose felt a lump forming in her throat. She straightened her shoulders and asked, "Would you like to see the painting, Your Excellency?"

Maria Theresa settled on her settee, and her ladies gathered around her.

"I've been waiting for a long time, Miss Estes," the Duchess said. "Let's see it."

Rose signaled two servants to bring the painting in front of them, and then she stood at the Duchess's right, waiting until the silk cloth fell from the canvas. The Duchess gasped and started to cry softly.

"Those are tears of great joy, I presume," Rose said and handed the woman a napkin.

"Magnificent," Maria Theresa whispered. "Francis will find it especially appealing, a reminder of what happened so he could become the Duke of Tuscany."

Holding the folds of her dress with one hand, the Duchess crossed the distance between her settee and the canvas and stopped in front of the painting. She scanned the entire picture and sighed.

"Your Grace," Rose whispered when she saw the sparkle in the Duchess's eyes.

"How can I ever repay you for your work?"

Rose beamed with pride, and she knew the moment was right. She felt a sharp ache rise in the pit of her stomach when she dared to say, "Grant my family the sole right to the porcelain market in Tuscany, Duchess. That is my father's dream, and if it comes to pass, then I can concentrate on opening an art gallery in Florence."

"You're the first woman to be a historical painter, isn't that right, dear?" Maria Theresa asked while she sat on an elegant armchair, waving her fan. "So, be it," she said and signaled her lady-in-waiting to approach. "Draw the document for Count Estes, and let it be known that his family will be the sole manufacturer of all porcelain things in Tuscany."

"What about the Duke, my lady?" the lady-in-waiting asked.

"He'll agree, like always, my dear," the Duchess said, shooting her a sharp look.

The lady-in-waiting took a step back and began writing. After she had bowed to the Duchess, Rose left the room. She couldn't wait to return home and send her father a letter to inform him of the Duchess's decision. On her way out of the door,

Rose managed to hear the Duchess say, "I'll see you at the masquerade ball, darling. I'll give you the documents then."

Rose left the palace. The months she had spent in Siena had been productive, and her father had agreed to let her go to Florence and paint after his return to Siena. He decided to build another factory in Florence and to hire workers, and he needed her help. Rose agreed to remain in Siena for as long as her father wanted her to stay. And then, there was Alex.

The change in his appearance wasn't unnoticed. Alex wasn't the pale, lanky man that had come months ago. He was now tanned and fit, and he was helpful to the staff, especially around the stables. He was good with the horses. His riding skills had improved from practicing every day, and Mr. Benito still worked with him on his shooting skills. He had shot most of the pots by now, and they were scattered around the garden. Day after day, Alex watched over her, and everywhere she went, he had to come too. She was never alone. They talked about philosophy, and Alex taught her how to tend to superficial wounds. He let her use the laser pen, and Rose practiced on him. When he came to her with a scratch, she cleaned his wound with water and then passed the laser pen over it. It never seized to amaze her how fast the wound closed as if nothing had ever happened. Rose could barely remember her life before him, and the thought of his imminent departure left her gasping for air.

Rose looked out the window when she heard a carriage stopping in front of the villa. It was already time for dinner. She descended the flat of stairs and noticed that Alex was already there, waiting for her in the main hall. The clock chimed six o'clock when Viola entered the villa.

"Alessandro Santini, meet my best friend, Viola Monti," Rose said.

Alex's short, dark locks were still damp from bathing, and the gentleness of his touch on her arm made Rose wonder how his hands would feel running over her body. She stopped breathing when he looked straight at her. His eyes, a dark blue, mesmerized her. A few seconds had passed before she breathed again.

"I'm delighted to meet you, Doctor," Viola said, her hand lingering a little too long in his.

"Viola Monti, a beautiful name for a stunning woman," Alex said. "Violets stand for loyalty, did you know that?"

"A quality every woman possesses, doctor," Viola added, shooting him a piercing glance.

The meeting between Mr. Matteo and Viola had left him wary. Alex had never considered himself a good judge of character, but the more he stared at the woman, the more he wondered what terrifying experience had made someone of her social position resort to extortion. Viola chuckled, and grabbed Rose's arm, heading toward the dining room.

"I'm starving, and you've promised a good meal, my dear."

"But of course, everything is prepared. Mr. Benito, you may serve," Rose told the butler after everyone had been seated, Rose next to Alex, and Viola across from them.

"Rose said you were in a duel with my brother-in-law, doctor. What was the disagreement about?" Viola asked.

Alex sipped from a glass of Chianti and played with the chicken on his plate.

"Personal matters," he answered.

"He wasn't very pleased that he wounded you."

"I find that hard to believe," Alex said. "He threatened to kill me the next time we meet."

Alex pulled his gaze from Viola and looked at his plate. The food smelled of garlic, and he pushed a full spoon of it into his mouth. With friends like Viola, Rose had no need for enemies. At least the link between Fabio, Mr. Matteo, and Thomas had been established, although the motive still escaped Alex's understanding. Fabio was still in love with Rose but decided to marry Annabella. Viola was Fabio's mistress and her sister's supposed friend, but she extorted money from Mr. Matteo, Rose's administrator. Alex couldn't decide about Thomas's role into their plan, but Lucia must have knowledge about her brother's affairs. He made a mental note to ask Lucia in the morning.

"Enough of this discussion about duels, and shooting, and wounds. Are you ready for the masquerade ball?" Rose asked, and took a bite of the cheese soufflé the cook had prepared. "It's delicious. You must try it."

"Of course I'm ready. The balls are the most exciting festivities of the year. First, it's the Palio, then the masquerade ball. I can't wait for them to start. Are you going to attend?" Viola asked, looking at Alex.

"I wouldn't miss it," Alex said. "Are you not well, my lady?" he asked, turning toward Rose when the pink left her cheeks.

Rose sighed. "Too many problems and a slight dizziness that doesn't want to leave."

"What's going on?" Alex asked.

"How disappointing it is to discover the people you trust the most are the ones to betray you in the end," Rose said, placing the spoon back on the plate. She had barely touched her food and, although soufflé was her favorite, she pushed it away after just one bite. Her large eyes, the color of freshly cut grass, shifted to meet Alex's, and she startled him when she pressed her hand against his clenched fist under the table.

"Who betrayed you, Rose?" Viola asked, resting against the back of her chair.

"My administrator might be involved in stealing money from our factory," Rose added.

"How can you be sure Mr. Matteo is involved?" Viola asked.

"I had him followed."

"My dear," Viola gasped, wiping her hands, "that's awful news."

After Viola had finished her wine, she rose from her chair and approached Rose.

"Thank you for a lovely time tonight, but I must leave. It's rather late, and you've had a long day." Viola kissed Rose's cheek and waved to Alex. "It's been a pleasure, Dr. Santini. Until we meet again, just be safe."

"But you just got here, Viola," Rose protested. "Please, stay a little longer with us. We haven't talked about your plans for the future."

"Another engagement requires my presence, my dear. I'm sure you understand," Viola said, breathing in her ear.

Rose walked Viola to the front door and waited until she entered the carriage. When the sound of the wheels on the cobblestones had faded, she returned to the dining room where Alex waited. She stood in front of the fireplace, finishing her wine, and Alex joined her.

"Viola's acting strangely too. I've known her all my life. We grew up together," Rose said.

"I don't believe in her innocence. Hours ago, she was asking Mr. Matteo to pay her one thousand scudi to keep his affair with someone called Rafael private," Alex said.

"Is this what you wanted to tell me in the carriage? I wonder why she needs the money. She should be concerned with finding a new protector now that her husband is dead. With Fabio's wedding around the corner, she will have to create a new life for herself."

"What do you mean by a protector?"

"A man who has money and influence. Don't tell me your world is different than this one," Rose said.

Alex nodded. "Nothing has changed. The world functions on basically the same principles in my time as in yours." He encircled her waist. "Could you live in my world if I take you with me?" Alex waited for her response.

"Five months until the portal opens again and I'm still alive. See, no one has killed me yet," Rose said.

"When the time comes, I will ask you to go with me," Alex said. "Will you give me your answer?"

"Maybe I will ask you to stay," Rose said before she pulled away from his embrace and left the dining room with Alex following close behind.

CHAPTER 15

Night fell over the villa on Strada Della Montagnola. Lamps burned at each corner of the residence, and the barking of a dog pierced the quietness of the late hour. Rose was on her way to her chamber when she caught the hem of her dress on a nail protruding from the old staircase. She lost her balance and waved her arms as if she was swimming before collapsing in Alex's arms.

"You're safe now," Alex said.

"I'm never safe, but thank you for breaking my fall."

Rose turned around and faced him. She stood on the top step, her hands resting on her hips. Alex chuckled at the sight of her, but his laughter died when she kissed him. So sweet was the taste of her lips on his tongue. Ignoring all the warning sounds in his brain, he lifted her in his arms and climbed the rest of the floors.

"It had to be the top floor," Alex laughed. "An elevator would be a real lifesaver right about now."

"An elevator? What's that?"

"Come with me to the future, and you'll find out for yourself."

Alex pushed the door to her room open with one foot and closed it with the other, setting Rose in the middle of her bed. Her hair spilled all over the ruffles of her pillowcase, and Alex inhaled the aroma of her curls.

"Just like your name," he said. "Goodnight Rose."

"But, Alex," Rose said. "Why?"

"Because I'm not worthy of what you're offering me," Alex said, closing the door behind him.

Alex tossed and turned in his bed all night, but he knew that he had made the right decision. They had no future together. He would have to leave, and Rose needed her chastity. Her family would disown her if she went against their wishes. How he had wanted to run his fingers through the fire in her curls and tilt her head back until the only sight was her smooth, creamy white neck. Alex braced himself and closed his eyes, sinking into a dream where Rose was his bride.

***

At dawn, Alex peeked into her room through the half-opened door. "Are you decent?" he asked, closing the door behind him, and holding his eyes tightly shut.

"Look at you, my knight in shining armor. Your concern for my reputation is touching," Rose said.

"If you weren't so sweet, I would have had you on your back with your heels in the air a long time ago," Alex said, closing her open mouth with a kiss and leaning on the bed. "What's the plan for today? Are we going for Fabio and Lucia's brother at last?"

"Elio is following both of them. But today, there is a competition between the contrades. It's a horserace held in Piazza del Campo, the main square of the city," Rose said.

Alex lifted an eyebrow. "So, the last days' preparations were for this event," he said. "I totally forgot about it."

"Indeed. One week before the event, people lay dirt around the track. Then they set up the stage, the bleachers, and the captain's stand."

"Is it called La Terra in Piazza?" Alex asked.

Rose nodded twice.

"Fascinating," Alex said.

"Do you still celebrate Palio in your time?"

"Of course, we do, in July and August."

Alex smiled, remembering the look on her face the previous night. Rose inhabited a part of his heart, which left him confused. Regardless of how charming she was, he couldn't deny that he would have to make a decision when the portal to his world opened again. He followed the movement of her lips without paying attention to what she was saying. Alex was happy that she was excited about the upcoming festivities and that she had decided to live her life as if nothing had happened. The past months had brought them close. Now, Alex understood that he would spend the rest of his days alone in his time and wonder how his life would have turned out if he decided to stay the eighteenth century.

"Alex, are you listening?" Rose asked, shaking his arm.

"To every word," Alex said, kissing her cheek.

"So, the captain is in charge of the Contrada, and he chooses the jockey. After the race ends, we have a ceremony to honor Madonna of the Assumption. I'm sure you'll like the celebration."

"Time to get up, unless you want to keep me captive in this room," Alex said, rising from her bed.

Rose laughed. "See you in the library. I want to show you one of Master Da Vinci's books," she said, pushing him toward the door. She twisted her hair into a bun at the nape of her neck and, when he didn't move from the threshold, she blew him a kiss.

***

In the afternoon, Rose felt slightly lightheaded. She grabbed the frame of the door when she entered the library, resting against the wood frame.

"What is it?" Alex asked, hurrying to her side.

"Nothing serious," Rose answered. Alex helped her to the sofa, and she rested her head against the cushion and closed her eyes. He took her hand into his, checking her pulse. *It's too fast.*

"You're running a fever. I will ask Mr. Benito to bring some laudanum. It'll help you," Alex said. He rang the bell, and as he waited for the butler, hundreds of thoughts crowded his mind.

"Don't worry, Alex, the dizziness will pass," Rose whispered and touched his face ever so gently. He was holding her hand when the butler entered the library.

Mr. Benito surveyed the room, coughed to attract their attention, and stopped two feet away from the door.

"What happened?" he asked.

"Mr. Benito, stay with Miss Rose. Her sickness has returned," Alex said, leaving the room.

"Of course, Doctor," the butler whispered. He approached the sofa and pulled up a chair. "Poor girl," Mr. Benito said as he stroked her hand.

A weak smile had crossed her face before she drifted off to sleep. After a few minutes, Rose opened her eyes. Alex had returned to the room, carrying a cup. He lifted her head, touching the cup to her lips.

"Here, drink this," Alex encouraged her. "Hell doesn't want beautiful girls like you."

Rose listened to him, and she swallowed the entire potion, her head falling back on the pillow after she emptied the cup. She touched Alex's cheek, and he grabbed her hand, holding it in his own. His concern showed in his eyes, which had turned a darker shade of blue than she remembered. Even if he tried to cheer her up by telling jokes from his time, the smile didn't reach her eyes, and this realization made his heart ache. For a while, he had forgotten about the threat on her life. He had been caught up in feelings he didn't know how to handle.

"We have to return to Luce Del Sol," Rose said. "The wedding is just around the corner."

"We have to stop the wedding. Annabella can't go through with it," Alex said.

"I must tell Annabella about Fabio and Thomas. I need you there with me."

"Count me in," Alex said.

Alex remained silent as he watched Rose doze off again on the sofa in the library. He dropped into a chair, dozing on and off himself. Then, Alex got up from the chair and picked up a book from Rose's desk, noticing that it was about Leonardo Da Vinci. He remembered about their chat, in the Estes's garden, about

Leonardo's disappearance for fourteen months in the same cave that Alex had come through. Could it be possible that the cave connected different worlds? The news on TV had talked about the supermoon, and the girl in the lobby had implied that a portal would open when the earth, the sun, and the moon formed a straight line. If he hadn't seen it for himself, Alex wouldn't think it was possible. Perhaps Da Vinci had experienced the power of the portal, and upon his return to Florence, had created his most well-known pieces.

It was evening when Rose opened her eyes, looking healthier than hours before. Without a word, Alex lifted himself from the chair and crossed the distance between the desk and the sofa where Rose lay.

"Welcome back to the world of the living," Alex said, running a hand over her forehead, noticing the dark circles under her eyes.

"I don't know what happened," Rose said, stretching her arms. "I was dizzy, and my heart pounded in my ears. I'm much better now." She rose to her feet and asked, "Are you ready to go?"

"Do you think it is wise?" Alex asked with concern in his eyes.

"I'll inform Mr. Benito that we're going to be late tonight," she said, ringing the bell.

***

Piazza Del Campo buzzed with horses, folks of every age, merchants selling their goods, and music. A white flag fluttered at the main doors of Palazzo Publico, the drummer tapped his instrument, and the captain signaled the starting of the race with one shot. People covered their ears as the loud noise shook the foundations of the nearby buildings. Alex felt his eardrums explode, his ears ringing for the next few seconds.

"Each Contrada has a flag with its own colors," Rose explained. "The combination of orange, green and white is for Selva, while the red, blue and yellow for Chiocciola. I am from Civetta or the Little Owl, and the flag with red and black stripes with white is ours."

"We use the same colors even in my days. Tradition," Alex said.

When the competition started, it seemed everyone stopped breathing for about a minute and a half. The horses and their riders ran three times around the Piazza Publico. Shouts and cheers merged in the Piazza, and Alex covered his ears.

"The first horse to cross the finish line still wearing its face emblem is the winner. With or without a rider, the horse is the one bringing pride to its Contrada," Rose shouted.

Selva won the competition, and people from its Contrada ran on the track, crying. Men and women, young and old embraced each other, hugging the horse and the jockey. The captain lowered the Palio, and the winning contradaioli took it. Followed by a mass of people, the winning jockey brought the Palio to Duomo to thank the Madonna, and they sang in unison "Te Deum." It was profoundly moving and beautiful, a feeling of solidarity in the air. Like many others present at the celebration, Alex and Rose held hands. Rose's voice filled his ears with sweet verses, and Alex sensed his spirit lifting. The ice surrounding his heart had melted a long time ago, and he had discovered he wanted to live, to laugh, and to love. The anger he had felt for the past three years had now become a sad memory.

"The partying starts now," Rose yelled over the noise. She dragged him with her, sneaking between the wall of bodies, and she didn't stop until they reached the food stand. She picked fruits, cheeses, and pastries, and Alex did the same.

People started to dance in the streets, crying out the sound of victory. Rose grabbed Alex's hand, and she spun around as her laughter filled the air. Her face flushed, and her body warmed from excitement. Her voice rose above the ground along with the hundreds of other voices. Complete strangers embraced and kissed each other.

"What's that?" Alex asked when he noticed that two or three men flanked some of the women.

"The cicisbei," Rose answered.

"What?"

"Lovers," Rose said, laughing. "It's a shame for a married woman to show herself in society without them. It's the norm."

Alex laughed hard, the bursts shaking his stomach. "I've never heard anything more outrageous."

"The women in your world do not have them?"

"In my world, it's called degradation if you have them, and leads to divorce and shame."

Rose stopped her spinning and held his face between her hands.

"I think I'll like your world. Will you take me with you?"

"Anytime," Alex said.

Alex pushed some people aside and, with Rose on his left side, he walked away from the crowds and commotion. Rose pirouetted in front of him, resting her palms on his chest. They were hot, and he circled her body and danced with her. Everyone else was dancing, and kissing, and laughing aloud. Alex kissed the side of her neck. He winked at another woman standing two feet away from them looking shocked. He moved to the other side and kissed her again. The woman's face turned red, and Alex giggled.

"Run away with me. If you dwell on the past, you'll miss your future," Rose said, squeezing his shoulders. "You are my future, Alex."

"We can't run away every time we're scared, Rose. And I know you are as scared as I am. We can't hide our entire lives, pretending to live. Not anymore," Alex said.

They left the ceremonies and the parties in the streets, along with the total mayhem of their mixed emotions. Hand in hand, they walked toward the end of the road where they found their carriage waiting. Alex's thoughts traveled miles away, turning to the rogues on the loose who wanted to hurt Rose. He would discuss the matter with Count Estes as soon as they returned to Luce Del Sol. For the rest of their trip, they talked about the Palio festivities and, when they stepped out of the carriage, Rose pushed open the front door and signaled Alex to follow. He hesitated, and she stretched her hand toward him.

"I want you to be the first to see it," Rose said. "Come with me, come!"

"Slow down," Alex said. "You're giving me a hard time, woman."

Their laughter awoke the staff in the house. Rose shushed Alex when a light appeared in Mr. Benito's room. They hurried to the main stairway, chuckling and teasing each other. She dragged Alex with her.

"Where's the fire? You're going to kill me one day," Alex said, out of breath.

Rose turned toward him. She winked, and then said, "It's a surprise."

"You don't go easy on me," Alex said.

When they reached the third floor, they passed his room and stopped at the end of the corridor, in front of her studio. The room was lined with silk wall coverings and had huge French windows overlooking the town, the garden, and the hills in the vicinity. Canvases, brushes, and colors covered every inch of the room. Her painter's apron hung on the easel. Rose stopped in front of a painting covered in a white cloth.

"Are you ready?" Rose asked.

"I am," Alex said.

Rose pulled off the cover. Alex covered his mouth. The finished painting was as beautiful as the unfinished portrait he had discovered in the hotel basement back in his time. Shades of ginger curls, a hint of sadness in her eyes, the curve of her neck were painted in the smallest detail. Even the frame looked similar to the one in his time. Alex looked at Rose and took a step toward her.

"This painting is the bridge that led me to you."

"What do you mean? I don't understand," Rose said.

"I saw this painting back in my time. It had your name, Countess Rose Estes, and the painting wasn't finished. You held a rose in your hand while the other one rested over your heart. It was in a storage room in the basement of the hotel where the portal opened."

"How did it end up there?"

"How would I know?" Alex asked. "Because it wasn't finished? Otherwise, it would have been displayed in an art gallery."

"So, that's how you knew who I was when we met in the garden? That's why you called me by name?"

Alex raised her hand to his lips. Adrenaline spiked through his veins. With his heart in his throat, he smiled.

"That's how I knew who you were, and I was delighted to meet you," Alex said. "You've completely charmed me."

"You have a bizarre way of showing it. Do you like the painting?" Rose asked, pointing at the canvas.

"It's lovely, but why should I like a painting when I can admire the original?"

Rose didn't say a word, as Alex searched the impressive historical paintings hanging in different corners of the room, some representing Siena during the plague, some depicting men fighting wars. The picture of her parents stood on an easel in the heart of the chamber, and another one of Annabella leaned on the wall.

"This one was a gift for her wedding," Rose said, pointing to her sister's portrait. She sighed, and a shadow crossed her face.

"What are you thinking?" he asked.

"Before your arrival in my time, a gypsy stopped at the estate. The gypsy asked for shelter. Papa didn't want to have anything to do with her, but I took her to the cottage. I gave her food and water. Before she left, the gypsy grabbed my hand and read my palm. She said that my destiny would come from the future. The future would save me from death."

Alex pulled her into his arms, holding her close to his body, and Rose buried her face in the warmth of his chest. His heartbeats drummed inside his ribcage. He longed for her, his body aching to be close to her. It took all his control to push her away and to move to another corner of her studio.

"We need to confront Fabio and Thomas with our findings. We should do the same with Mr. Mateo and Viola. We have to make them confess," Alex said.

"It'll break Annabella's heart."

"I'll break anyone's heart rather than lose you. Do you think we can find Thomas? Lucia might know about her brother's whereabouts. He's the key."

They left her studio, Rose struggling to keep up with Alex. He slowed down enough for her to catch up. Then, in one instant, he swept her off her feet, and carried her in his arms, dancing in the hallway.

"You are crazy," Rose scolded. "Put me down. Servants will see us."

"Let them see."

"Mr. Benito will tell my father."

"I'll tell him myself when we return to the villa."

"Papa will kill you."

"He'll certainly try."

Alex lowered Rose to the ground as gently as he possibly could, and he walked with her to her bedroom. He stopped in front of the door and leaned toward her.

"Rest tonight. We don't know what tomorrow will bring," Alex said, kissing her lips ever so gently.

"I had a great time with you today," Rose said.

CHAPTER 16

"Doctor, wake up," Mr. Benito said from the doorway.

Alex looked around. It was still dark.

"What is it, Mr. Benito? Is Miss Rose sick?" he asked, pushing the covers aside. His toes felt cold on the floor, and he jogged to the door, rubbing the sleep from his eyes. He shrugged his shoulders to release the beginning of a throb forming in his head, and then he yawned.

"It's an emergency. My cousin needs you," Antonio said, standing next to Mr. Benito.

"What happened?"

"His wife can't give birth," Antonio said. "Dr. Guillermo doesn't know what to do. Please, help them, Doctor."

"Give me a moment," Alex said. "Wait in front of the house."

Alex pulled on his pants and buttoned his shirt as he descended the stairs and walked to the driveway where Antonio waited with the horses. They rode together until they reached a sector of the city where the poor lived. Two barefoot girls and a man sat in the dirt, crying softly, with their heads on their knees. Alex dismounted and entered the room where two midwives tended to a woman who was screaming in pain. Another man watched helplessly, and he covered his ears every so often.

"Who are you?" Alex asked, looking at the man standing next to the woman's bed. He had the olive skin of the people in Siena and an aquiline nose. He shook his head, and then he looked at Alex.

"I'm Dr. Guillermo," he said. "There's nothing I can do for her other than pray."

"I need warm water and all of you out of here," Alex cried. "Give me your lancet and stand by to help." He turned toward Antonio, and said, "Go back to the villa and tell Miss Rose to give you my laser pen."

"I'll be right back," Antonio said.

Alex listened to the sound of hooves beating against the road until they dissipated into the night.

"Bring more candles," Alex said to the first midwife, a woman old enough to be his grandmother. The woman nodded.

"You," Alex said, pointing to the younger one, "be prepared to cover the baby. The water should be warm. Light a fire."

Alex examined the woman's belly. The baby wasn't turned. He realized that if he wanted to save both mother and child, he had to perform a C-section.

"Why isn't he back yet?" Alex asked.

"Coming doctor," Antonio said, busting into the room with Alex's laser pen in his hand.

"Madam, it'll hurt, but stay strong. If I don't cut your belly, both of you will die. Do you hear me?" Alex asked as he touched the woman's shoulder.

"Do what you must, Doctor, and soon," the woman whispered. She grabbed a small pillow and bit into it while two women immobilized her legs. Dr. Guillermo went behind her and held her shoulders, and Alex made an incision right below the belly button. He asked Dr. Guillermo to keep the muscles apart, and by the time he had separated them, the woman had fainted already.

"Wipe the blood," Alex said to the older midwife. He picked up the baby who had the cord around his neck. The child's face was purple, and he hung motionless. At the sight of him, the women covered their mouths, praying silently. *I could use a prayer or two*, Alex said to himself. He hadn't performed a C-section since medical school.

"He's stillborn," one of the women said.

"Silence," Alex said, cutting the cord and holding the baby upside down while hitting his bottom. No sound came from him.

"It's too late," Dr. Guillermo said. "You killed them both."

"No one is dead yet. Keep quiet."

Alex laid the baby on the bed and leaned toward him. He massaged his heart, small strokes in the beginning and harder when he received no response. He opened the baby's mouth and pinched his nostrils as he blew air into his lungs. His chest began to rise, and the baby finally cried.

"How's my baby, doctor? I can hear him crying," the mother, who had regained consciousness, whispered.

"The doctor is with him, woman," the younger woman said.

Alex covered the baby with a clean towel and raised the boy in his arms before giving him to one of the midwives. The mother smiled, and she lowered her head to the pillow. With the baby out of danger, Alex turned to the mother. He wiped the area around the incision, held the two sides of the uterus, and passed the laser pen over the incision. He did the same with the abdominal muscles.

"Let me see that thing," Dr. Guillermo requested after Alex was done with his task.

"Another time, Doctor," Alex said. He prepared laudanum for the mother and gave the glass with the tonic to the younger midwife. "Give it to her, and then let her rest. I will stay with her overnight."

"Doctor, the husband is asking about his wife and baby. What shall I tell him?" the older midwife asked.

"Let him in," Alex said.

"Let me see him, woman," the husband said when he entered the room. He leaned next to his wife and kissed the baby's dark hair.

"A boy, finally," he said. "What should we name him?"

The mother looked at Alex, and she asked, "Doctor, what is your name?"

"Alessandro," Alex answered.

"Then we shall name him after you," the mother said between sobs. She kissed her boy and looked at him. "Do us the honor to be his godfather, Doctor. He wouldn't be here without your help."

The unexpected request left Alex shaken. He had never had a godson or anyone of his own, and the baby he had brought into the world was the first person connected with him in a tie stronger than blood. He had tears in his eyes when he looked at the baby sleeping peacefully in his mother's arms.

Alex spent all day and the next night with the newborn and his mother. It was dawn when he returned to the villa. He managed to take his boots and his trousers off before falling asleep.

***

"Halt right there!" one of the four guards invading the villa commanded.

Awakened by their bangs, Rose gasped as she watched the cardinal's men destroy her home, searching through the chambers and breaking fine china. She pulled a robe over her nightdress and trembled. The guards stopped in front of Alex's room and demanded to see the doctor.

Alex had just enough time to pull his pants on before the guards invaded his room.

"What is the meaning of this?" Alex asked as he buttoned his shirt.

"You're accused of witchcraft," one guard said, "and for being in possession of dangerous objects. We must investigate."

Rose jumped in front of Alex, pushing the guards away from him. She tried protesting, but when the guards pointed their weapons at her, Alex grabbed her shoulders and shook his head.

"No," he said, stepping in front of her and shielding her from the men.

"I'll call Elio," Rose said while the guards escorted Alex down the stairs. Their long guns pierced the chemise, hurting his spine. Alex remained silent. If he tried to escape, he would endanger Rose, and the thought of her in a detention cell made Alex livid.

"Are you going to hurt us, witch?" a guard asked, pointing the gun at him. "Your accuser claimed that you possess strange powers, and you practice sorcery with a magic wand."

"What magic wand?" Alex asked, frowning. He tried to open the door and jump from the carriage. The guard caught him, pinned him to the floor, and tied his hands behind him. The rope cut through Alex's skin, and he ground his teeth.

"The Grand Judge will hear your case," the guard continued.

Alex tilted his head, hearing that he would face trial in front of the High Council. His only hope was that Rose would find a way to help him escape. Perhaps, Elio would find a way. His heart raced and a knot formed in his throat, forbidding him to breathe properly. He managed to take in a few gulps of air, its coolness piercing his chest.

When they reached the jail in the town square, the guards pushed him through the doorway. Long hallways without windows stretched to the left and right, and men in long, burgundy robes walked fast, keeping their heads down. They held books and beads in their hands and looked at the floor as if it held the secret to immortality. A scream came from the pits of the dungeon beneath his feet, and Alex swallowed hard. His mouth became dry, and he could barely move his feet. The guards dragged him to a cell smelling of urine and locked him in. Alex fell to the stone floor. Hours passed and the night replaced the day. Regardless of how much he beat on the door, no one came to talk to him.

***

After the guards had carried Alex away, Rose ran frantically up the stairs toward her bedchamber. She wrote a note and asked a servant to deliver it to the police station. While she waited, she requested Lucia to help her dress.

"Mr. Marotto is here to see you," Mr. Benito said shortly.

"Let him in," Rose said and sprinted toward Elio. She fell into his arms and sobbed.

"Can you help him, Elio? Alex is innocent," Rose said between sobs.

Elio led Rose to the sitting room and took her hands into his. The room was bright, in total contrast to the gloom of the situation.

"They came in the morning and arrested him for witchcraft. He's innocent. He's only a doctor who uses things we have no knowledge about."

"Child, I'll do what I can for Alex. I sent word to your father."

"I'll beg the Duchess to intervene if I must. She owes me an enormous favor," Rose said.

Elio rose from the settee, and said, "Have faith."

***

It was midnight when Alex heard movement on the other side of the door.

"Alex?"

"Yes," he answered. He glued his ear to the door and listened. "Elio?"

"Miss Rose sent me. She said you were in need of assistance," Elio whispered.

"You've no idea. How do I get out of here?"

"Let me handle the problem," Elio said. "It may take a while."

Alex sat on the only chair in the cell, and the waiting seemed without end. He dozed on and off as he prayed for a miracle. He stretched his arms over his head and squatted a few times to keep the blood flowing. A slight movement caught his attention, and he asked, "Are you back?"

"Not so great now, are you? Let's see how you explain the things in your possession, Doctor, if you are indeed a doctor."

The man on the other side of the door laughed.

"Fabio," Alex said, punching the door. "I'm not a damn magician. You know I'm a doctor. I saved your father-in-law."

"But I didn't see anything," Fabio said.

"Damn you!" Alex yelled. "I'm only a doctor."

"It hasn't be proven yet. One thing is sure: you are not from around here."

Alex listened to Fabio's quick steps fading until he heard nothing at all. His thoughts went to Rose, who was alone in the villa and at the mercy of her future brother-in-law. The gardener was missing. Lucia hadn't heard from her brother in weeks, and he hadn't returned to Luce Del Sol either. Regardless of how hard they had tried to find the connection between Fabio and Thomas, they had failed. Elio said that Rose should return to Luce Del Sol, and Alex agreed with him. Only Rose totally disagreed and remained in Siena to supervise the factory as her father had asked.

Late in the evening, a guard brought Alex a tray with a slice of black bread and stale water. He took a bite and chewed on it, and the taste was even bitterer than his state of mind. Alex pushed the food away and fell asleep with his head on his knees.

***

After Elio had left, Rose ran up the stairs toward Alex's chamber. His bed wasn't made, and his clothes were scattered all over the floor. She picked them up and basked in their scent. She missed him already. Then she searched for the briefcase he had brought from his time, and when she discovered it in the wardrobe, Rose embraced it as if it were Alex himself. The brown leather case looked expensive, and she opened the latch, searching inside. First, Rose grabbed the phone and examined the screen. It was black, and as much as she pressed the button on the side, the phone didn't wake up. She hid it in the pocket of her skirt and put the bag back where she had found it.

Rose ran to the stable and locked the door behind her. After she had searched every stall, she grasped a hammer, gripping it so hard that her fingers turned white from the pressure. Alex would understand her decision. She closed her eyes and hit the phone a couple of times until it broke into tiny pieces that littered the floor. She brushed them away and mixed them with dirt. Her thoughts turned to Alex, alone and scared in jail. *How terrified he must be,* Rose thought while walking back to the house.

The glass of water barely satisfied her thirst. Hadn't she warned Alex about using his advanced medical procedures in a time when people were still using simple, primitive practices? They weren't prepared for medical advances. Her own family considered her desire to paint history instead of sticking to the portraits and static objects unhealthy. They weren't ready for new ideas yet. Rose curled her legs under her. The last rays of sun penetrated through the silk curtains, and after she had closed her eyes for a few moments, Alex's face came to her mind.

***

As soon as he woke up the next morning, Alex stomped around in his cell. It took a minute for his brain to register where he was, and the recollection of the last day's events left him exhausted. He glanced at the cell's bars forged from iron and tried to bend them. Even if, through a miracle, he managed to create an opening, the jail was on the second floor. He bit his lips, the salty taste of blood oozing into his mouth from the cracks in his skin. With no idea of how he would escape, he dropped to his knees and prayed for a miracle. *What was Rose doing this early? Was she worried about him?* If he hadn't helped the woman and her baby, he would have prevented all this nonsense about witchcraft. In four months, the portal would open and take him back to his world and everyone he had ever met in this world would be dead—even Rose.

Days and nights passed, and Elio came every day to visit and lift his spirits. Because of his position in the secret police, the guards allowed Elio to talk to Alex. He told Alex that the date of his trial was scheduled for the end of October. Elio prepared the witnesses for the day of the trial, and he encouraged Alex to stand firm and not say a word that could be used against him. Two months had passed, and although the guards treated him fairly, Alex was on the verge of madness. He paced the cell and punched the walls until the guards had to tie him to the bed. They fed him laudanum, and Alex slept most of the time. The days when he was awake, he practiced the relaxation techniques he had learned after Sophia's death. At the end of the second month of his imprisonment, Rose told Alex that he would appear in front of the High Council. Rose instructed him to say he had studied at Oxford, and that he purchased the laser pen in London. Her father agreed to testify at the trial and the woman whose baby he had saved decided to appear as a witness.

It was only two months until the portal would open again, and Alex had to escape. Rose was alone, and she wasn't feeling great. She had refused to meet Viola and had sent her mother back to Luce Del Sol. She had lost weight and wasn't sleeping, the dark circles under her eyes a testimony to her pain. The day before the trial, Rose came to visit Alex.

"I have something to say," Rose said.

"Go on, tell me. It can't be worse than this," Alex said, pointing at his surroundings.

"I smashed your phone with a hammer." When Alex said nothing, Rose continued. "I was terrified. They came and searched the house. When they found nothing, they left and said it had been a mistake."

Alex grabbed the iron bars that separated them, while his body shook violently.

"The phone was important to you, I know. But I couldn't allow the guards to find it. I'm convinced that Sophia would agree with me. What if Fabio were to testify against you? He had seen the phone."

"I remember," Alex sighed and cupped her face in his hands. "None of this is your fault, Rose," he said. "I should have listened to you and gotten rid of the things I brought with me."

Unexpectedly, a part of his life had closed. Sophia had become the past, and Rose, his present. He couldn't imagine phantom a future without her, and the reality of her life being in danger because of her association with him hit him full force.

"Leave now, Rose, and never come back. If they convict me tomorrow, say that you knew nothing of my past, that I was a liar who lured you because of your innocence. Pretend madness, if you must. Can you promise me this?"

Rose gasped and shook her head. "No, I can't," she said. "It's not true."

"Nobody cares about the truth, Rose. Hundreds of years will pass before the justice system listens to the accused." Alex shook her shoulders. "You must live. Do you hear me?"

Rose nodded, and she hugged Alex through the iron rails, kissing his lips. She turned around and left the jail, running on the streets until she saw the cathedral. All night Rose prayed, on her knees, with her head bowed, and hands folded. Elio came looking for her, but she didn't move when he insisted she should go home. When the first rays of sun touched her cheeks, she rose from the floor and went back to the villa. She grabbed the pistol, the one she had bought for Alex, and hid it between the creases of her dress. It was the morning of his trial, the day when Alex's fate would be decided. More than twelve months ago, she had promised that she would keep Alex alive until his return to his time, and she intended to do just that.

"Are you ready?" Elio asked when Rose came out of the villa.

"Whatever I may do, stand by me Elio, and save Alex if you have to choose. He must live at all costs."

"Rose, child, what are you saying?"

"It's best if you know nothing. Promise me you will save Alex and take him back to Luce Del Sol."

Elio nodded, and they went toward the Palazzo where the trial was due to begin in less than an hour. The court was packed. Attracted by the unusual accusations of witchcraft, the people of Siena arrived at dawn and waited in front of the Palazzo for news. Elio pushed Rose into the palace through a side door. She was holding his arm and kept her gaze pinned to the floor as she walked through the building. The trial was in full session when they entered the courtroom. Three judges formed the High Council, and Alex represented himself.

"All I know is that the doctor saved my life, Your Honor. Without his intervention and the use of the new medical device, the one Dr. Guillermo believes to be the instrument of witchcraft, I wouldn't be here today," Count Estes said.

"Count Estes, we appreciate your deposition. You're an esteemed member of the Duke's Court, so there is no reason we won't consider your testimony. Return to your seat," the Grand Judge said.

Count Estes sat next to Rose. She linked her fingers with those of her father's and waited for the next witness to come.

"Count Monti, what have you to say?" one of the judges asked.

"I don't know much about the doctor. But I know this. One day, I discovered a silver case among his things, with a strange picture on top."

"We found no such thing in his possession," the guard who arrested Alex said.

"He hid it somewhere. Search again," Fabio said.

"Your statement doesn't stand Count Monti. The guards searched the villa where the doctor stayed, and they didn't find anything resembling your description."

"But Your Honor," Fabio pleaded with the judges.

"Return to your seat, Count. Bring the last witness," the judge ordered.

The woman whose life Alex saved took the stand with his godson in her arms.

"What is the meaning of this?" the Grand Judge bellowed. "Children are not allowed in my court."

"Your Honor," the woman said, "I meant no disrespect. I merely wanted to show my child. He wouldn't be here without the doctor. And this," the woman added, holding the boy with one arm and pulling her skirt down her belly to show the mark on her abdomen.

"This is an insult. Cover yourself, woman. Guards, take her out," one judge yelled.

"Let her stay," the Grand Judge requested. He left his place in the tribunal and went to the woman. He looked closely at the woman's belly and touched the thin scar on her skin. It was a pink line, and the people in the room gasped. The Grand Judge shook his head. The woman went to the back of the chamber where her husband waited. He put an arm around her shoulders and played with the baby.

"Dr. Santini, where did you learn the fine art of medicine?" the Grand Judge asked. "Your skills are remarkable."

Alex, who took the stand, looked at Rose. She shook her head. He smiled at her, and then he turned toward the judges.

"Your Excellency, I studied in Oxford and spent many years developing new medical instruments too. They are still experimental, not used in hospitals yet. When I left London, I was allowed to take the laser pen with me, to use in the practice I intended to open in Florence. On my way, I was attacked by thieves and forced to stop at Count Estes's residence and ask for help. It happened the night when Count Estes was wounded, and I saved him. As payment for my services, Count Estes offered me a position among his staff."

"He is no witch, Your Grace!" Rose yelled from her seat. Her father put a hand over her mouth and pulled her down. She put her hand inside the hidden pocket of her dress and touched the pistol. Just then, a scream pierced the room. A guard fell.

"This man needs medical attention," Alex cried, kneeling by the man. He opened the man's pupils and then checked for a pulse. Dr. Guillermo, who was also in the courtroom, knelt down beside Alex. He checked the man's vital sign and starred at the Grand Judge.

"He's dead," Dr. Guillermo said.

"Move over," Alex said, and pinched the man's nose with one hand and opened his mouth to the other. He blew breaths into the man's mouth a couple of times, and there was still no response. He began chest compressions. He pushed hard and fast to the center of the chest for thirty times, and then he tilted the man's head back and blew again into his mouth until he saw his chest rising again. The man opened his eyes and started to cough, and the people gasped at the sight.

"This man is no witch," people in the attendance yelled. "He's a miracle! He brought the guard back."

"Remarkable, doctor," Dr. Guillermo said, shaking Alex's hand. "Your Honor, I must drop all charges. I owe this man a public apology."

"The court is dismissed, and the case closed. The prisoner will be liberated at twilight."

The Grand Judge signaled the guards to take Alex back to his cell, and everyone vacated the courtroom.

"Now what? " Rose asked.

"Now we wait," Elio said, escorting her out of the courtroom. "Were you willing to risk your life to free him?"

"Excuse me?"

"Rose, were you ready to use the gun you had hidden in your dress to release Alex?"

Rose blushed and said, "If necessary."

CHAPTER 17

Alex jumped to his feet when the cell door opened, and the Grand Judge himself entered. He barely recognized the judge without the wig and the black cape around his shoulders. He was about five feet, shorter and less imposing than Alex had imagined him to be, with a trimmed beard and snow-white hair that curled above his pointy ears. He could have easily fit under Alex's armpit.

"Dr. Santini, I must ask you a favor," the judge said.

"A favor? I was hoping to be out of here before nightfall."

The judge shook his head and sat on the wooden bed that had been Alex's companion during the long hours of silence and waiting, his face pale.

"Your Excellency, what is it?"

"You have brilliant skills, I saw for myself. I was wondering if, maybe, you could stop at my house before returning to yours."

"I rather go straight home, if you don't mind," Alex said, rubbing his hands.

"My daughter is suffering from a sickness no doctor knows how to cure. She has pain right here," the judge said, pressing over the right side of his abdomen. "She has a fever and throws up a lot. Do you think you can help her?"

Alex grabbed the judge's arm, pushing him out of the cell. "We have no time. Let's go. I need Dr. Guillermo's help and his medical instruments."

The judge turned toward the two guards standing in front of Alex's cell. "Fetch Dr. Guillermo and bring him to my house. Hurry!"

They left the jail and entered the carriage waiting for them at the front door.

"Home!" the judge yelled.

The coachman took off, crossing the entire Piazza Publico. He took a sharp left on the first crossroad, and the judge's house came into view. It was a two-story villa covered in gray bricks, with white shutters on the windows, which gave it an elegant appearance. The coach bumped over the rocks on an alley shadowed by citrus trees. Marble statues stood among the trees, and two lions were posted on each side of the villa.

As soon as the carriage came to a stop, Alex and the judge sprinted inside the house.

"Where is she?" Alex asked.

"Follow me, Doctor," the judge said and took him to a room overlooking the gardens.

A girl, no older than sixteen, lay on a bed. The dark circles under her eyes contrasted with the whiteness of her skin. Alex pulled the covers off and lifted her chemise. He pressed his palm against the right side of her belly, and the girl screamed when he touched her.

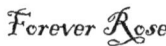

"When did this start?"

"A few days ago," the girl answered between sobs.

"It's your appendix," Alex said. "If I don't operate on you soon, you'll die."

"Do what you must, but save her," the judge said. "She's all I have."

Two servants put the girl on a table, and Alex opened the windows to let the light inside.

"Help me, doctor," Alex said when Dr. Guillermo entered the room.

"We must put the girl to sleep first," Dr. Guillermo said, pulling a bottle from his medical kit and squeezing three drops on a napkin. He held it close to the girl's nose and waited until she fell asleep.

"What was that?" Alex asked.

"I'm surprised you don't recognize oil of vitriol. What do you use as anesthesia in London, doctor?"

"Later," Alex said. "Now, I need a knife."

Dr. Guillermo handed Alex a knife with a straight razor blade.

"Wash your hands and help me hold the muscles apart. I must reach the appendix," Alex said and waited for Dr. Guillermo, who cleaned his hands in a bowl of cold water and returned to the table, not letting Alex out of his sight.

Alex made an incision on the lower right side of the girl's abdomen, and Dr. Guillermo held the muscles open with his bare hands as Alex reached for the appendix. The judge, who planned to remain close to them during the entire surgery, fell on his back when he saw the blood squirting from the cut Alex had made on his daughter's abdomen.

"What do we do with him?" Dr. Guillermo asked.

"He'll have a bump." Alex ignored Dr. Guillermo, removed the girl's appendix, and dropped it on a plate. Then, he sewed her wound with a needle he found in the surgical kit that Dr. Guillermo had brought and pretended not to notice the curious way Dr. Guillermo studied the appendix.

"I've never seen one before."

"It's an experimental practice back in London, and not yet released to medical practitioners."

"That means you haven't done it before?"

"There is a first time for everything, Doctor," Alex said.

"And the girl?"

"For the moment, she's out of danger."

"Is she going to live?"

Alex patted the doctor's shoulder. "Give her laudanum for the pain. I'm not going to lie. She'll feel like a thousand knives have cut into her body. But she'll live. Keep her still. If she moves, the wound will open, and I must stitch her again."

The maids had prepared clean clothes for the girl, and Alex and Dr. Guillermo put her on the bed. The judge instructed the servants to remain with his daughter while he accompanied Alex to the door. Dr. Guillermo offered to stay and watch the girl overnight.

"I'll be in your debt forever," the judge said. "How can I repay you?"

"By keeping an open mind to advances in science," Alex said. "The world needs visionaries, not adversaries, Judge."

Alex turned around and entered the carriage parked in front of the villa. He was anxious to get home where Rose would be waiting for him. He had spent more than two months in jail, far from the woman he loved and not knowing if he would make it back alive. He had less than two months until the portal was supposed to open and he hadn't yet found Rose's enemies. It was dark by the time Alex arrived at the villa since it was now November and night came early. When the Estes's residence came into view, he knew he was home.

Rose was waiting for him on the threshold, and Alex jumped from the carriage before it came to a halt. He pulled her into his arms and kissed her.

"I missed these sights," Alex said, looking around as they entered the villa.

Just then, thunder rumbled nearby, shaking the entire foundation of the house. Rose turned around and looked at the sky.

"It's going to storm," Rose said, closing the door.

***

Alex turned over on his side, tracing the contours of her face while she slept next to him.

"Good morning," he whispered when her eyelids started to quiver, and her eyes opened.

"Good morning to you, too," Rose answered. "I guess you're wondering what I'm doing in your bed."

"Something along those lines," he said. "Not that I am complaining."

"It's because of the thunderstorm."

"Thunderstorm?"

"Yes, storms give me the creeps. Last night was awful. Branches pounded my windows, and the wind's howling made me run to the only place I knew I'd be safe," Rose said.

"What an interesting story," Alex said with mischief in his voice.

"When I was little, I used to run to my father's room and fall asleep next to him. He'd carry me back to my room after the storm had passed."

"I'd be scared too," Alex said. He leaned on his elbow, twisting her curls around his fingers. "Hmm, I like the way they feel."

Without giving her time to respond, Alex placed a kiss on her mouth. He sensed her pulse rising and dropping, her breath speeding up when he played with her lower lip. With her arms around his neck, Rose surrendered herself to his game. When he bit her earlobes, her body arched toward him.

"Rose, I haven't kept the promise I made," Alex said, pulling away from her embrace. He rose from the bed and walked toward the window. With his back toward her, he said, "It's almost time for the portal to open. We must return to Luce Del Sol and tell your father about Thomas and Fabio. Elio needs to question Mr. Matteo, and then, we're left with Viola."

Rose stepped in front of him and put her arms around his waist. Thin lines that weren't there before he went to jail now cut his face.

"I asked Lucia if she's heard from her brother," she said.

"And has she?" Alex asked, leaning toward Rose.

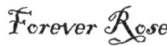

"No, but she thinks Thomas may be in Florence visiting his family."

"We should ask Elio to check."

"I already did." Rose grabbed a wool blanket from the edge of her bed, wrapping herself in it as she walked around the room. "His family hasn't stepped foot in the city."

"In other words, no one knows where his family is."

Rose nodded. "I'm happy you're home."

"It's good to be back," Alex said, kissing Rose again before he opened the door and pushed her into the hallway.

"He adores me. He does," Rose said as she twirled on her heels, passing Lucia on her way back to her room. She turned around and grabbed the maid's arms, dancing with her.

"Miss Rose, did the demons burst over you this morning?" Lucia asked.

"Dr. Santini returned. He is free. Tell me, Lucia, isn't this morning more radiant than other mornings?"

Lucia shook her head and pulled her arms away. She grabbed Rose's hand and ushered her into her chamber, closing the door behind them. A single rose lay on top of her pillow. Rose threw herself on the bed, picked it up and kissed the petals.

"So sweet," Rose whispered.

"All right, Miss, now stay still so that I can help with your dress," Lucia said. "This one's perfect," she said, holding a velvet dress in front of Rose. "What do you think?"

"Don't you think this rose is much prettier than the others?" Rose asked.

Lucia started to laugh.

"He wants me, but he pushes me away. Why must it be so complicated?"

Lucia brushed Rose's hair, clipping it back into a stylish French twist.

"You must meet Mr. Matteo this morning. The new orders are ready to ship, and he needs you at the factory to sign the release papers. Mr. Benito asked me to remind you."

"I'm ready," Rose said, leaving the room.

"And don't forget about the ball!" Lucia yelled from the threshold.

***

By now, it was the beginning of January, and the air had turned a bit chilly. It rarely snowed in Siena, and the rose bushes still decorated the gardens. Three weeks had passed since Alex had returned from jail, and Rose spent every spare moment in his company, researching Da Vinci's book, especially the events surrounding his disappearance in the cave where the portal had opened thirteen months ago. If their calculations were right, they had less than a month before the portal opened and Alex returned to his world. Mr. Matteo requested a leave of absence to tend to his failing health, which left Rose in control of the factory. Alex grew restless as the night of the masquerade ball approached. Alex and Rose talked about returning to Villa Luce Del Sol after the ball.

Rose only talked about how pompous the ball would be, about the people they would meet and, especially the Duchess who would bring signed contracts granting the Estes family the supremacy over the porcelain business in all of Tuscany.

"It's time to get ready," Lucia said on the evening of the ball.

"It will be amazing," Rose said, looking at her new dress.

Her headdress was made up of a lace handkerchief trimmed with a border of pearls. Lucia pulled Rose's hair on top of her head in thick curls separated by a band of diamonds, leaving two small curls down each side of her face. A dress with very short sleeves and a train of lilac spider web adorned with pearls and a star in the middle completed her Egyptian-themed outfit. She put on gloves and looked in the mirror.

"Remind me again why we must attend a masquerade ball?" Alex asked.

"I promised the Duchess that I would be there. She convinced the Grand Judge to shorten your detention and hurry the trial. She was in the audience when you saved the guard's life, Alex. She said she will bring the contracts tonight."

"Enough reasons to last a lifetime." Alex sighed. "There go my hopes for a quiet evening."

Rose didn't answer, just stared at her reflection in the mirror. "Splendid!" She clapped her hands, spinning around the room.

"Not yet," Alex protested. He tied her lace mask on and turned her around. "Now you're perfect."

"You look like an angel of the night," Rose said, arranging his mask. "With your black cape and a tricorn, you're quite a sight, Alessandro Santini."

As he checked his attire in the mirror, Alex laughed. "I feel ridiculous."

"Well, you're not." Rose giggled, running down the stairs with Alex following close behind.

***

Palazzo Sansedoni, a majestic castle built from red bricks, facing Piazza del Campo, was the venue for the ball. The beautifully decorated interior featured expensive polychrome marble and inlaid stones. Carriages stopped in the driveway, and people dressed just as Alex and Rose made their way through the grand hall. Alex and Rose followed. Rose couldn't take her eyes off the elegant tapestries and elaborate food arrangements.

"These statues are characteristic of the Medici court to which the Sansedoni are devoted," Alex said, touching the statues that lined the grand hall. "These frescoes with mythological topics were painted by the members of the Florentine school."

"I'm impressed by your knowledge," Rose said, taking his hand and pulling him as she wove her way between the people in the ballroom.

"My Italian heritage," Alex said.

"Along with my lessons," Rose added.

Waves of welcome came from all sides. Rose moved graciously from one group to another, embracing close friends and kissing them on the cheeks. An atmosphere of excessive eating, drinking, and flirting combined with dancing and gambling dominated the extravagant town hall where Oriental clothing and Domino costumes were by far the most popular disguises.

"These are the only balls where women can go unattended," Rose shouted in his ear. "Women can approach strangers and strike up discussions inappropriate at any other gatherings. Here, the masks provide independence."

"Interesting solution," Alex laughed, "the masks."

"Alex Santini, you are full of mischief," Rose said, giggling.

The enormous chandeliers cast a cheerful light over the ballroom while music, plentiful food, and drinking brought the most intimate desires into plain view. A smile spread across Alex's face, as he swallowed a glass of Chianti and looked from one mask to another. Despite his disguise, he felt hideously exposed and couldn't wait for the night to end. In the solitude of the villa, he would have Rose to himself, away from the noise and praying eyes.

"The success of these parties depends on discretion," Rose said.

"Nothing in here suggests discretion, Rose," Alex replied.

Alex looked at the couples in the far corners of the ballroom, masked by the shadow of curtains, kissing while their hands rested in all the inappropriate places. He opened his mouth in surprise when a man raised a woman's skirt and touched her leg while she leaned on an iron staircase.

"You're doing it again," Rose said.

"What?"

"You're staring."

Rose pulled Alex next to a window. "One of the men wearing a Medico Della Peste costume tonight is Fabio. Maybe this one," she said, pointing to a man in an ankle-length coat wearing a mask that looked like a bird, who passed them on his way to a group of noisy people.

"How do you know?" Alex asked, scanning the ballroom.

"I don't. I just assumed it because he'd never wear anything less than impressive. Just wait until midnight when the masks come off."

Rose picked a slice of orange from a server's tray and stuffed it in Alex's mouth.

"This will keep you occupied," Rose said. "Do you have masquerade balls in your time?"

"Not that I know of," Alex said, blinking rapidly. "My world is far more modern than this."

"You are still set to return to your time. Is my world challenging for you, Alex?"

"I'd be lying if I said it is easy."

No one would notice his disappearance in his world, other than his friend, Renaldo, and even he might think Alex had just followed his advice to take a vacation.

"Look," Rose said, pointing to a man and a woman next to a marble staircase, who had removed their masks as soon as the clock struck midnight. "Those two are the Duke and the Duchess of Tuscany," she said. "I must talk to the Duchess about my contracts."

"Go, now," Alex said. "I'll find something to do."

Rose went to the Duchess, and Alex leaned on one of the pillars. His gaze fell on Fabio across the room, who had just taken off his mask before he opened a door beneath a winding marble staircase connecting the floors. A woman looked both ways and followed him.

"I'll find you," Alex said as he passed Rose on his way to the spot where he saw Fabio and the woman disappearing.

Alex pulled the curtains apart and craned his neck. A narrow corridor flanked by rooms on both sides stretched as far as he could see. The sound of departing footsteps made him hurry. With his back against the wall, his heart stopped when he heard voices coming from a room nearby. The door was open a crack, and the pale glow of a candle offered enough light to help Alex get around without hurting himself. Fabio's hands were resting on the woman's shoulders, and Alex would have given anything to be close.

"I'm pregnant, Fabio," the woman confessed. "I can't go on by myself. Here, hidden in Mr. Matteo's cane, you'll find the contracts you need. Give them to Lord Remington to settle your debt tonight."

"Wonderful news, Viola. I couldn't ask for a lovelier partner than you. As for the child, it's unexpected," Fabio said, kissing her cheeks as he held the cane.

"Are you still going through with your wedding?" Viola looked as though she was about to cry. "I can't raise a child by myself. What shall I do, Fabio? What?"

Viola started sobbing and pounding his chest with her fists. Fabio grabbed her hands by the wrists and kissed her fingers ever so gently. He hugged her and hummed to her until Viola stopped crying.

"All we need is money. Then we can leave Siena behind and move to London where no one knows or cares about us. Can you keep this secret a little longer?" Fabio asked.

"Mr. Matteo threatened to reveal our plan if I asked him for more money. He made it quite clear in the afternoon after I met him at the cathedral," Viola said.

"He won't. After you had sent me your message, I instructed Thomas to finish him off. He should be as quiet as a fish by now."

Alex shuddered. He remembered what Rose said about the secrets and the plots concealed behind stone walls.

"And what are we going to do with Rose?" Viola asked.

"It's been taken care. She won't know what happened. No one will figure it out. Even the doctor, who's her shadow, won't be able to save her," Fabio said.

"You pushed Dr. Guillermo to accuse him of witchcraft, and still, he escaped. He has powerful friends."

"Enough of him," Fabio cried, pushing Viola away from him. "We must leave Siena and return to the villa. But we must travel separately."

"I'll meet you at home."

Alex shook his head and stepped away from the door, hitting a statue with his back. It shattered into hundreds of pieces as soon as it reached the floor, its noise echoing through the hallway. He saw their shadows approaching and ran toward the exit without looking back.

***

Ladies-in-waiting and an army of lords, all decorated for the special ceremony, surrounded the royal family. Their hairstyles, adorned with sparkling diamonds and dresses that revealed more than they covered, were the main attractions of the evening. Rose bowed as soon as she stepped before the Duke and Duchess.

"Have you received the contracts, Miss Rose?" the Duchess asked.

Rose paled. "No, Your Grace, I came prepared to ask about them. I'm set to leave Siena at dawn."

"I sent them to your factory, and my servant told me he had released them to your administrator," the Duchess added.

"I'll check with Mr. Matteo in the morning, Your Grace. And, many thanks for saving my doctor's life."

"I want him to come to Court. His skills are admirable," the Duchess said, waving her feather fan and turning her attention to the dancing in the hall.

Hearing that Mr. Matteo had received the contracts and had said nothing about their arrival made Rose dizzy and weak. The room began to spin, and she grabbed the back of a chair to steady herself. She had been right to suspect Mr. Matteo, and Alex had been wrong that Fabio wanted her dead. She bowed to the Duke and the Duchess as she retired to a corner of the ballroom, away from the curious gazes of her acquaintances. She searched the hall for Alex and jumped when she heard someone whispering in her ear.

"I know you," a man in a domino costume said. "Do you know me?"

"I would recognize you anywhere, Count Asante," Rose answered, still looking for Alex, who had disappeared behind a door under the staircase. Count Asante pulled her toward the center of the ballroom. He twirled her around, among the other couples.

"Tell me, my dear Rose, have you given my wedding proposal any thought?" Count Asante asked.

"My answer is not the one you desire, my lord."

"Then, the rumors are right. You are considering someone else."

"It's a long story, Count, one I would like to keep private. A woman's heart is filled with mysteries, and reason has nothing to do with her decision."

"You are cruel, milady," Count Asante said, stopping in his tracks.

"You lost this battle. The woman gave you her answer, so leave," Alex demanded, grabbing Rose's hand and pushing people out of his way as he marched toward the exit.

"What happened, Alex?" Rose asked, running to keep up with him. "Why are we leaving in such haste?"

"Fabio has the contracts you said the Duchess would give you," Alex said. "Viola gave him Mr. Matteo's cane along with money and your documents, and she told him to pay Lord Remington. They even mentioned something about finishing off Mr. Matteo and about you, Rose."

"Me? What could they possibly say about me? And what about Viola?"

"She said she is carrying his child," Alex said.

"Fabio's child? That means Viola was the woman you saw the night when my father was hurt. I thought she was my friend." Rose came to an abrupt stop. She covered her chest with her hand. "My poor sister, she's clueless. We must warn her about their dishonesty, Alex. We can't let her go through with the wedding. We leave at dawn."

"Look, Fabio is moving. Maybe we can persuade him to return your contracts."

"If we can catch him," Rose said, looking at Fabio, who was sneaking out of the ballroom with the cane in his hand. They picked up speed, pushing people out of their way. Rose turned back to apologize, but Alex tugged at her arm, pulling her toward the door. The night was clear, the sky filled with stars, and the moon full. They ran to the carriage, not losing sight of Fabio, who mounted his horse. He crossed the square, leaving the city's gates behind, and they followed him.

"He's leaving Siena," Rose said. "Hurry, Alex, we're losing him! If he passes over the bridge, my contracts are forever lost."

"I'm doing my best," Alex said, while he drove the horses, following Fabio.

"He's over the bridge already," Rose shouted while she looked out the window.

"He noticed us," Alex said. "It would be much faster if I rode alone."

"We're going together. He has my contracts, and my future depends on them."

"He lost it!" Alex yelled, halting the carriage in the middle of the stone bridge.

"Lost what?" Rose asked.

"Look! The cane is being carried away by the river. There is no time," Alex cried out, jumping into the water and following the direction of the stream.

"Be careful!" Rose shouted from the bridge.

The river was high after the previous day's storm, and Alex fought the currents threatening to subdue him at any time. He swam, and the water carried him farther away from the shore. The cane was a few laps in front of him, and Alex doubled his efforts. His muscles were cramped, but he managed to grab the cane. Alex held it above the water while he swam toward the shore. At a turn in the river, a current caught Alex. His head went under the waves, while he fought to escape.

"Help! Someone help!" Rose cried from the center of the bridge.

Rose ran along the bridge. She threw her dress shoes away and grabbed the edge of the stone fence, preparing to leap into the river when a man ran past her and jumped into the water, swimming toward Alex. He fought with the waves, and the current pushed him farther from the shore. The man reached Alex and grabbed his collar. Rose tried to make out the swimmer's face, but the water and the darkness hindered her efforts. When the man reached the shore, he left Alex on the grass. Alex turned toward him, wanting to thank him for saving his life.

"You!" Rose shouted.

Fabio tilted his head, staring at Rose before he ran toward the bridge. She thought she saw compassion in his eyes. He didn't look back, and minutes later, the hooves on the road were the only sound they heard.

Rose kneeled next to Alex and hugged him tightly.

"You are the craziest person I've ever met, Alex. You could have drowned in the river, save for Fabio, who surprised me," Rose said, kissing him repeatedly.

"I'll do it anytime for your kiss," Alex laughed and rolled Rose next to him on the grass. "I've got your documents." Alex gave Rose the cane as he continued to kiss her.

"Alex Santini, stop this."

"I can't," Alex said. "I'm addicted to you."

Alex moved his hands to the back of her neck, and she felt every cell tensing with expectation, her body shaking with desire. This man had swept her off her feet, and every ounce of resistance she once had, it melted away when she lost herself in the blue of his eyes.

CHAPTER 18

Rose and Alex left Siena early in the morning. They decided to return to Villa Luce De Sol and confront Rose's parents with their findings. Alex wasn't looking forward to meeting Count Estes and explaining why he had to duel with Fabio. He helped Rose climb inside the carriage and signaled the coachman that they were ready for the five hours journey back to the Estes's manor.

"Why didn't you sleep last night?" Alex asked Rose.

"You're worried about me. Don't be," Rose said. "We must tell my father about Fabio's plan."

"We need proof to accuse people."

"Papa must know what is going on."

"Of course," Alex said, staring at her. "It's the work of your sister that brought Fabio's wrath upon all of us."

"Love doesn't listen to reason. Annabella has been fascinated with Fabio since we were young. Luckily, marriage wasn't in the cards for me," Rose said, remembering the day when her sister simply told everyone she would marry Fabio, and everyone accepted her decision, although it came as a surprise, especially because Fabio didn't show signs of affection toward Annabella. Not once did she imagine her sister as the object of his romantic attention, but Rose loved Annabella and wanted her to be happy, so she accepted her choice.

"I find everything about this very strange," Alex said, scratching his head.

"I guess he fooled us all."

Rose was convinced that the deep purple circles under her eyes and their sunken looks told the story of her sleepless night. She breathed in the smell of his skin, a mixture of the wind and lemon, and thought of asking him to stay, although she knew that she had no right to decide his fate.

"We shall tell Papa where you came from."

"I don't know, Rose. My presence here is not justified by the laws of physics. He won't understand."

Rose shrugged her shoulders, looking out the window. The rusty leaves spread on roads as a reminder that nature followed a predestined path. The wind nudged a pile of blood-red leaves and swirled them into the chilly January air. Tucked inside the comfort of her cape, Rose remained quiet for the rest of the trip. That night, when Alex kissed her by the river, she realized she would never look at another man the way she looked at him. Rose followed the rhythmical rise and fall of his chest for the remainder of the trip from Siena to Villa Luce De Sol.

"We're here. Your mother is waving and Annabella too," Alex said, looking out the window all groggy from the nap he had taken in the carriage.

When the carriage came to a halt in front of the villa, Rose didn't wait for the coachman to open the door. She jumped down, running toward her mother and sister.

"I've missed you," she said.

"What's all this nonsense about stopping my wedding?" Annabella cried.

"Papa should explain to you why you can't marry Fabio."

"Behave, girls," their mother snapped, pushing them inside the house.

Rose looked over her shoulder at Alex, who stood by the horses, waving to her and winking. She closed the door behind her, hoping that he would be all right by the time she finished talking to her mother. Her heart skipped a beat. She wished Alex would be next to her when she talked to her mother about their findings, just as he had promised her back in Siena.

"Good morning, Dr. Santini," Count Estes said, dismounting. "Thank heaven the trial is behind us."

"An experience I have no wish to repeat," Alex said, and a shudder passed through him. "Thank you for pleading my case during the trial."

"Easy, boy, easy," Count Estes said, patting the horse who was restless after the long trip from Siena. "You should thank Rose and her powers of persuasion. Come with me!"

Count Estes signaled Alex to follow. They passed through the foyer and waved to Rose, who was climbing the stairs along with her mother and Annabella. Count Estes opened the door toward his studio, and the smell of leather joined the aroma of spirits.

"From the look on your face, I gather the news you bring is not all that great," Count Estes said, handing Alex a glass of brandy and pouring one for him.

"You'll be as surprised as I was when you'll hear it."

Count Estes stopped in front of him.

"Did you discover who wants Rose dead?"

"None other than your future ex-son-in-law," Alex answered.

"Fabio," Count Estes said. His dark eyes fixed on a spot on the opposite wall. Although he didn't seem a dangerous man, Alex was glad they were on the same side. He passed his hand through his hair, looking every bit as confused and distracted as Count Estes.

"It was a conspiracy. Your gardener, Thomas, and Viola helped too," Alex continued.

"Viola?"

"That's not all."

"There is more?" Count Estes dropped into a chair. "What now?"

"Viola is expecting Fabio's child. She told Fabio at the masquerade ball."

"What?" Count Estes asked, smashing his fist on the desk. "Unbelievable."

"At least, I've retrieved the contracts he had stolen from you, and if we find Thomas, we've got our key to bringing light to the events of the past months."

"I must talk to my daughter before I decide what to do next."

"Thomas tried killing me to get to Rose. He wounded you at her birthday party. He was the man I fought in your garden the night we stumbled over the note," Alex said, raising his voice as a vein throbbed on his temple.

"There is no need for you to get all fired up. We must think before acting," Count Estes said.

"And something else, Count if I may." Alex coughed, a dry, irritating cough, knowing the moment was as good as any to talk to her father. "Rose doesn't want to go against your decision to send her to Siena to oversee the factory, but she misses painting."

"I know, son. I'll set things right. By God, I will do it."

***

"Sit, Rose. We should talk," Countess Estes commanded when they reached her bedchamber. "Countess Asante said you were dancing in the piazza during the Palio festival, and that you kissed a very handsome man. Can you fancy what embarrassment came upon me?"

"Mother, I," Rose tried explaining the circumstances for the kiss, her voice breaking under her mother's stare.

"There is no time for excuses. I hope nothing happened between you and the doctor. He will never raise to our social position, child."

"Hearts choose for themselves whom to love," Rose said, fixing her eyes on her mother's.

"Rose, I can't believe what I'm hearing. He doesn't possess ranks or wealth."

"He has something more precious than that, mother."

"What?"

"He has a heart. A man who will lay down his life for you is hard to come by," Rose said, leaning back in her chair. She grasped the arms of the chair tightly and counted.

"Who is going to sacrifice his life?"

"Alex, mother, he would gladly sacrifice his life for me. He fought Fabio when he knew he would lose. He jumped into the river to retrieve the contracts and almost drowned."

When her mother rose from the couch and went to the armchair where Rose sat, Rose braced herself. Once again, the same sensation of nausea she had experienced in Siena gave her a throbbing headache and a slight pain in her heart. As gently as her mother could, she took Rose's hands into hers, her voice soft when she talked.

"You are heir because Annabella is naïve. I've told your father that it's not proper for a woman to run into town and handle the challenges of a factory by herself. You need a man by your side."

"Are you suggesting I shall marry to satisfy some vanity, some old norms in our society?" Rose asked, raising her voice and pulling her hands out of her mother's.

"Rose Estes, mind your manners. You can't repeat the same mistake your own mother did," her mother said, grabbing her shoulders.

"When did love become a mistake?" Rose asked, turning pale.

She jerked from her mother's clasp and slammed the door behind her. Her biological mother's love story was a subject the family held private at the estate, and after her death, her grandmother, the old Countess Estes, blamed Rose. If Rose hadn't been born, her daughter would still be alive. Years passed, and her grandmother didn't kiss her even once. On the other hand, Rose understood her adoptive mother's reasoning. History was bound to repeat itself, and Rose, like her biological mother before her, chose to follow her heart. But on the other hand, there was no way she would part with a man who had made her a priority in his life. He was different from the men of her century, who saw women as means of satisfying physical needs. As soon as she located Alex, she would tell him that she was prepared to go with him when he left through the portal. His century couldn't be worse than hers.

"I gather that you talked to your mother," her father said, catching Rose in his arms.

"Yes, I did," Rose answered between sobs. She threw herself into her father's arms, the only place she had always felt protected.

"So, the rumors are true," Count Estes said. He seized her arms and stared at her. Although she tried to control the trembling of her chin, she failed miserably, and a fresh set of sobs shook her body. After she had pulled herself from her father's grasp, Rose turned her back toward him, facing the wall and standing on tiptoes. "You're doing it again," her father said, " as you did it when I caught you in the stables, by the horses, and you pretended you lost your earrings."

"I was ten at the time," Rose said, sketching a smile. "And what rumors are you talking about?" Rose asked.

"About your affair with the doctor," Count Estes added.

"There is no affair."

"Of course there isn't. I know my daughter well. Come with me," her father ordered, leading her to the library. He locked the door behind them, pulled a book out of the second shelf of the bookcase and took out a bottle, pouring a glass of brandy for Rose and one for himself. "Here, drink this."

Rose took the glass from her father, swallowed, and the brandy burned her throat. She patted her stomach, licking her lips, and then she tilted her head, listening.

"Rose, we'll discuss your future after I talk to Fabio."

"So, Alex told you about Fabio and Thomas."

"And their intent to kill you. Yes, he did. He told me about that and much more."

"What did he say?"

"That your heart aches because you want to paint," Count Estes said.

Rose put the glass down and touched her forehead.

"Are you tired from your trip?"

"A little," she said, although not entirely sure if she felt dizzy because of the journey or the brandy she just drunk.

"Go back to your room if you're sleepy," he suggested. "Oh, by God, I'd better take you," her father whispered.

The comfort of his arms when he picked her up reminded Rose of her childhood. Hearing her screams, how many nights did her father run to her bedroom and stay with her until the nightmares disappeared? Storms terrified her, and her father provided comfort with his stories. As Rose grew up, she learned to control herself, but, from time to time, like that night when she ran into Alex's room, Rose needed the closeness of another person to make her feel safe.

"You're the best part of my life," Rose whispered when her father covered her with a quilt.

"Never forget it."

***

"Summon Elio Marotto. As soon as he arrives, lead him here," Count Estes ordered the butler as soon as he returned to the studio where he had left Alex.

"Yes, my lord," Mr. Ciccio said, closing the door behind him.

"Elio saved my life in Siena," Alex said.

"Elio and I studied law, debated the issues of the social classes, and chased after girls in our youth. One night, after many bottles of red Toscana, we concluded that women have the right to choose their husbands instead of allowing their parents to determine their fate. They are entitled to pursue their dreams," Count Estes said, falling into a chair.

"Then, you're aware Rose wants to be a historical painter, not an heir to a factory," Alex said.

"I know, and I am ready to grant her wish to live in Florence and paint. I'll let her become the pride of my old age," Count Estes said.

"Rose can come with me."

"Come where?"

They looked toward the door when it slammed. "It's been a long time," Elio said, stopping by the cabinet where Count Estes

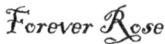

kept the spirits and pouring a glass of Chianti. "Anyone else cares to join me?"

"You came fast," Count Estes said, nodding. He took the glass Elio poured him and sipped.

"I bring unfortunate news," Elio said.

"I know that look," Count Estes added.

"I have to deliver a letter." Elio pulled an envelope from his coat.

"A letter? In blood? From whom?" Count Estes asked.

"Mr. Matteo left it for Rose."

"Why in God's name?"

"He had it in his hand when he died," Elio said.

"Mr. Matteo is dead?" Alex asked.

"I found him dead in his home."

Count Estes covered his mouth. Alex snatched the letter from Elio's hand, and after he had read it, he flopped onto a nearby sofa. Count Estes took the letter from his hand and read it aloud.

"*My Dear Rose,*

I never meant to hurt anyone. But what a man won't do in the name of love? Yes, love, the feeling that's shaking your core and pushing you to do unbelievable things, hoping that one day you will undo the wrong you've done. I don't know where to begin or how to end. The words are scarce and my time is running out. I loved someone with all my heart and protecting him blinded me. I broke your trust and, even if it's too late, please, accept my sincere apology. One day, I hope you'll find the strength to forgive me.

Viola is not your friend, but a woman who is using your kindness to accomplish her plans. Along with Count Fabio Monti, she is planning to take over the Estes' domain by eliminating everyone who stands in her way. I can't stop her plan, but someone has that power. Keep the doctor close, for he is the key to your salvation.

My kind regards,

Mr. Matteo"

Elio filled three glasses with Chianti and slid into the seat across from Alex. After he had drunk his wine, he looked at Alex and then back at Count Estes. "Any thoughts?" he asked.

"So, Viola, Fabio, and Thomas planned to kill Rose," Count Estes did the math. He had tapped on the cherry desk before he continued. "We agree that Fabio is the villain. Now we need a plan to stop him before he stops us."

"Was Rose the reason for your duel with Fabio?" Elio asked Alex.

Alex nodded. "Thomas acted at Fabio's command. He tried to kill Rose on her birthday, but the knife struck her father instead. I asked Lucia about her brother's affairs, but she has no clue where he is," Alex said.

Elio knitted his brows. He leaned on the wall, cracking his knuckles.

"Are you sure he's mixed up with the villains?" Count Estes asked, with disbelief in his eyes.

"I fought him in Siena," Alex said. "He was on the roof of the building across from the inn where Fabio stayed. He tried to kill me with arrows."

"We need a strategy, Giulio. No time to waste," Elio said.

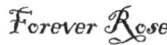
"I have a plan," Count Estes said.

***

Rose woke up refreshed after the nap she took in the afternoon. She helped Annabella sort among the gifts received over the past months, now scattered over the floor and still wrapped in colorful boxes. They filled five wooden trunks with the household goods that Annabella intended to take away to her new residence after the wedding.

"I still have much to do, and there are only two weeks left until the wedding," Annabella said.

"Fabio can't marry you," Rose said.

"Why is everyone telling me that Fabio can't marry me? Is he in love with another woman?"

Annabella laughed, taking a bite from a sugar cookie. Rose grabbed her shoulders, forcing her to sit on the sofa. Causing her sister pain was the hardest thing she had to do, and Rose took a deep breath before she whispered.

"I'm not sure about his feelings for you, but one thing is clear. Another woman carries his child in her belly."

"Impossible!" Annabella shouted, pushing Rose away. "You're jealous. Isn't it enough that you are the heir? I thought it was a joke when Papa said that you were going to stop the wedding."

"Dr. Santini heard them. Fabio wants me dead," Rose said.

"Fabio? A murderer?"

"I'm not allowing Fabio to take advantage of you!" Rose yelled.

"I don't believe you."

"He loved you for your inheritance when his heart belonged to another." Rose choked on her words, and the entire room began to spin. Her words reached her ears as if she were in a dream. "He's not the one for you. I will stop him, by God, I will," Rose said before she fainted.

CHAPTER 19

"Rose, look at me," Alex said. Alex's touch was soft on her shoulders, like the touch of a feather. He wiped the sweat from her forehead and gave her lemon water to drink. Rose took a sip and pushed the glass away, her sentences losing coherency while she shook from head to toe with fever. She continuously whispered one word.

"Supermoon? What is she talking about?" her mother cried out. Countess Estes dropped to her knees, touching Rose's face, and Alex wondered if he would be forced to treat both mother and daughter.

"What's wrong with her? She was all right while we unwrapped the gifts, only to collapse a second later. Is she faking it to get your attention?" Annabella asked, looking over her mother's shoulder.

"Annabella," her mother gasped, a shocked expression settling on her face, "your sister is sick." Countess Estes rose from the floor, turned to Alex, and grabbed his shoulders, shaking him with all her strength. "Do something, Doctor," she pleaded.

"First, we must lower her fever and stabilize her temperature," Alex said, and no one but him noticed the slight tremor in his voice. He rang the bell, and when the butler arrived, Alex said, "Bring a bucket of cold water to Miss Rose's room."

Alex turned to Rose, who lay on her bed as white as a sheet, and he took her hands into his. The same thing occurred while they were in the house in Siena. It happened too when they were in the cabin in the woods before they had reached Siena after the archer had tried killing them, but Alex hadn't acknowledged those signs. This time, Rose's seizure lasted longer than the previous ones, and Alex thought that she might need heart surgery. Without the aid of modern technology, it was impossible to diagnose her condition. He turned toward the door when he heard a knock.

Lucia entered the room first, followed by two of the house's servants and Mr. Ciccio. They sat the oval wood bathtub with cold water in the heart of the chamber and stepped aside, waiting for orders.

"We have to put her in the tub and fast," Alex commanded.

Rose whispered, moving her head from left to right and repeating one word: roses.

"Does she want roses? Why is she asking for them?" Annabella queried, looking at the vase filled with roses that were on the writing desk.

"I'm not sure," Alex answered, raising a brow.

Lucia stripped the clothes off Rose until she was left wearing only a chemise. "She's ready, Doctor," she said, stepping away from the bed.

Alex lifted Rose into his arms and lowered her into the water.

"It is cold," Rose whispered.

"I know, but it'll help you," Alex said.

It was the end of January, and by his calculations, the portal would open soon, and he would take Rose to his century. A test would be enough to discover the cause of her sickness. Back in his time, Alex would have access to all that he needed to heal Rose, and if a heart surgery were imminent, he would make sure the best surgeons cared for her. He looked at the face of the woman he loved and kissed her forehead.

"You'll feel better soon," Alex said. He flattened the mess of ginger curls dripping with water and ignored her relatives' stares. He wouldn't let her die like Sophia.

"Dr. Santini," Countess Estes said, "there are people here."

"Yes, I know, and they shouldn't be here. Rose needs space to relax. Go away, now, all of you," Alex said, pushing them out the door.

"Let's go, Eleonora. Dr. Santini knows what to do," Count Estes said and grabbed his wife's arm, pulling her out of Rose's chamber. "Come with me too, Annabella."

After everyone had left, Alex fell to his knees, holding Rose's hand and splashing cold water on her cheeks. It took more than an hour for her fever to come down. The candles shone brightly in the chamber, making her skin translucent. Wet curls dangled over her body, floating on the water like tongues of fire.

"If something happens to me, I won't want you trapped in my time," Rose whispered.

"In my time, a test would suffice to find out where the problem is. I lack many things here," Alex said.

"How I wish I could go with you." Rose paused, looking at Alex.

"I'm not leaving you here."

Alex leaned toward Rose and kissed her. She laced her arms around his neck and rested her cheek on his shoulder.

"May I come in?" Count Estes asked after he cracked the door open.

"Papa, I'm not appropriately dressed for a visit," Rose hollered, and her cheeks flushed up to her ears when her father entered her room.

"Don't drag your heels."

Count Estes turned his back, waiting for Rose to dress up. Rose took her wet chemise off before putting on a robe, and then she took a blanket, covering her legs and resting on a rocking chair by the fire.

"Come closer," Rose said, reaching for her father's hand.

"Did this happen before?"

"Yes it did, on our way to Siena," Alex said.

"And then, in the library, after your release from prison," Rose added. She lowered her head because it felt like lead, and her chin trembled. "I feel a weight pressing on my chest. It burns when I breathe," Rose explained, her voice thick and slow. "It always comes after I smell roses."

"Roses?"

"Do you think they used roses?" Count Estes asked as he turned to the vase with roses sitting on top of the table. He checked the petals, turning them over. He smelled them too.

"Don't touch them, Count!" Alex yelled. "Whoever sent the roses was familiar with her preference for the yellow ones." Alex's eyes grew wide, and a thought crept into his mind. He snatched a napkin, picked up the flowers, wrapped the napkin around them, and laid them on the writing desk. At first glance, nothing seemed out of the ordinary. He turned the roses on every side, but other than a few small globules on the inside of the petals, they appeared healthy. "There is an unusual pattern of drops on petals. But it can be a plant illness," Alex said, turning one stem around and checking every leaf with a letter opener he had discovered next to the writing pads.

"Are you certain about this?" Count Estes asked.

"No, not really," Alex continued. He checked another one, and a similar pattern of drops appeared on the petals. Every flower had the same taint. "They poisoned the flowers and brought them to Rose. My belief is that the toxin affected her over months," Alex said, shaking his head.

"They poisoned her by smell and touch, not by taste," Count Estes said, looking at Rose.

"Papa, I don't want to die," Rose cried, tightening her grip on her father's arm.

Count Estes embraced her. "You won't." He opened the door, looking both sides. "Eleonora! Annabella! Come here at once!" He paced in the room until a few minutes later Countess Estes and her youngest daughter entered the room. "Stay with Rose! Don't let her out of your sight," Count Estes said. He turned toward Alex, his voice thundering when he spoke. "I'm going after Fabio!"

"And I'm getting Thomas," Alex said, running out the door with the count at his side.

***

Alex dismounted in front of Thomas's house, letting the mount loose on a field nearby. The grass was damp with evening dew, but Alex didn't care if his feet got soaked. The house was the last one in a village of no more than thirty, and every one of the village's inhabitants was asleep at this late hour. A narrow road separated the stone houses perching atop a steep hill overlooking deep ravines crowded with olive trees.

Alex approached the house and noticed the door was open a crack. No other sound except those of crickets. He pushed the door a little wider, with his foot, and entered into a small foyer. A mantle hung loosely on a chair that had seen better days while a bow and two arrows rested in a corner. Shadows from the disparate pieces of furniture grew on the wall. Alex pulled the pistol he carried with him since his duel with Fabio and walked into the bedchamber where a window banged against the windowsill. He breathed heavily as he searched through the room, not entirely sure what he was looking for.

Alex jolted when he heard the neigh of a nearby horse and ran outside in time to see a rider running across the field. He slammed the door shut and looked for his horse with a strange desire to gallop. He squired his horse across the dirt road while the wind blew his hair over his face. He chased the horse and the rider in front of him through groves of olives and orchards of lemons separating Estes and Monti properties, and after an hour of riding, Fabio's estate appeared on the horizon. Alex was out of breath when he reached the front of the villa. He kept his distance from Thomas, taking into view the only carriage parked in the driveway and a horse grazing in a nearby garden.

Thomas let his horse loose in the fields and then lifted his chin toward the sky where menacing clouds covered the face of the moon. The wind picked up speed, blowing through the empty branches that hit each other. A powerful storm was coming. A gust of wind scattered raindrops in every direction. When the first drops of rain struck the ground, the wind's howling grew steady. The night became darker than when they had left Villa Luce Del Sol. Terrifying clouds buried the stars and the moon, and the only light came from small lamps guarding the mansion's entrance. Threads of wavy mist crept over the ground while raindrops seared the fog, ripping it apart like vicious, silver bullets.

After Alex had dismounted, setting his horse free in the garden, he watched as Thomas opened the front door. Alex followed him in. The corridor was quiet and dimly lit. Alex advanced, hiding behind the columns and expensive furniture. Thomas reached a massive door, his knock resonating in the silent house. He pushed it open enough and squeezed inside a room where a fire burning in the fireplace tossed shadows on the walls. Alex heard Fabio marching in the room, his steps heavy on the wooden floor. He peeked inside the bedchamber through the cracked door. Fabio's hair was disheveled, his blouse open. He looked ghostly in the night, a disturbing image of a man haunted by thousands of demons.

"Come closer, no reason for you to stop." Fabio's sharp voice sent shivers down Alex's spine. "They know about us, Thomas," Fabio said.

"Lucia sent word that Count Estes is looking for me," Thomas said.

Fabio grabbed a glass and threw it across the room. Hundreds of sharp pieces scattered in every corner of his studio.

"My wedding is ruined, and Rose is still alive. My estate is a mess, and you are incompetent." Fabio sighed, shaking his head. "Had Rose accepted my proposal, none of this would have happened," he continued, gritting his teeth and spitting on the floor.

"My Lord, it'll be over soon," Thomas said, and Alex touched his gun when he heard him.

"For once, you're right," Fabio said, tousling his hair. After a couple of steps, he turned toward him, staring him in the eye. "What about the other task I gave you? Is it done already?"

"He is as good as a dead fish," Thomas added. Hearing his words, Alex peeked into the room in time to see Fabio nodding.

"Go now, before anyone catches you in here," Fabio commanded.

"How about my family, Lord? Can I see them?"

"They'll be free as soon as Rose is dead."

Fabio spat his words so fast that Thomas backed away. Alex ducked behind a statue, one of Fabio's ancestors, by the name engraved on the marble, and he waited for Thomas to depart. The gardener walked toward the door, resting his back against the wood frame. He rubbed a hand against his chest with short, jerky movements, gasping for air.

"How did I get involved in such nonsense?" Thomas muttered, rushing out of the house.

Alex waited until silence settled over the hallway and followed Thomas outside. The clouds began to disperse as Thomas turned onto a side alley bordered by citrus trees, then he turned back, hiding in the shadow of a bush. He lifted a hand and grabbed the windowsill, swinging his leg over the edge and jumping inside the empty library. Alex was right behind him, staying out of sight. Thomas walked toward the far wall and raised one corner of a velvety curtain, slipping into a hidden passage. Candles placed at equal distances lit the tunnel. It was silent inside, wet and terrifying, the air stuffy and unhealthy. The water leaked through the rock, dripping to the ground. Bones of thousands of people filled the crevasses, the small ones piled against the walls. Alex shuddered at the sight of the urns and crosses scattered among the bones. The eerie feel of the place gave him goosebumps and Alex half expected to see ghosts and demons from the underworld. He followed the passageway, touching the cold stones, and he jumped when rats ran over his feet. Thomas was ahead of him, and Alex advanced, guided by the man's steady movement. The underground channel descended after a few steps, and Thomas reached a narrow, stone spiral stairway that led to the heart of hell itself. After about fifty steps, the tunnel grew larger, so that Alex didn't have to bend over anymore. Voices coming from nearby pierced the tunnel, and all his senses became alerted at the smooth movements around him. A chamber with high ceilings and wide columns appeared at the end of the passage. The guard touched his arm when he passed by him, and Alex jolted from the rush of adrenaline. He jumped back, out of the guard's way and a stone from the wall behind him pierced through his spine. He bit his lip to stop from crying out.

When Thomas hid in a gap in the wall, Alex did the same. They waited for a few seconds, and Alex forgot how to breathe. Then, Thomas picked up a torch and shined it in each cell he passed. Some were empty; some had the remains of stinky feces, while others held prisoners in rags along with mice and rats. Alex's heart drummed in his ears, threatening to explode from the growing tension. Alex watched Thomas stop at the last cell, in the farthest and darkest corner of the dungeon.

"Iulia, Justina! It is Papa," Thomas cried softly, squeezing his hands between the bars of the cell.

"Papa!" the girls yelled in one voice.

One of the girls pushed her skinny arm through the bars. Thomas grabbed her hand and kissed it repeatedly.

"Where's your mother?" he asked, and his voice cracked.

"Mama died last week. She was sick, and they didn't bring a doctor. She coughed hard and spilled blood before dying." The girl wept, her sobs shaking her chest.

"Papa, why are they keeping us here? I want to go home," the second girl pleaded with her father.

"Where did they take her?" Thomas asked.

"I don't know. Men came in the morning, kicked her and covered her with a sack. They carried her away," the first girl said.

Thomas ground his teeth as he pulled the bars apart. Alex felt the man's desperation. "Damn, Monti. Die in hell," he whispered between his teeth.

"The guard is coming back. If he sees you, he'll kill you. Go and hide, Papa."

One girl pushed her father away from the cell and grabbed her sister's hand, moving to the farthest corner of their prison cell and falling to the ground, not letting out even the faintest of sounds. At the sound of approaching footsteps coming from the opposite side of the dungeon, Thomas jerked away from the bars. He signaled the girls to keep quiet while he pushed his back against the wall. Alex touched his pistol, ready to shoot if he must.

"Well, what do we have here?" the guard asked after he stopped in front of the girls' cell. He was a stout man, with arms like knots of old branches. He passed his hand through his thin hair while he wiggled the cells' keys. "Soon, we'll meet in the whores' house."

Alex watched Thomas, who pulled a knife from its sheath, and the knife looked menacing in the dim light of the dungeon. With one move, Thomas covered the guard's mouth, passed the blade over his throat, and threw his body to the floor. He wiped his hands on his breeches and put the knife back in its sheath. Alex gasped, touching his own throat. Thomas grabbed the keys, trying them one by one until he found the one that opened the door. The girls ran to him, crashing into his chest. He kissed each girl a couple of times before they all rushed out of the dungeon.

Alex leaned against the cold stones of the wall, watching as Thomas and the girls hurried up the stairway. When they reached the top of the stairs, Thomas pulled open the velvety curtain, peeked inside the room, and signaled the girls to follow him. Alex was three feet behind them.

"I'll lower you to the ground. Run and hide in the bushes, then wait for your sister to come," Thomas told one of his daughters as they approached the window.

He held Iulia first and lowered her over the ledge and did the same with Justina. Thomas was preparing to jump when the door leading to the library opened. He had barely enough time to hide behind the curtain. Alex remained hidden behind the curtain, half in the passage and half in the chamber.

A woman hummed as she tossed her cape on the sofa. She took her time taking off her gloves and danced around the room.

"You seem happy today," Fabio said, and his voice made Alex shudder. He wanted to strangle the villain, and he clenched his hands, his fingers digging into his palms.

"Why shouldn't I? We're closer to our goal than ever. You'll inherit the Estes' fortune when Rose dies. And Annabella is an easy errand."

"Don't jump to conclusions too fast, Viola," Fabio said. "We're still far from reaching our goal. I must find a way to alleviate Count Estes's suspicions and to continue with the wedding preparations."

Viola moaned when Fabio twisted her arm behind her back, kissing her neck gently. He bit the delicate skin of her flesh, and when she cried, he covered her mouth with his own.

"What are we doing with Thomas?" Viola asked, breaking off the kiss and turning to embrace Fabio. "We don't need witnesses left behind."

"He'll disappear when he finishes the job."

"And his family?"

"They'll join him."

Fabio's voice was cold, calculated, raising goosebumps all over Alex's skin. Fabio lifted Viola's chin, and Alex wished he could shoot them both.

"Fabio," Viola moaned, as she kissed him and ran her hands up and down his back. "We could have moved to London with the money I gathered from Mr. Matteo."

"That wouldn't last long with your expensive tastes, my lady," Fabio said, biting her neck. "Come with me!"

Fabio lifted Viola and left the room, their playful giggles spreading along the hallway. Alex left his spot behind the curtain and jumped to the ground, running toward the back of the garden. He could see Thomas and his two daughters running too between bushes and trees. Alex stopped two feet away from them and dropped to the ground. Thomas grabbed his daughters' arms and said, "We can't go home. Count Fabio will find you there."

"Papa, what are we going to do?" Justina asked.

Thomas searched inside his shirt and drew out a leather purse. He put the bag into Iulia's hand.

"Iulia, you must care for your sister. Tell your aunt that your mother is dead. I'll join you as soon as I finish what I must do."

"Yes, Papa," Iulia said, lacing her fingers with those of her sister's.

"Go now. You have a long trip ahead," Thomas said, watching his daughters walking away from him before he headed back to Fabio's estate.

CHAPTER 20

As he paced in front of Fabio's Villa, Alex braced himself. He had been right all along to suspect Fabio as the mastermind behind the conspiracy to kill Rose, but Rose didn't want to accept his theory. The mere thought of how Fabio had played the injured party and had provoked him to a duel brought a bitter taste to Alex's mouth. He lifted his chin when he heard horse hooves approaching, his eyes widening when Count Estes and Elio descended next to him.

"Doctor, are you well?" Elio asked Alex, shaking his shoulder.

"We have no time. Rose is dying," Count Estes said.

"Keep quiet," Elio said. Count Estes grabbed his shotgun from the saddle bag before he walked toward the villa with Alex and Elio right behind him.

"Fabio and Viola are inside the library," Alex whispered. "Thomas rescued his daughters from Fabio's dungeons. But his wife is dead."

"What did you say?" Count Estes asked, shrugging his shoulders.

Alex told Count Estes how he had followed Thomas from his house to Fabio's villa and down the tunnel that connected the library with the prison below, and how he had witnessed the guard's murder. Elio touched his own pistol, his brows knitting above his eyes.

"Thomas is inside the library now, with both of them, Viola and Fabio, and I'm afraid of what he will do to them if we don't stop him in time," Alex said.

"I'll go first," Elio said, pushing open the front door and entering inside the foyer.

"I'll watch your back like in the old days," Count Estes said.

"Old days, my ass," Elio muttered, a puff escaping his mouth. The thick carpet muffled their footsteps. Soon, they reached a corridor with floors covered with Venetian marble. They stopped when they heard the shouting and the shattering glass coming from Fabio's library.

"Tell me where she is? I swear I'll kill you, you bastard. What did you do to my wife?"

"Thomas?" Count Estes gasped, covering his mouth with the tip of his fingers. "I've never heard him yell at someone before. He's a quiet man."

"Your gardener?" Elio asked, looking at Count Estes. "What is he shouting about?"

Count Estes raised his shoulders as he glanced at Thomas through the cracked door. Thomas was pointing a pistol toward Fabio. Rage distorted his face, and his chin trembled.

"Your wife is safe, Thomas. I promise. Now, put the gun down and let Viola go. She doesn't have anything to do with this," Fabio pleaded with him.

"Oh, but she has everything to do with it. Isn't she your woman?"

"Watch your mouth, peasant, and leave her out of our business. I'm warning you," Fabio shouted.

"You're warning me?" Thomas yelled. "My daughters are safe from you, but I can't say the same about my wife."

"That's nonsense. Your wife was sick, she spat blood, but she's well now," Fabio said, seemingly unaffected by the man's threats or Viola's sobs. Thomas stopped midway, studying Fabio.

"Tell me, then, where is she? Take me to her," Thomas demanded, poking Fabio with his gun.

"Let Viola go, and I'll bring her to you."

Thomas looked from Fabio to Viola, who was shaking next to him on the sofa where he was keeping them captive.

"She's coming with us, and if you lie, she dies!" Thomas roared, signaling them to rise and to step ahead of him.

He didn't notice Count Estes and Alex by the wall or Elio, who grabbed his wrists, twisting them behind his back until he groaned. Count Estes seized the pistol from Thomas's hand as the color on the gardener's face drained.

"How fortunate to catch all of you," Elio said. "We're going to have a chat." He pushed the three prisoners back into the library, closing the door behind all of them. Alex and Count Estes flanked each side of the sofa, eyes fixed on Elio. "Sit down, all of you." Fabio, Viola, and Thomas sat shoulder to shoulder, inches apart. Elio leaned toward Viola and whispered, "Countess Monti, we meet again, although the circumstances are blurry. They escape my understanding."

Viola averted her gaze, her pallor emphasized by the fire burning in the fireplace. With her hands clasped in her lap, she leaned back on the sofa, closing her eyes.

"By the end of this interrogation, you'll get to know me well. In short, I like keeping matters simple, so answer every question as honestly as you possibly can," Elio suggested.

"You have no right to keep us here!" Fabio yelled.

"I don't think you understood me very well, Count Monti. I'm in charge here. You only speak when spoken to," Elio said, leaning toward Fabio, his nose an inch away from his face. "Count Fabio, Countess Viola, and Thomas, I accuse you of plotting to kill Rose Estes, and stealing her business contracts."

"Don't you have any scruples, my lord?" Fabio yelled from the depths of his lungs. "Are you accusing innocent people?"

"Innocent?" Thomas laughed. "There is not one bit of innocence in your body, not even the tiniest spot. You are a liar, a cheat, and a fraud."

"Bad times," Viola whispered, closing her eyes.

Alex touched Viola's shoulder, and she jerked away. She sobbed, trembling in her seat. She seemed to be in a state of shock. Alex knew all about terror since he had experienced it himself when he was shot, and Sophia was killed.

"What were you doing in such bad company, Viola?" Count Estes asked, stopping in front of the girl. "My daughters considered you their friend. Your father will be devastated to learn what it has become of his daughter," Count Estes said.

Viola straightened her posture, and her words were hesitant when she talked again.

"What can I say, Count Estes. I am sorry," she said.

"You're a slut," Thomas said, staring at Viola, who moved closer to Fabio and pushed Thomas away from her.

"Wait your turn to talk!" Elio hollered, forcing Thomas back to the sofa.

The wind opened the windows, a gust of wind and of rain whipping the floors. Lightning hit a tree in the gardens. Thunder rumbled at regular intervals, its sounds shaking the villa. Somewhere, in the back of the house, a door banged against a wall, while the fire burning in the fireplace died. The few tapers on the walls flickered, dispensing a warm light over the entire chamber, its softness in contrast to their faces.

"Is it true what Thomas says?" Count Estes asked. "Are you Fabio's woman?"

"Of course, I am," Viola answered.

"No, she isn't," Fabio argued.

Elio laughed, and Count Estes shuddered. Alex kept his lips tightly shut, staring first at Viola, and then at Fabio.

"I guess you didn't get your stories straight. Yes, no, what's the truth?" Count Estes asked.

Fabio lowered his chins and stared at the floors, while Viola fidgeted in her seat, lacing her fingers in her lap and rocking back and forth.

"Stop doing that," Fabio whispered, "you're making me dizzy."

"And you, Thomas, what reason did you have to bite the hand that fed you all these years?" Elio asked as he tightened his grip on Thomas's shoulder, who was trembling in anger. They were all silent which sent Elio into a rage. "I suggest you start talking if you want to make it out of here alive," he said.

"Sir, I only followed Count Monti's orders. He held my family in his dungeons and forced me to poison Miss Rose," Thomas cried. "Poor, Miss Rose!"

"Shut up, Thomas, if you want to see your wife again," Fabio said.

"She's dead already!" Thomas yelled, kicking Fabio in the leg.

"No, she's not," Fabio said, trying to avoid his kick by lifting his legs off the floor.

"Fabio, you know that's not true," Viola said, weeping. "Thomas, I'm sorry, but your wife died a week ago."

"You're sorry! You'll be ruined when I'm done with you!" Thomas yelled.

"What do you say in your defense, Count Monti?" Count Estes asked Fabio.

"Nothing at all," Fabio answered.

"All right, then. Let's start at the beginning and try to make sense of this whole mess. Thomas, tell us why Count Monti asked you to poison Rose," Elio demanded, sitting down on a nearby chair as he waited for Thomas's answer.

"I didn't ask him to poison Rose," Fabio said.

"Count Monti," Thomas started, "asked me to deliver poisonous flowers to Miss Rose. After I had refused, he kidnapped my family: my two daughters and my wife. He threatened to kill them if I didn't do what he wanted me to do. He locked them in his dungeon, and I didn't know if they were dead or alive."

"Why would he do that?" Count Estes asked Thomas.

"For the money," Thomas answered.

"Is what he says true, Count Monti?" Elio asked.

"I don't have to answer any of your questions. Think whatever you want," Fabio snapped.

Thomas coughed to clear his throat before he continued. "The knife I threw on the evening of Miss Rose's birthday was intended to end her life quickly. When it didn't, Count Monti decided to use poison."

"And how did he deliver it to Rose?" Count Estes asked.

"I sprayed it on the rose's petals, and when Miss Rose touched them, the poison went into her skin. Eventually, once the poison built up in her system, her heart would stop beating."

Alex gasped, while Viola cried softly.

"I'm sorry. My love for Fabio blinded me. I wanted him to stop, especially after he decided to marry Annabella. I stole Count Estes' contracts for him so that he could pay his gambling debts to Lord Remington, then I insisted we move to London to get away from everything and everyone. What a fool I was!"

"Keep quiet, woman," Fabio said.

"I threatened Mr. Matteo so he would assist me. He skimmed the money from the factory to keep his affair with Rafael out of the public eye. A scandal involving a relationship with a man would have ruined his reputation as an esteemed member of the church." Viola turned toward Fabio and said, "I did it for you, for us, Fabio."

Elio leaned toward Viola, and he said, looking at her in disgust, "Mr. Matteo is dead. He left a letter, telling Rose about your involvement in the theft. What a wonderful friend you were to Rose!"

"It wasn't my idea," Fabio said. "It was hers."

"Hiding behind a woman is not honorable, Count Monti, although nothing about you is noble at all. I don't know what Viola or my daughter ever saw in you, you bastard!" Count Estes shouted, slapping Fabio's face. A trace of blood appeared in the corner of his mouth, and Fabio wiped it with the back of his sleeve.

"Nothing like this would have happened if Rose had accepted my marriage proposal. I loved her, but I was left with no option other than marrying Annabella because I thought you would make her an heir to the estate, knowing that she is your rightful daughter. You're the one responsible for your daughter's condition, not me," Fabio said.

"You're saying it's my fault? You make me laugh, son," Count Estes said.

"All I ever wanted was to save my estate from ruin."

"I thought you loved Rose," Count Estes said, staring at Fabio. "You rascal, why didn't you tell me about your situation? For your parents' sake, I would have helped you to recover."

"I was desperate and didn't know what else to do."

"You shouldn't have used my family to settle your scores. You made a laughing stock out of me and used my daughters like pawns in a chess match."

"I told you it was a bad idea to marry Annabella," Viola whispered, gazing at Fabio. Then, she looked at Thomas. "I was wrong to go along with any of this. When Fabio suggested trying the poison on your wife, he said he had the antidote."

Thomas wept, his cries piercing the night. He flew out of the chair, and before anyone could do anything to stop him, he grabbed Viola by her neck.

"Thomas," Alex shouted, as he tried to pull Thomas away from Viola.

Thomas' fingers tightened around Viola's neck, while the woman choked and fought to escape from his clasp. She put her small hands over those of Thomas, gasping for air while Alex watched her eyes jutting out from their sockets.

"Let her go!" Elio screamed as he detached Thomas's hands from around Viola's neck. Alex pulled Thomas away from the woman's limp body and threw him to the floor.

"Viola? Answer me!" Fabio cried, trying to rise from his spot on the couch where Count Estes held him at gunpoint.

"She's dead," Alex said.

"No!" Fabio cried. "Viola, answer me!" His screams echoed through the room, drowning out the thunder.

Elio grabbed Thomas from the floor, forcing him to the wall while Count Estes helped him tie his hands behind his back. Thomas didn't fight them, and his face looked peaceful.

"She is avenged now. One life for another is the right thing to do," Thomas said, lowering his head between his shoulders.

"You should have let the law prevail, Thomas," Elio said, shaking his head.

"Where the hell is Fabio?" Alex asked, compelling them to stare at the empty sofa where Fabio had sat just minutes ago.

Alex ran to the window in time to see Fabio running away from the estate and becoming one with the night.

"I'll get him, Alex, I promise I will. No hole in the earth will hide him. I'm not going to lose my daughter," Elio said.

"Your daughter?" Alex asked.

"It's a long story," Elio said.

Alex looked at Count Estes, waiting for an answer.

"What are we going to do with Viola?" Count Estes asked, pointing to the body on the coach.

"We'll take her to Siena with us. I must fill out a report about the conditions surrounding her death, and then we will burn her body," Elio said.

"Is Rose your daughter, Elio? Does she know it? Are you aware how much she wants to find out who her real father is?" Alex asked. He grabbed Elio's shoulders and shook him until Count Estes pulled him away from his friend.

"It was a pact we made a long time ago," Count Estes said. "Let's get the woman and put her in the carriage."

"And Thomas?" Alex asked.

"He'll join us," Elio added.

Elio and Alex picked up Viola's body and wrapped her in a blanket they grabbed from the sofa. They left the villa in silence, and when they had reached the edge of Monti's estate, Count Estes turned onto the road going to his property, while Elio, Alex, and Thomas headed straight to the city.

"There is only one place where Count Monti feels safe," Thomas offered. "At Three Lilies, in Siena, his hiding place. The landlord will do anything for money."

CHAPTER 21

It was midnight when they left the Monti estate. The pounding of hooves on the dirt road leading to Siena echoed in the night. Elio urged the horses through a dirty mixture of water, fallen leaves and broken branches spread along the road. He checked each side of the road, scanning the woods.

"Count Monti could be anywhere. He'll do anything to protect his life, even kill," Elio said, casting sidelong glances into the woods.

"That monster killed my wife!" Thomas cried from inside the coach where Elio and Alex shoved him before they had started their journey to Siena.

"Time will ease your pain," Elio said, coughing to clear his throat.

"That's easy for you to say. You haven't lost anyone," Thomas said, poking his head through the window.

"The woman I loved died in childbirth," Elio whispered.

Alex glanced at Elio, and his eyes filled with tears. When he lost Sophia, the recovery period had been long and painful. And now, as if coming full circle, Alex couldn't shake the bad feeling he had since the previous morning. He thought of Rose, fighting for her life, and his blood boiled. He whipped the two horses, and their neighs pierced the night.

"Are you all right, son?" Elio asked Alex.

Alex nodded.

"I'll help you catch Count Monti, and then you can do what you must to me for killing the woman. I know that they'll hang me for it," Thomas said from inside the couch.

"If people walked around taking the law into their hands, there would be no reason for people like me to exist," Elio said.

"I thought of going to the police, but Count Monti had connections. I was scared of what he would do to my daughters if I accused him of kidnapping."

Elio shook his head and didn't say a word until the first buildings of Siena's outskirts appeared on the horizon. The cobblestone streets were deserted at midnight, aside from the few stray dogs that found refuge between ruins. The men followed the winding road passing through the center of the sleeping city until they reached the police station. Elio unlocked the door while Alex helped Thomas carry Viola's body inside the station. Elio pointed to an office with an oval wood table, two chairs, and a bed. The body was rigid and cold. By looking at Viola, no one would have guessed her troubled existence or the sacrifices she had made in the name of her love, so peaceful she looked when they had sat her on the bed. Then, they returned to the foyer, waiting for Elio to fill out the death certificate. When Elio finished, he shoved the certificate inside a drawer and returned to the entrance where Thomas and Alex waited.

"I met Dolores Estes twenty years ago when I accepted her brother's invitation to spend a summer at his estate. We finished the law examinations, and I didn't want to go home. One evening, when Giulio and I went for a walk in the gardens, I laid eyes on a lovely redhead with porcelain skin. For the first time in life, I found myself incapable of articulating one word," Elio began his story.

"Did she say anything?" Alex asked.

"Yeah. She asked me if the cat had my tongue," Elio laughed, and Alex chuckled too. "We married in secret, and we told her family when we discovered she was expecting a child."

"Rose," Alex said.

Elio nodded. "The Estes's sent Dolores to live in a convent until the child was born while they settled her marriage to an old count whose wife had passed away. With Giulio's help, I kidnapped her from the convent, and we lived at my home. It stormed the night when the baby came, and Dolores died from complications."

"Rose deserves to know that you are her biological father," Alex said. "She's been searching for you all her life."

"I promised Giulio that I won't interfere in her life," Elio said. "I was content to watch her grow from afar."

"We must hurry if we want to find Fabio and the antidote," Thomas interrupted Elio's story. "Let's go!"

Alex opened the door and checked the street. He waited in the middle of the road for the others to join him while Elio locked the door behind him. They passed through the piazza where Alex had fought Fabio, stopping across from the inn illuminated by a single light that hung above the entrance. All windows were dark, except for a candle shining on the second floor.

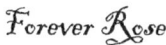

"I'll knock. The landlord knows me," Thomas said.

"I'll go too because the innkeeper thinks I'm Fabio's friend," Alex added.

Elio stared at them, and Thomas rested his hand on Elio's shoulder, his words soft when he spoke.

"I want him behind bars for what he has done to my family. Because of him, I became a murderer."

Elio nodded, and he hid behind boxes with vegetables in the inner court of the inn. He watched as Thomas knocked: two long blows followed by three short ones and a whistle. He repeated the signal until the landlord appeared in the door frame.

"Is it you, Thomas?" the innkeeper asked.

"Yes," Thomas answered. "I'll sleep in my room tonight."

There was no movement for a few seconds, and Alex searched for his gun. Then, he remembered he had left it at the Estes's home. The landlord yawned while he urged them inside the foyer.

"You know the way," the landlord said before he retired to his own room.

"No one will hear a thing," Thomas told the landlord, and he meant every word.

They climbed an old flight of stairs, and when Thomas avoided two steps, Alex followed. It was quiet in the corridor, every guest in the inn long asleep, and only a candle shone in a candlestick on the wall. They stopped in front of Fabio's room, and they watched as shadows danced on the floor when he passed by the door.

"Not every day the hunter becomes the game," Alex whispered.

Thomas grinned. He touched his pocket, and then he knocked. When Fabio opened the door a crack, Thomas wedged his foot between the door and the wood frame, and they entered the room. Fabio leaned against the wall, his hands gripping the back of a chair.

"Listen, Thomas. I didn't intend for any of this to happen. Doctor, make him understand."

"Do you have the antidote?" Thomas asked.

"I had every intention of freeing them once the task ended. I was in Siena when the guard tested the poison on your wife," Fabio said in one breath.

"Murderer," Thomas hissed. "You're a far cry for a human. You wanted to marry one woman when you loved another, and in the end, you lost both."

Fabio's chin trembled, and he seemed to have aged years in a matter of a few hours.

"Give me the antidote to save Rose," Alex said. "It's the least you can do."

"I broke the bottle when I fled. Nothing is left," Fabio said. "Work your magic now, Doctor, if you can."

Alex grabbed Fabio's jaw, and he squeezed until he heard the crack of his bones. When he threw him across the room, Fabio landed on the floor where he remained for a couple of seconds. Alex bent over him, and Fabio's kick sent him in the other corner of the room. He looked at Thomas, who raised a knife, and he shook his head. Thomas seized Fabio by his collar and prepared to slit his throat, as he had done with the guard when the door hit the wall, and Elio stormed inside.

"Let the law prevail, Thomas," Elio yelled, snatching the knife from Thomas's hands. He turned toward Fabio, twisting his arm behind his back, while he searched through his pockets. He turned each one upside down, pushing Fabio into a chair and forcing him to stay still.

"He broke the bottle when he fled from us," Alex said.

"Is that right?" Elio asked.

"Lads, I never had an antidote," Fabio said, laughing. "It bought me time to escape."

"No!" Alex shouted. Pain ripped a fiery path in his chest, and Alex couldn't breathe. All was lost. Without the antidote, Rose would die, and he would never hear the sound of her soft voice nor feel her touch again. Just like he had never touched or felt his wife again after she had been murdered.

Elio shook Fabio's shoulders. "You, villain if anything happens to Rose!" he cried out.

"I know, you'll kill me," Fabio said.

Fabio lunged to his right and grabbed a letter opener from the table, stabbing Elio in his liver. Then, he took a step back and circled the table, keeping his eyes on the door. He was half in the hallway when Thomas grabbed him by his shirt. He passed the knife over his neck, dragging Fabio back inside the room.

"Just shut up, rogue," Thomas said, throwing Fabio to the floor.

Elio fell too, looking at Fabio, who choked on his own blood. Alex checked Elio's wound and then shook his head.

"Thomas, go to your family and never return to Siena," Elio whispered. He turned toward Alex, and he said, "I need to ask you a favor, Doctor."

"What can I do for you?" Alex asked.

Elio panted as he pulled the necklace with the pendant from around his neck. "Give this to Rose. Tell her it is from her father. She'll understand," he said. "Go now," he urged Alex before he leaned to one side. A tear had trickled down his cheek before he took his last breath. Alex closed his eyes and covered Elio's body with a quilt he had retrieved from the bed before storming out of the room. Thomas was right behind him when Alex jumped on a horse, threw a last look at the inn, and rode out of Siena and into the night.

Alex arrived at Luce Del Sol when the first rays of sun touched the ground. He dismounted and ran up the stairs toward Rose's room. He was out of breath when he stopped in front of her chamber door. The old clock's pendulum rang six in the morning, its echo traveling through the entire house. Alex knocked and when no one answered, he opened the door and stepped inside the room. Rose's parents were with her and Annabella too.

A bird hit the glass, and Annabella opened the window and chased it away.

"Go away you stupid bird. There is nothing to your liking in here," Annabella said, wiping her eyes.

"What is it, Bella?" Rose asked weakly.

"Only a bird that hit the window," Annabella said, turning around. "This is all my fault, Rose. If I didn't want to marry Fabio, none of this would have happened." Her voice broke, and she sobbed uncontrollably.

"I remember the day you arrived, Bella. You were a pink doll with beautiful eyes. I fell in love with you the moment I held you. You started to suck on my finger, and I laughed. I made you a promise then."

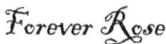

"Please, Rose, don't talk. Save your strength," Annabella said, kissing Rose's hands.

"Alex will find a way. You'll see," Rose whispered.

"I hope you're right," Alex said, entering the room.

All turned toward him when they heard his voice. Rose gasped when she saw him. He looked tired and dusty, and his beard had grown overnight, gray blending with the black.

"Did you find the antidote?" Rose asked, trying to lift herself up between the pillows.

"Not really," Alex answered.

"I don't want to die, Alex. Find a way."

Alex approached Rose's bed, signaling Annabella and Rose's parents to leave them alone. As soon as they left, Alex leaned on his elbow and kissed Rose's hair.

"It was one of Fabio's lies," he whispered. "He never had an antidote."

"Am I doomed?"

Paralyzed, Alex stared at Rose. He had been too blinded by his emotions to notice her failing health, her dizziness, and loss of weight. Had he paid attention, he wouldn't be condemned to witness her fight for her life.

"Forgive me for all I've done. I never meant for any of this to happen," Annabella said, opening the door and approaching the bed.

"Don't worry! Alex will find a way out," Rose said.

"Dr. Santini, do something," Countess Estes said, entering the room and approaching the bed.

"Rose?" Annabella screamed when Rose closed her eyes, and her head fell to one side.

"Sooner or later, death comes to us all," Rose whispered, her voice breaking. She fell asleep and a couple of hours passed before she woke up again.

"You can't die. I won't allow it," Alex said, shaking her shoulders and pulling her into his arms. He rocked her close to his chest.

"I'm sorry to make you go through this pain again. Return to your time. You don't belong here," Rose whispered.

"Hush, woman, don't say anything else," Alex shushed her while Rose pushed him away with the last of her strength. She tried lifting herself from the pillows, and after he had arranged one behind her head, a huge and the most beautiful smile ever spread over her face.

"The portal to your world opens tomorrow," Rose began. "Leave me here and go, and don't ever look back. Your safety is more important than my life."

"You're coming with me. I won't leave you here to die," Alex said, a shudder coursing through his body.

"What portal?" Count Estes asked from the chair where he had sat quietly since he entered the room. "What world is Rose talking about, young man?"

Alex grabbed Rose's hand, checking for a pulse. Satisfied that he could still feel a weak throb in her vein, he got up and walked toward the window. He peeked outside, but there was no trace of the moon, only a strong wind carrying silver drops of rain and the old branches smacking against each other.

"Don't worry, Alex. The storm will pass by tomorrow, and you will return to your time," Rose said.

"What are you two talking about? What time?" Countess Estes queried, joining her husband's concern.

"Do you care of explaining what is going on here?" Count Estes asked too.

Countess Estes grabbed Alex's arm and forced him to look at her. Alex knew it was time to tell her parents the truth. Annabella kneeled by Rose's bed and folded her hands together in prayer. The discreet motion of her lips made Alex consider the last time he had prayed, and he couldn't remember when it was. He looked as if a thousand winds slashed his face, his hair scruffy, and his eyes burning bright.

"Is this what you think bothers me now?" Alex asked, turning away from the window to face Rose, ignoring her parents. "It's you, Rose, you are the one I'm thinking about."

"Dr. Santini?" Count Estes asked again, crossing the distance between the chair and Rose's bed.

"Can we speak in private?" Alex asked, looking at Count Estes expectantly.

"Stay with your sister," Count Estes said, nodding and then signaling Alex to go with him toward the door.

"Without the antidote, Rose will die," Alex said when he stood face to face with Count Estes. "I should apologize for not being truthful with you."

"Do you care to explain to what extent you weren't truthful with me?" Count Estes asked, raising an eyebrow and twitching his lips.

"You see, I came from the future," Alex said and let the words sink in, noticing how Count Estes started to cough. Countess Estes, who joined her husband turned white and leaned into the door, covering her heart with her hand. Her chin began trembling, her legs giving in. She slid to the floor, and she gasped.

"Mother, is everything all right?" Annabella asked, rising from the floor where she stood praying for Rose.

Countess Estes nodded, incapable of articulating a word.

"Excuse me?" Count Estes asked.

"My time is three hundred years apart from yours," Alex continued.

"So, you've traveled three hundred years into the past," Count Estes said, his jaw dropping. Annabella rose from the floor, stopping next to him. "You look like one of us," she said, checking him out.

"Did Rose know?" Count Estes asked.

"Yes, she knew. She found me in front of the cave in the gardens," Alex answered.

"But how is it possible? How?" Count Estes asked again.

"I went through a portal created by a supermoon that happens every fourteen months. A few people know about this phenomenon, and no records exist of these events in your time. Scientists of my time discovered that Leonardo Da Vinci disappeared in the same cave through which I arrived in your world."

"Master Da Vinci, you say," Count Estes said. "Yes, I remember reading that he went away somewhere for months. Nobody knows for sure where he went."

"Fourteen months ago, a swirling vortex opened, and I passed through it. Actually, it sucked me in. That is how I got here on the night of the first attempt on Rose's life," Alex said in one breath.

"So, how do you plan to return?" Count Estes asked.

Alex swallowed a glassful of water he found on a table, and his voice was calm when he spoke.

"The same way I came, through the portal."

"This explains your medical skills. They are way ahead of our time," Countess Estes said, leaning on her husband.

Remembering Rose's words about the supermoon's occurrence, Alex said, "The next window opens tomorrow."

"How do you know?" Annabella asked.

"Calculations," Alex said. "I will take Rose with me. In my world, it's a simple procedure to analyze the poison. One shot, and she'll be fine."

The amazement in the count's eyes was evident, and for the first time, Alex saw himself as a stranger in a foreign land where anything in the name of love was interpreted as madness.

"I can't let her go with you. She's my daughter," Count Estes said.

"If she stays here she'll die," Alex said, pacing up and down the room and gazing out the window every so often.

The first lines of light stretched passed the horizon. The clouds cleared, and the wind died. Nature shone under a sky refreshed of all impurities, and Alex had the urge to open the window and let the fresh air inside the room. He inhaled, held his breath, and then pushed the air out of his body before turning toward the count.

"I found a way." Alex paused and raised his chin up. He locked stares with the count in an intense, acute, painful moment when both realized their options had run out.

"Continue," Count Estes managed to say.

"I will pass through the vortex and return with the medication before the portal closes again."

CHAPTER 22

After her father had left the room, Alex took Rose's hands into his and kissed her delicate fingers. She was pale and shaking, and barely breathing.

"Tell me about my options," Rose begged.

"Tonight is the supermoon when the portal opens. Your father doesn't want you to come with me to my world, so I must go alone, although I wish I can stay here with you," Alex said, shifting from one foot to the other.

"You can't stay here. You mustn't," Rose said. "If I die, they'll accuse you of murder. You can't be trapped in a world that's not yours. I can't condemn you to death."

"It's not your decision, Rose," Alex said.

"I can't stand or walk or run. Father was right. I'll be a nuisance to you if I'm coming," Rose whispered.

"Then, I'll run through the portal, grab what I need from the hospital and return through the vortex before it closes again."

"What happens if you don't make it back?"

"That's not an option."

Alex's voice became a little more than a whisper, and Rose didn't say a word for what seemed like an eternity for him. When she spoke, her voice was clear and stronger.

"What are you waiting for? Go!"

"I'm not losing you like I lost Sophia," Alex muttered, kissing the palms of her hands and smoothing her hair.

"I will make it until your return. I know I will," Rose said, picking up his chin and forcing him to look at her.

"Stay strong," Alex said.

"Was I not strong for the past months?"

Her chuckles echoed throughout the room, and Alex loved the sound of them.

"I will go through the portal tonight," Alex said.

"Promise me that you won't take any unnecessary risks."

He couldn't tell her that he had no intention of living in his world without her. The past months had made him see clearly, where his future lay, and his world had nothing to offer but the grief of losing a woman he once loved. During the past fourteen months, Alex had tried to deny it, lying to himself that, as soon as he returned to his time, everything would become a distant memory. He shook his head, knowing how empty his life would be if Rose weren't a part of it. Alex was aware that he would start looking for her again, passing through the portal every fourteen months for one more chance at happiness. No way could he lose the woman he loved. Alex kissed Rose and prepared to leave the room.

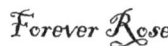

"Don't worry about me, Rose."

"I can't stop worrying about you," Rose said.

"I'll be back in time with the drugs you need. You are a strong woman," Alex mumbled.

Alex had been down the same road when Sophia was killed. He learned to survive, and he managed to become a thriving surgeon. He only failed to fall in love again. In the beginning, he had denied his attraction to Rose. He kept telling himself he was drawn toward her because she reminded him of his late wife. Day after day, he discovered that he was in love with Rose, not the memory of Sophia. And Rose had protected him and always found a way to keep him safe. He had made it thus far because of Rose, and he could only be worthy of her love if he saved her from her fate.

"You'll come with me to the portal and wait at the mouth of the cave. I'll run to the hospital and get what I need. I'll be back before the portal closes," Alex said.

The strength in her eyes, her willpower to live, gave him hope. He had to return to her time before the portal closed again.

"Let's do that, Alessandro Santini," Rose whispered.

"Here, hold this," he told her, pulling the necklace Elio had given him before he died. "Your father wanted you to have it."

Rose looked at the necklace, and she gasped. "And Elio?"

"He loved you very much," Alex said going to the door and asking her father to enter the room. Count Estes didn't move from the threshold, and Alex sensed his agony too.

"Papa, come here," Rose said, extending her hands toward her father.

"You just became the famous historical painter you planned to be. You can't die on me," Count Estes said.

"Make sure that Alex passes through the portal. Promise me that you'll force him to go if you must."

"I promise," Count Estes said.

Rose touched her father's hand, and she followed him with her gaze as he left the room.

"Take me to the window," Rose said, and Alex did as she requested. He lifted her from her bed and stopped in front of the window where her gaze took in the view of the entire garden. The last storm had scattered petals of her beloved roses over the whole garden.

Rose sighed. "Before you leave, tell me some more about your world, Alex," she begged while they returned to the bed and lay next to each other, waiting for the evening to come. Her head rested on his shoulder, her hand on his chest, and she counted his heartbeats. She thought they were too fast. Her eyes were getting heavier again, and her fever was rising too.

"My world is filled with people, like here. We struggle to make it better. We love, and we die. We fight for what we believe in, and we strive to improve. There are bad people and good ones. Sometimes the wrong people win. We explored the universe, and we went among the stars to discover new worlds."

Rose moaned in her sleep as sweat covered her body. Alex wiped it away and forced her to take a few sips of cold water. Her head rocked from one side to the other.

"I will show you my world. I'll take you with me through the portal after you heal and let you discover wonders people in your time have never imagined. You will paint in a studio, and display your paintings in famous art galleries all over the world.

Renaldo will witness our marriage on the beach, just as you've always dreamed."

Alex told her about his favorite books and the places he planned to take her to visit while he watched her fight the fever. His voice was steady, his tone firm. The day passed, and the first stars shown in the sky, playing hide-and-seek with the clouds. A gray blur covered the face of the moon. Rose didn't wake up, and the night spread its wings over the entire estate. Her temperature was high, and he remembered the aspirin he had brought from his world when he passed through the vortex. Alex searched the room, and his gaze rested on the aspirin bottle on the table. It had been there since he had given the bottle to Countess Estes after he had treated his wound with the laser pen. Alex picked up the bottle, and he gasped.

"Only two," he groaned, as he unfastened the lid, shaking the pills into his palm. He went to bed and looked at Rose. She muttered something he didn't understand. After he had put the pills into his mouth and crushed them with his teeth, he leaned toward Rose and opened her lips, pushing the crushed aspirin into her mouth.

Rose swallowed the aspirin, and Alex forced her to drink from the cup he held to her mouth. He didn't hear the door opening, or Count Estes approaching him until he touched his shoulder. Alex jumped.

"It is time. Rose asked me to make sure you did it. Her mother will stay with her now."

"I can't leave here and go," Alex argued.

"Don't worry. Rose is a strong woman, Alex," Count Estes said. "We had better go now if you want to make it in time."

"I am coming back," Alex said.

"Of course you will, and she'll be right in front of the cave, waiting for you," Count Estes said, pushing him out the door.

They left the room without looking back and, with every step he took, Alex felt like dying. He turned around, but Count Estes stopped him with a shake of his head. He pushed him forward, toward the back of the garden where the cave was. Alex looked back to Rose's window one more time, and then he turned around. Her father grabbed his shoulders.

"I made a promise, son, and I intend to keep it," he said.

Alex didn't know what was harder: leaving Rose behind without knowing if she would make it or the fact that he would have to live his entire life in search of her if the portal closed before his return.

"I can't keep my promise, sir. I can't live my life without her. Why can't I stay?"

"You must go. She asked you to go. You said you could bring medicine from your time, drugs that could save her. Stay true to your word and hurry," Count Estes said, pushing him inside the cave.

"The moon is full," Alex noted as he searched the sky, "but the portal isn't opened yet."

"Patience, son, patience," Count Estes said.

They waited for what seemed like hours, and when Alex decided to give up and return to the villa, circles filled with blue light grew broad around the cave, and they looked impressive. Count Estes stood by the mouth of the cave, and his jaw dropped. He chuckled and wanted to touch the blue energy rings. Alex pulled him back.

"The portal could suck you in, as it happened to me," Alex said.

Alex tore a late rose from a bush before he entered the tunnel connecting the two worlds. He covered his eyes with one hand and felt his whole body decomposing in particles of matter while he passed through the vortex. There were crackling sounds all around him, a gust of wind blowing his garments, and the air he breathed was hot. When Alex opened his eyes again, he was standing in the middle of the basement back in Florence where everything had begun fourteen months ago. A security guard doing his rounds walked in his direction, and Alex waited for him.

"Are you lost? A storm is on its way. Hurry, before the blizzard gets the best out of you," the security guard said, and he pointed the way up the stairs and to the front exit where other visitors were looking out the window.

"I'll be right back," Alex said.

The guard shrugged his shoulders.

Alex stepped outside the hotel, and when he looked at the sky, he saw gray clouds moving in. Snowflakes covered sideways and roads, and the street lights made everything silver. He pulled his collar up around his ears and stuck his hands deep into the pockets of his coat with golden buttons. A thorn pricked his finger, as he pulled the rose from his pocket and looked at it. He had furrowed his eyebrows before he put the bud back in the pocket. He walked as fast as he could, and in about ten minutes, he reached the hospital. Alex ran up the stairs toward the pharmacy and slammed the door. He grabbed a bag and began dropping bottles and boxes with antibiotics into it, and then he searched for the section with treatments for poisoning.

"What are you doing in here?" an intern asked when he saw him stuffing the drugs in his bag. "You need permission to retrieve drugs from the pharmacy."

"Oh, yes, I'm Dr. Santini. Doctor Bruno is on his way, and I'm in a hurry. He'll bring it to you."

Before the intern could say anything more, Alex pushed past him, ran back downstairs, and sprinted outside. By this time, the snow was thick on the ground. He pulled up his collar and headed toward the hotel. He gasped as he fell to his knees, slipping on a patch of ice. A frigid wind stung his cheeks. He bit his lip as he took into view the full moon still hanging in the sky. *It is the only way*, he thought. He rose from the sidewalk and approached the front door. He entered the hotel, and the manager on duty stopped him when Alex turned toward the basement.

"You can't go there," the manager on duty said.

"I must get into the basement," Alex said.

"It's impossible at this hour. Return tomorrow."

"You don't understand. Tomorrow is too late. I must get through now."

"Leave, or I'll call the police, sir," the manager on duty said, lifting the phone and beginning to dial the police number.

"Only for a minute, please," Alex begged.

Attracted by the commotion in the front lobby, a security guard approached and pulled his gun, pointing it at him.

"Step away from the premises, sir," the guard said.

"Can I make a call?"

The manager on duty passed him the phone, and Alex dialed the only number he remembered. Renaldo would be asleep and probably in a terrible mood to be awakened at this late hour, but Alex needed his friend's help fast. He thanked the manager on duty before he exited the hotel, walking up and down the street and waiting for Renaldo to come.

It didn't take long, about ten minutes at the most, and a car stopped right next to Alex, and Renaldo hopped out.

"Alex?"

"Renaldo, my friend," Alex said, "I'm happy to see you."

"What happened to you, man?"

"It's a long, crazy story."

"Where have you been?"

"I need your help."

"What is it? What's up? Sounds serious."

"I need to get to the hotel's basement, and the security guard won't let me pass, Renaldo," Alex said.

Renaldo touched Alex's coat and looked at his hair that became longer since they last met. "You're acting weird. What's wrong with your clothes? And this hair? And where have you been for months?"

"You won't understand even if I tell you. I have no time."

"Why don't you try me out?"

"Very well," Alex replied. He told Renaldo the entire story of the supermoon opening a portal toward another century, about saving a count's life, learning to ride a horse and to shoot a gun. Alex also mentioned about falling in love with the count's daughter, who was the spitting image of Sophia and who was about to die from poisoning if he didn't return in time with medicine.

Renaldo listened, and he didn't move or breathe until Alex finished. Then, he cleared his throat.

"If I didn't know you, I'd consider you crazy."

"Wait," Alex paused, remembering the rose he had with him. He put the flower in Renaldo's hand. "How do you think I have this?"

Renaldo checked Alex's face and the rose he held in his hand. "What's your plan?"

"I have to go back."

"You have to do what?"

"I have to go back to her, Renaldo," Alex said. "I must pass through the portal before it's too late."

Renaldo shook Alex's shoulders. "Are you nuts? Do you plan to live three hundred years in the past for a woman?"

"She is no ordinary woman, Renaldo."

"She's not Sophia, pal."

"I love her for who she is, not because she reminds me of Sophia."

"I suppose I can't talk you out of this."

"I've made my decision, Renaldo, "Alex said. For a very long time, he had denied himself intimacy with a woman because he was afraid of being hurt again. But Rose was right. Life didn't offer guarantees. He had to take a chance and fight for his right to be with the woman he loved. Nothing in his world would hold him back. Apart from his friend, Alex had no one waiting or worrying about him.

"What about your career, Alex? You are an amazing surgeon. You've worked hard to get to where you are. You can't give that up."

"Nobody will notice my absence. And you, my friend, you can come with me too. She has a sister named Annabella."

"You're mad, man. I can find lots of Annabella here. I don't intend to travel into the past. Look at us, talking about time travel as if it's an everyday thing," Renaldo added, rolling his eyes. "Are you ready to leave?" Renaldo asked.

"I am," Alex said.

"Are we going to meet again?"

"Probably not in this life," Alex laughed.

"What if she doesn't want you, and you find yourself trapped in her time for the next fourteen months?"

Alex shrugged his shoulders. "I'll take my chances."

"Alex, can't I talk you out of this craziness?" Renaldo insisted.

The air was fresh, the sky clear and a cold wind blew the snow on the sidewalks. Colorful wreaths decorated the hotel's front doors.

"I want you to promise that you'll never say a word to anyone about the portal. In the wrong hands, that information could be dangerous," Alex said.

"After this frenzy passes, you may want to return," Renaldo said.

Alex stared at his friend, winking. He wouldn't return. Rose was there, and she was waiting for him.

"She has to be an amazing woman to make you lose your head."

"I've lost myself to her, Renaldo, completely," Alex declared.

"Have you already forgotten your friend?" Renaldo asked.

"You can come too. Why don't you join me?" Alex teased him, but his eyes were pinned on the sky. He followed the trajectory of the moon which hadn't moved from its spot.

"And do what?"

"With your knowledge of psychology, they'll treat you like royalty if you cure their minds."

"Hell, no, I like civilization."

They had known each other for a lifetime, and the thought of spending their lives apart showed in the strain on their faces.

"I'll miss you, buddy," Renaldo said, and he paused to catch his emotions and his breath. "Are you sure the portal will take you back to the same period? What happens if you end up in a different century?"

"I'll never know if I don't try. I owe it to Rose. My heart tells me she's waiting for me and that everything will work out."

Alex surveyed the gray clouds covering the face of the moon, and his heart started to beat faster. Snowflakes began to fall, burying the city under the heaviest snow in Florence's history, and Alex was anxious.

"Are you ready?" Renaldo asked.

"As ready as I can be," Alex answered.

"How are we going to enter? It is locked," Renaldo said after he checked the side door.

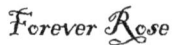

"We'll find a way," Alex assured him. They waited for an opening in the sky and the full moon to shine once again.

"It's time," Alex said.

He approached a lower window close to the ground level and broke the glass with the bag he was carrying. Hundreds of tiny pieces spread onto the basement's floor, and Renaldo opened his eyes wide. He looked around for signs of police, and he whispered, "I don't want to spend Christmas in jail."

"You won't. By the time they figure out someone broke into the basement, you'll be long gone," Alex said, looking around.

"Go now, before the moon disappears. Look, the clouds are hastening," Renaldo urged him, and after he had hugged his friend one last time, Alex pushed the bag through the window, and he jumped down onto the floor.

"Take care of you!"

Alex waved one more time, picked the bag up from the floor, and looked for Rose's portrait. He saw it in the corner. It was then that he noticed the inscription—To Alex with love— and he remembered the time he had spent in Siena recovering from the gunshot. He grabbed his temples and closed his eyes for a few minutes. He still couldn't believe that he had gone through a chain of events that would terrify anyone in their right mind, and yet he couldn't wait to go through the portal again. He had to save Rose. He couldn't let her die. Sophia died because of his carelessness, and he wouldn't allow history to repeat itself. He turned around when a cracking noise filled the room, and he laughed. Blue circles of light formed where they appeared fourteen months ago, and Alex passed again through the swirling vortex, taking his bag with him.

The twenty-first century remained behind as Alex stepped once again into the time he had longed for. It was still night when he emerged from the mouth of the cave. He had made it. There stood Villa Luce Del Sol, bathed in the brightest moonlight of the month, and Alex breathed a sigh of relief.

He had to find Rose. She said she would wait for him in front of the cave. It was after he calmed the pounding of his heart that he called for her.

"Rose?"

No one answered. Alex looked around, growing impatient. What if she had died while he was away? He prepared to return to the villa when he heard Rose humming, and he smiled when she spotted her next to an aged, bare oak. Wrapped in her heavy cape, she rested her head against the trunk of the tree. Alex stopped in front of her, blocking the moon's light and waiting for Rose to open her eyes. She gasped when she saw him and swallowed hard.

"I made it," Alex whispered.

"I knew you'd come back," Rose said. "Papa brought me here after you left. He just went back to the villa to fetch a hot tea."

Alex kissed her hands and pulled a syringe from the bag. "It'll hurt a little," he said.

"Hurry and do it," Rose whispered. "There isn't much time left."

Alex administered the serum and sat next to her on the cold ground. Rose laid her head on his chest, and he held her close.

"I'm here to stay," Alex said, nodding firmly after he had checked her pulse. It began to slow down, and Rose started to breathe regularly. Her temperature went down, and the color returned to her cheeks.

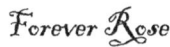

"It's going to be over soon. This shot will make everything right."

"How long are you going to be here?"

"For as long as you'll have me."

"Do you think forever will work for you?" Rose asked.

"Forever is a splendid idea," Alex said, kissing her lips.

Lost in the moment, they only had eyes for each another. The swirling vortex had disappeared, and they both jolted when they heard a voice saying, "I guess I made it in time for the fireworks."

"Renaldo? What are you doing here?" Alex asked as he rose from the ground and went to his friend.

"I thought you might need a best man for your wedding to this beautiful Countess," Renaldo winked, pushing Alex away and kissing Rose's hand.

Rose stared at Renaldo, and Alex sighed.

"Rose Estes, this is my best friend, Renaldo Bruno."

"Countess, you're more beautiful than I ever imagined," Renaldo said. "Now, I understand Alex's fascination with you." Renaldo leaned toward Alex, and he asked loud enough for everyone to hear. "Didn't you say she has a sister?"

"Renaldo!" Alex shouted, looking in Rose's direction, embarrassed by what his friend said.

Rose only laughed, and she said, "Welcome to the eighteen century, Renaldo Bruno. I hope you'll find my time to your liking."

"And so our story begins," Renaldo sighed.

"And it will be one hell of a story," Alex added, embracing Rose.

ABOUT THE AUTHOR

Writing is very important to me, but there are other things I do and care about too.

I have a boy, who is sixteen. I do fun things with him and am deeply involved in the issues that preoccupy him. He is my life. I am a full time, hands-on Mom by day, and write at night. The hardest thing that ever happened to me was when my mother died. She was an extraordinary, wonderful, fantastic mom, and everybody loved her. We still miss her. You don't stop missing someone you lose, but you learn to live with it. We have all tried to go on and lead good lives. Sometimes the lessons we learn are hard. In my experience, perseverance wins the prize. I'm stubborn about not giving up on most things and people.

I love fashion and do interior design every chance I get. It is very exciting to plan a home and see it all come together. It's like a fantasy come to life. Laughter definitely keeps me going when life gets tough.

I'm bi-cultural Romanian and American, grew up in Romania and speak a little bit of French. I went to Romanian schools through high school and American colleges. And now I live in Nashville, TN.

I enjoy cooking and baking. I'm not good at relaxing and having nothing to do. I love to keep busy. I'm good at multitasking and get antsy if I have nothing to do. I love projects and keeping super busy and when forced to "relax" I read, or start a new book. I always want to write.

I'm a great believer in making marriage work if you undertake the commitment. There is nothing more pleasant than being in a good relationship that both people work at and nothing worse than being in a bad one.

So that's me, what I do, and where I've been. I look forward to continuing to share my new books with you.

Love,

Carmen Monica